THE SWORD AND THE SECRETS

SECRETS ~ BOOK 2

JAN DAVIS WARREN

WILD HEART BOOKS

ISBN-13: 978-1-942265-30-6

To my friends and family for their support and encouragement.
Thank you all. I love you dearly.

"*A*arrgh!" A second too late, Lord John Stanton III pivoted to the left, and swung his sword in a tight arc to deflect the sharp blade that grazed his midsection. The coppery smell of blood and the sting of pain triggered the battle rage of the warrior he once was.

Using the flat of his blade and an aggressive downward thrust, he disarmed his sparring partner. Heart pounding, he was thrust into the memory of his last battle. He raised his sword to follow through with lethal force. Instead of the echoing screams of battle, silence and a staying hand of restraint held back his blow. He blinked and was once again surrounded by the peaceful meadows of home.

Shaken, John threw down his sword and took three steps back.

But for God's grace...

"I..." John swiped his hand across his eyes. Exhausted from too many sleepless nights, for his dreams plunged him into never-ending bloody battles. His last encounter with the enemy, ten months ago, had left him near death and ended his two year service in the king's army. Memories he would give anything to forget. So much death, destruction…and guilt. The large, raised scar on his side burned with fresh intensity.

"By the saints!" His best friend, William, rubbed his bruised knuckles and released a string of unsavory curse words. His gaze met John's, then dropped to John's torn tunic with its growing stain of fresh blood. William motioned to the crimson-stain with an expression of horror and regret. "I tripped." He ran his uninjured hand through his hair and hung his head in defeat. "Is it bad?"

"No!" John snapped, raising his tunic to examine the wound. He swiped away the blood, then cleaned his hand against the ruined fabric.

"I'll replace your tunic."

"Hang the garment! A hair's breadth closer and you would be explaining to my family why you killed their only son." John's voice rose in anger, not because of his wound, but at how close he'd come to ending William's life. He retraced his steps, picked up his sword and, with a shaky hand, shoved it into its battle-scarred scabbard.

"That would not be a conversation I'd likely live to finish." William paled as he swiped the sweat off his brow. With a groan of frustration, he bent down, retrieved his fallen sword, and gave it an angry swing, lopping off the tops of a patch of tall weeds. "It's all the fault of…" He didn't finish his thought and, instead, pushed his sword into its war-worn sheaf, and then picked up a woven bag from the ground. "I must not be the only one distracted to allow my blade to come so close."

"Aye." John slapped his friend on the back to show there were no hard feelings. Neither were of a mind to continue their sparring, so they shouldered their equipment and ambled back toward Brighton Castle. "I'm glad the glen is far from prying eyes, or the whole village would be ablaze with embellished details of our swordplay." John glanced around to confirm there were no witnesses.

"Your sister…" William waved his hand at John's torn tunic. "I should have never yielded to her last request."

"I assume you refer to Elise." He checked his wound and found the scratch had stopped bleeding. "I am more inclined to blame our injuries on our equal lack of focus." John's desire to help William keep his skills honed was the only reason he would wield a sword again. Boastful pride and arrogance on the battle-field had cost many unnecessary deaths, including the hostages they'd sought to free. Their screams still tormented his thoughts.

"John?" William raised his voice to get his friend's attention.

"What?" John rubbed his hand across his brow, then glanced over at William to show he was listening.

"I said, certainly 'tis Elise I'm speaking of." William sent him a look as if John were daft. "Your eldest sister, Sarah, is long married and lives near London, and I cannot imagine someone with aught against quiet, little Hanna." He loosed a deep sigh. "How can three sisters be so different?"

"So what has Elise done now?" John adjusted his pace with William's slower, more awkward, gait. His energetically inventive middle sister was full of good intentions, but her creative mind often led her into trouble.

"This." William tapped his right leg with his scabbard, receiving a dull thump.

They had met at the glen, and John had been so consumed with his own problems he hadn't noticed until now. William's pant leg was usually tied just below his knee, exposing a pine peg, but now the garment fell to his ankle where a shoe appeared.

"See?" William paused and raised his pant leg. A carved wooden leg, with an attached foot enclosed in a leather shoe, was visible. "It's heavy and awkward. This thing caused me to stumble, and 'tis the reason my blade came close enough to strike you."

William's limp became more pronounced the longer they walked. He stopped at a tree stump and sat. "I can't stand it another moment." He unstrapped the wooden leg, held it up, and pulled off the shoe to show John.

"Hmmm." John barely suppressed his laughter at the detailed sculpting of the foot with individual toes and toenails. It must have taken his sister weeks to carve such a life-like foot. "'Tis a work of art. What don't you like about it?"

"It's too heavy and, in spite of the padding, it rubs a blister when I wear it." He lowered his bag and pulled out a simple, lighter-weight piece of carved pine, which was wide at the top, then narrowed to a dull point. It was scarred and discolored from daily use, quite a contrast from the smooth and polished limb he'd removed. The pine peg had a hollowed out top, lined with a thick pad of wool to cushion his stump.

He folded his pant leg and used the straps to attach the well-worn peg leg in place. "I know she means well, but why she insists on trying to invent a better leg is beyond me." He tapped the wooden peg. "This works fine and I'm able to do most anything I did before."

"She just wants to help. Besides, I think she's a bit smitten with you since you saved my life." He waited while his friend stuffed the carved masterpiece inside the bag and stood.

"Smitten?" He shook his head and walked on. "She's destined to marry someone with a title, a lord or maybe even a prince. Not a low-born, crippled soldier." His protest hinted at his regret.

"You earned your knighthood in battle. I heard the Earl Marshall give the scribe orders for your commendation." John wondered if those orders had been lost, since no mention was made about a ceremony after the Earl Marshall was killed in battle shortly after.

"It doesn't matter. I don't think anyone thought either of us would live long enough to receive such honors after our last battle." William adjusted his bag to his other shoulder. "Being knighted still wouldn't make me a noble."

"I don't think my parents are as determined to find a suitably royal husband for Elise as you apparently are." He sympathized with his friend's dilemma, but he knew of his parents' concern that Elise's unorthodox interests and refusal, as she put it, *to being bartered off to a stranger in an arranged marriage,* had already made the process of finding her a suitable husband a challenge.

"When I think of what I heard happened to the last candidate who came to court her...something about singed hair and beard." John's humor could no longer be withheld, and it bubbled out in undisguised laughter. "Elise's version of the matter was simply that the pompous windbag got less than he deserved after he tried to take liberties with her while she was in the middle of a volatile experiment."

"If I'd...*we'd* been there, the scoundrel would have suffered far more than singed hair." William's angry tone and scowl confirmed John's suspicions.

His friend was indeed in love, or at the very least, in danger of falling deeply in love with Elise. The thought lightened John's mood. The man who saved his life would make a worthy husband for his uniquely talented sister.

"William, we grew up together, and are close as brothers, but I still do not understand your fascination with Elise. I love my sister, but she has been taking things apart and inventing contraptions since she was able to use tools." John allowed another chuckle to escape. "My parents never knew if the furniture would hold together after she'd been around."

"Aye. I remember an incident involving a visiting dignitary." William's scowl was replaced by the crinkle of laugh lines.

"I think that was when she was twelve. After the wheels came off the king's magistrate's carriage, she confessed to the vandalism. All because she wanted to see how the blacksmith had fashioned the new brackets that attached the undercarriage. That cost my father a new carriage to replace the broken one and a lot of futile promises of keeping my sister in hand in the future." John smiled at William's lighter gait. "My mother finally insisted Elise be given a tutor to direct her inventive passion and a shop of her own to experiment to her heart's desire, safely away from anything in and around the castle."

John stopped as the sound of thundering hooves headed their way. "Looks like we're about to have company."

Two riders galloped toward them, slowed, and then stopped a short distance away. His mother, Lady Evangeline, and the subject of their discussion, Elise, waited as the men approached.

"Good day, gentlemen." Lady Evangeline nodded to William, then focused on the bloodstain on John's torn tunic. Her gaze met his, and he smiled with a slight nod of assurance for his wellbeing.

She frowned, making it clear there would be further discussion as she examined and doctored his wound when he arrived home. "Son, we must start for London first thing in the morning. The girls are almost packed, but your servants said you've done nothing in preparation for the trip. They said you've decided to travel later. Is that true?"

Her expression of disapproval stirred John's conscience, but did nothing to dissuade him from his decision.

"I've decided to wait and leave in a week or so. Before I leave, I'll help William track down the predators killing our sheep." It wasn't exactly a lie, for he had intended to offer his help with the hunt. A glance at William showed he was avoiding eye contact with either woman. As an honest man, he wasn't a good liar, and John had not discussed his decision to leave later, or about helping him with the hunt, something he would address once the women had gone.

"I heard you have a gift for me?" John turned his attention

toward his sister, hoping to avoid being questioned further. His mother had an uncanny way of knowing when her children were hiding something from her, and he wasn't ready to discuss his decision with his family just yet.

"Hanna told you?" When John confirmed with a nod, Elise smiled. "I wanted it to be a surprise, but that's all right. It's my latest invention. I'll give it to you when you get home." Excitement edged her tone, but Elise couldn't keep her eyes off of William. She frowned when she spotted him wearing the old peg leg, sending her gaze up to the carved foot sticking out of the top of his bag. Her mouth opened, and then closed without speaking as she glanced from William to their mother.

"This trip is supposed to be a family outing. I know Sarah will be disappointed when you don't arrive with us." Lady Evangeline was not to be deterred by idle conversation.

"Sarah will have much more important things on her mind with this being her first child. She needs you, not me, to be there to hold her hand when her time comes."

"Your father is not going to be pleased to be trapped in close quarters with three talkative females for such a long journey." Lady Evangeline smiled and straightened in the saddle. "We'll discuss this further once you are home." She gave them a dismissal nod. "Gentlemen."

"Mother, I could keep them company." Elise turned to her mother for approval.

John frowned and shook his head.

His mother smiled and gave him a slight nod of understanding. She turned to Elise.

"I'm afraid not. You've neglected the last of your packing and need to finish. That means bringing nothing you can not wear. Understand young lady? No tools, no—."

"But I..." Elise gave a big sigh, but then submitted to the lecture. His mother was still talking as they rode away.

John dreaded keeping his real reason for traveling separately from his parents, but it was necessary if he were to fulfill his plan.

"What's this about you needing to help me track down whatever is killing the sheep before you can leave?" William continued to watch Elise as she rode away. "I don't *need* your help for a job I've done plenty of times, but you're always welcome to join the hunt." Being the gamekeeper for the castle and surrounding two hundred acres kept William busy training the men in his charge to guard the estate against predators and poachers, a serious crime that would result in the death of man and beast if caught. "What is the real reason for not going with your family?"

"I have decided…" John rubbed the sweat off his brow and quickened his pace.

"Decided what?" William drew his attention from Elise to John.

"I'm going to become a monk."

"What?" William caught up to his friend and took John's arm to halt him. "You cannot! You're the sole male heir of your family line. You have a solemn obligation to marry." He smiled and released him. "Your mother will not allow it." As if the subject was closed, he turned and resumed the journey to the castle.

"I am serious." John walked beside his friend, his voice lowered to assure his words wouldn't carry beyond them. "I vowed that if you and I lived after being struck down in battle, I would devote my life to serving God and the church."

"I appreciate your earnest prayer on my behalf, and I am most grateful to God for His divine intervention, but don't tie *me* to your vow. I plan to marry and have many children to carry on my father's line." He slapped John's shoulder and laughed. "You would do well to follow my example."

"Would you marry to forget Elise? Or are you planning to

marry her in spite of your lack of title and numerous other objections?"

"Let's leave your sister out of our discussion, please." His laughter was once again replaced by a scowl. "I know she'll be waiting to pester me about this fool leg. There will be endless questions and demands to try it again after she does one thing and then another."

"Your protests are exaggerated. You're a free man who could say no without penalty. I suspect you love every minute of her fussing over you, simply to be in her presence." John's comments were met with continued murmurs of denial until they arrived at the castle, where William hurried off to the stables to escape Elise until he was ready to be found.

John slipped inside the castle by the servants' entrance to avoid running into his mother, then sought the sanctuary of his room. He would need to spend time in prayer before he met his family for the evening meal.

Deceiving his parents was not his intent, but the truth of his plan was his to keep until the right time.

The dread weighing heavy on his chest confirmed, this was not the time.

～

The family meal was filled with excited chatter about the trip to London and seeing his older sister, Sarah, and her husband, Trevor, the Duke of Denham.

As John focused on his creamy carrot soup, speculations swirled around the table about when the baby would arrive. Somewhere after he progressed to his well-seasoned venison steak and roasted potatoes, he vaguely remembered hearing someone mention something about a full moon or change of seasons, which were rumored to stir the baby into coming. It could be because the same theory applied to predicting the birth of livestock.

By the time the bread pudding was served the babble had turned to each person's favorite names for either a girl or a boy. The entire conversation about babies dulled John's senses, making him grateful he was able to give his sole attention to his meal.

The servants hovered about, collecting empty plates and utensils as the items were pushed aside. His mother signaled the end of the meal by placing her napkin on the table.

Now his parents would want to discuss his reasons for not accompanying them on the trip, something he had managed to avoid until now.

Earlier in the day, he'd kept his mother talking about the herbs she used to prevent infection while she doctored his wound. And before she could mention the trip, she'd been summoned to tend a servant who suffered a bad burn—fortunate for him, but less so for the poor injured girl.

"Elise and Hanna, I hope you've finish your packing." She glanced over at Hanna and smiled. "I will be up shortly to inspect what you've chosen to bring. It must fit into the two trunks you each have in your rooms." She turned her attention to Elise. "You will not persuade your little sister to include any of your things."

"But I need..." Elise halted her protest when her father stood.

"Listen to your mother." His stern tone was softened by a smile. He stepped around the table and gave Elise an affectionate pat on her shoulder. He paused and glanced at John. "Son, according to your mother, we need to discuss your reasons for missing our trip."

John followed his parents into his father's office, a dark paneled room across from the great hall, where male guests often retreated after a meal to discuss politics and business. As

children, when John and his siblings were summoned there, it usually meant a long discussion involving their latest youthful transgression.

Withholding the true purpose of his plans from his parents gave John the same guilty feeling as when he was eight and had hit Father Simeon's horse with a rock, resulting in the old priest getting thrown off. John's punishment had been doubled because he'd also lied, denying his guilt. After a long lecture about telling the truth and accepting the responsibilities for one's actions, he found out the extent of his punishment for his childish prank. It had cost him a much anticipated trip with his father to London to see the king's knights compete in a tournament. And he had to run errands for Father Simeon for a month until the priest's bruised hip healed. It was a harsh lesson in telling the truth and doing what was right that he'd never forgotten.

But not telling his parents *everything* now was not the same as lying.

In the office, a warm fire crackled in the fireplace. Placed nearby were large, wing-backed armchairs which beckoned any who entered to sit and relax. The walls on two sides were lined floor to ceiling with bookshelves filled with well-read books his family had enjoyed for years. A set of three large leather-bound books held the lengthy genealogy of each of his parents' lineage. His parents' marriage, John's and his siblings' births were all inscribed within the thick volume on the end, leaving room for each child's marriage and future children. The thought of his page remaining blank without wife or children to continue the Stanton family name filled him with a sudden pang of regret.

He chose his favorite chair and waited for his parents to settle into their places near him.

Many well-placed candles brightened the room, but couldn't lighten his dread for the conversation to come.

His father drew his mother down beside him in an oversized

leather chair made for two to sit comfortably. The affection between his parents had always filled John with a sense of security and love.

Once he had wished to find such a match. The longing in his heart was still there, but he fought to ignore it. He had made a vow and planned to keep it.

A servant put a decanter of sherry and small cakes on a side table, then left the room and closed the door.

"Would you please explain the reason for your planned absence in our family outing?" His mother's tone conveyed her disappointment. "I'm sure it has nothing to do with hunting predators."

"I need time alone." He had his parents' full attention. The flush of guilt caused him to drop his gaze to his hands as he twisted his signet ring with the Stanton crest carved into the silver. Crossed swords of valor with a war horse in full armor on one side, and an eagle clutching arrows on the other, painted on a black background with a gold cross in the center. As a part of his heritage, he would leave it and any items of his past behind when he left the castle. "I plan to take my leisure to travel to London, and then I'll continue on to Sarah's home. It might take several weeks to arrive, but I promise I'll get there."

"Are you still troubled with nightmares about the war?" His father's concerned gaze stirred John to tell the truth.

"I...yes, though not as bad as when I first returned home." Should he tell them more? How he only managed to calm the panic those dreams evoked with prayer and the Word of God? Would that help them understand his plans to become a monk?

"We want you to go with us, John." His mother leaned forward and took his hands. "But we, better than most, understand how important it is to get alone to heal and hear from God."

"I thought your mother had died, not knowing she had barely escaped an assassination attempt on her life." His father

stroked his well-trimmed beard, something he did to gain control of his emotions. John recognized the deep regret exposed momentarily in his father's expression when he spoke of that time.

"It was a miracle I escaped." His mother's voice caught with the words. "By taking me to their convent to doctor my burns, the good sisters saved my life. They also taught me the Word of God and how to heal using herbs and prayer." She flinched, but didn't pull away, when his father rubbed her burn-scarred back.

As a child, John had seen her ugly scars only once, but he'd never forgotten. Even now, he grieved knowing how much she must have suffered escaping the burning lodge, which assassins set ablaze after trapping her inside. He'd always admired his parents for overcoming the hatred for those who had caused them so much pain and grief.

He found the concept of forgiving his enemies no easier now than when he was struck down on the field of battle. Perhaps it was because of the nightly dreams of war that stirred his hatred. If he could rid himself of those, perhaps forgiveness for himself and his enemies would follow.

"It took much longer for my heart, mind, and emotions to heal than my body." His mother leaned back into his father's embrace and smiled. "God is able to restore your peace and joy too, son." Worry furrowed her brow. "My concern is that you'll be traveling alone. Won't you reconsider and take a castle guard, or even William, along for added safety?"

"Mother, taking anyone with me would defeat the purpose of seeking solitude. My wounds are healed and I'm able to make this journey on my own, thanks to your herbs and prayers." He raised his hand when she would have interrupted. "I'll take a small supply of herbs and oils and with the knowledge you've taught me, I can help others along the way." A prick of apprehension stirred at his words.

"That's wonderful, John." His mother's approving smile sent

the burn of guilt into his gut. She probably wouldn't have looked as pleased if he'd told her his whole plan. "We want you to share your knowledge, but don't be lax in keeping your other skills honed, as well, son."

"You've trained us well to take care of ourselves. Even ten-year-old Hanna knows what to do when attacked." John tried to lighten the mood. "Yesterday, I arrived in time to see her stand her ground and challenge a young wolf. She wielded a stick like a sword, waving it and yelling at the poor scraggly thing while protecting a small fawn she had followed into the woods."

"She did what?" His mother's posture became rigid, her eyes wide with alarm.

"Calm down, Evangeline." His father hugged her. "The wolf ran off when John arrived, and he brought Hanna home unscathed. I happened to be in the courtyard when they arrived and she begged me not to tell you, lest she get punished for going into the woods alone. She knows better and promised not to do it again. Everything turned out fine."

"I need to check on my girls." His mother scowled at him and stood.

John also stood, and she hugged him tight. He inhaled her familiar scent of lavender. Her love, prayers, doctoring skills, and a fierce determination to see him healed were the reason he survived his wounds. His family was a blessing he would cherish in his heart forever.

"I'm not happy about you traveling alone, but I understand your need to do so." She touched his face. He leaned down so she could kiss him on the cheek. "I'll be praying, but you need to use wisdom and take every precaution to remain safe. Listen to God's leading." With a sigh, she stepped back, then hurried out of the room.

"I agree with your mother in this." His father grinned and patted John on the shoulder as he headed to the door. "I think it

best to assure Hanna I wasn't the one who told on her." He turned and left the room.

John listened to his father's footsteps as he climbed the stairs to the second story, and then head toward the girl's rooms in the east wing. The murmur of voices floated down and surrounded John with memories of his childhood. A family life he would never know as a monk.

An ache he couldn't describe stirred within him.

CHAPTER 2

"Julianna Westerfield, someone might see you gazing out at the passing scenery. It's not what the *blind* Princess Roseanna would do." Lois Westerfield, Julianna's mentor tugged on the younger woman's cloak to gain her attention.

"I know. You're right, Lois. It's just..." Julianna took a deep breath, inhaling the scents of wildflowers and pine. "I love the outdoors. It smells like...freedom." She turned her attention from the picturesque peacefulness of green meadows and grazing sheep, to focus on her companion within the carriage. Even the impending danger of their assignment couldn't steal her enjoyment of being out of London.

"Freedom, indeed!" Lois straightened her posture to a rigid semblance of authority, though her five-foot diminutive frame fell far short of Julianna's five-foot-five-inch height. "Julianna, you are a special agent of the Crown and the Church. Over the last ten years, since you came to the Grand-fork Institute for Higher Learning, you've been granted many special privileges and taught all manner of skills no maiden of your nineteen years can boast." She crossed her arms and tilted her chin up. "Knowledge is the true measure of power and freedom."

"We have seven riders approaching." Everett, an experienced agent in charge of their protection and transportation, spoke to them from the driver's bench through a small sliding door. "And they don't appear friendly."

Julianna tensed. "How far are we from the earl's estate?" It took a good measure of willpower not to lean out the window to see what lay behind, but a *blind* princess would have no reason for such action. This assignment hindered her natural instinct to distrust details she couldn't see for herself.

"We're close, m'lady, but the horses are tired." Steven, a young agent in training, relayed the driver's message. There was a pause and murmurs of conversation between the two men. "Everett says we can't reach the estate before the riders overtake us." Fear reflected in every word.

"He knows what to do next, Steven. Stay calm and follow his lead." Lois Westerfield, the senior agent of their little band of spies, spoke to the young man in a tone meant to relay calm and authority.

"Aye, teacher." Steven closed the small door.

Julianna knew her mentor well. The concern etched in the furrows of Lois's brow spoke louder than her words of the potential danger the riders posed.

Lois turned toward Julianna and frowned.

"As for you, *princess,* you must call me *Aunt* Lois." The older woman's concern made her tone harsh. "Do not forget, child. Our lives depend on you playing your part perfectly."

"I'm sorry, *Aunt* Lois." Julianna had been locked behind closed doors practicing every move, gesture, and word for weeks in preparation for this assignment. She stretched. Every muscle was weary from the long journey to the Earl of Arnsberg's remote estate.

Adding a tilt to her head to listen to the sounds around her, she settled into her ruse of being blind. Their success or failure depended on her producing a flawless performance. "I promise, I'll stay in character."

"See that you do. Now we must prepare for the worst." Lois straightened her unadorned matron's traveling bonnet of soft gray felt and matching wool cloak. With a flick of her wrist she produced a pearl handled dagger and hid it within the folds of her cloak.

Following Lois's lead, Julianna smoothed the wrinkles from her high-waisted gown of pale blue satin, then adjusted her matching bonnet. She put her hand into the specially designed pocket of her gown and found her dagger. The king's personal weapons maker had designed the plain black handle to fit her hand. Her grip tightened when the riders drew near.

"Driver, stop the carriage!"

Julianna risked a glance. A large unkempt man rode hard to catch up to the carriage. He had a scar on his face and was wearing a filthy tunic, which was torn and ragged. His stench wafted through the carriage window as he passed by to reach the driver.

Following Lois's lead, Julianna pulled her lavender-scented handkerchief from her sleeve to cover her nose.

"Sorry, but the Earl of Arnsberg is expectin' us and we mustn't be delayed." Everett's voice sounded strong and confident.

"You haulin' the princess he sent for?" Scarface reined his horse back until he was able to see inside the carriage.

Catching a glimpse from her peripheral vision, it took more will-power not to react to the stinky man gawking at her than Julianna had expected, in spite of her training.

"She's a looker all right." Other riders surrounded the carriage, peering into the windows, hooting, and shouting out obscenities.

Thankfully, Everett kept the carriage moving, not allowing the horses to slow.

"The earl ain't goin' to like you speakin' to Her Highness that away." Steven found his voice and fell into character as he was taught. "What do ye think the earl might do to 'em, Mister Everett?"

"I heard he cut the tongue out of the last man who disrespected him and his orders." Everett's voice rose in warning. "Disrespectin' Her Highness is the same as disrespectin' the earl."

"We ain't doin' no such thing." Scarface shouted. "Get on with ye." He waved his hand at the driver and allowed his mount to ease back a distance to keep out of the dust the carriage stirred up on the dusty road. Yet, by the sound of the men's loud complaints, they still followed.

"Everett and Steven did well don't you think?" Julianna waved her handkerchief in the air to displace the stench Scarface and his men left behind.

"Well enough." Lois's tone was not as confident as her words.

Not facing the person to whom Julianna was speaking had taken countless hours to overcome, for she found she could tell more about a person by looking them in the eye and by the way they held themselves than by their words alone.

Julianna stole a glance at her mentor. Lois rarely showed her worry, but today the furrows that creased her brow remained in plain view. As a teacher, Lois was skilled at appearing passive and devoid of emotion, but Julianna knew she cared deeply for the young people she trained and worked them harder than any of the other teachers. Of late, too many of the trainees had not survived their first assignment.

"Get ready m'ladies. We're almost to the manor's gates."

"Thank you, Steven. Don't be nervous. Everett will help you remember your part." Lois's tone was calm, yet authoritative.

"This is your first assignment, but I have confidence you'll do us proud."

"Aye, teacher." The young man slid the small door closed.

Julianna chanced another glance and watched in amazement as Lois's countenance changed. Her mouth slacked until it drooped on one side. Her perfect posture slumped and tilted to favor her left side. She lost all semblance of the cunning and highly-skilled agent of the Crown that she was, as she slipped into her role as the princess's eccentric Aunt Lois in this plot to find out the identities of the Black Guard.

Julianna swallowed and closed her eyes. *Stay alert. Look, but don't react. You mustn't let them know you can see.* She whispered the words she was taught during her training. Resuming her blind persona, she focused on the empty seatback in front of her in case Scarface decided to make another visit.

"God, be with us and keep us safe." Julianna needed God's help if they were to succeed.

"*Amen.*" Lois whispered.

CHAPTER 3

"I don't like leaving you behind." Lady Evangeline stood before John, hugged him, then touched his shoulder. Her brow furrowed, as if she sensed something was amiss.

"The lad's a highly trained soldier who's been to war, dear. I have faith he can make his way safely to London on his own. Don't fuss." Lord Henry Stanton drew his wife toward the waiting carriage and handed her inside. He glanced back at John and smiled. "You're smart, son. If I could have thought of a reason to travel later with you, I would have."

"Henry…" Lady Evangeline leaned out the window ready to protest.

"I know. No highwayman would dare challenge the two of us…" His father raised his hand in surrender and grinned.

"The three of us." Elise yelled out from within the depths of the carriage.

"The four of us." Ten-year-old Hanna added, as she leaned her head out of the window from her place across from their mother and waved her small, wooden practice sword in the air.

"Yes, absolutely, the four of us. With our Lord's help, we are a formidable army standing for good and fighting against evil." He smiled and touched Hanna's cheek before he turned back to John. "We'll expect you to arrive, hopefully, before Sarah's child is born. But, if not, soon after." He put an arm around John and gave him a fatherly squeeze. "Work out your troubles. Be safe, son."

"I shall do my best." John's parents had reluctantly submitted to his need to make the trip on his own, not surrounded by well-meaning family or eager-to-help servants. John's nightmares were well known to the whole castle, but the deciding factor for his parents, he learned this morning, was the assurance from their priest, Father Alvin, that solitude and contemplation were often beneficial for overcoming trauma.

Elise leaned out the open door. "Promise you won't forget the gift I made for you."

"I won't forget." John had met with Elise last night after their mother's inspection of his sister's luggage. Any mention of London caused Elise to cringe, as if the word inflicted the pain of bad memories best forgotten.

He understood, for not all of his scars from the war were visible. As her big brother, he would have gladly slain her enemy, but since she refused to speak of what happened, he turned his attention to her gift. He received it with great exuberance and was glad to see the return of joy and excitement in his sister's eyes. Both emotions reflected in her voice when she gave him the crozier she'd designed and carved especially for him, though how she knew he would need a staff on his journey still baffled him.

With a grin and a teasing wink, Elise slipped back inside the carriage and settled in her place beside their mother.

"It's time to go." Henry stepped into the carriage but didn't close the door. "Father, would you please pray a blessing over our family and our trip?"

"Aye." Father Alvin was a large, formidable man who still

carried himself with a warrior's commanding stance, as the career soldier he once was before he obeyed the call of the ministry. "Father God, I humbly ask that You watch over this family for safe travels and give their daughter, Sarah, a safe birth and healthy child." He looked up at heaven. "And for Your guiding hand upon John as he sojourns later to meet them. In Your Son's precious name, amen."

The door closed and the driver snapped the reins. The family's carriage led the way from the castle, followed by a wagon driven by two servants, which was filled with supplies and gifts for Sarah, her husband, and the soon to be birthed first grandchild.

As John watched his family leave, an unexpected feeling of abandonment washed over him.

"I, too, must go. I have a young couple to counsel before their wedding bans are made public." Father Alvin slapped John on the back and smiled. "Making any vow to God is serious, but those made in haste without proper retrospect are subject to be amended as God sees fit."

"What do you mean, Father?" John turned his focus from his family's departure to the priest.

"I mean that according to His Holy Scriptures, God has a plan for each person's life. If His plan is for a person to marry, then they can best serve the Lord by raising a family to honor God and His commandments." He studied John. "I know you made a vow to serve God, but I am not certain that becoming a monk is God's plan to fulfill your pledge." Father Alvin's time as a soldier was confirmed by his personal knowledge of the cost of war, also evident by the numerous battle scars on his face and arms. "I pray our Lord speaks to you about your future along the way, but you must choose to listen."

"We've already discussed this, Father. My vow to serve God and the Church if we survived was answered when William and I lived. Isn't that a sign God accepted my vow?"

"I believe taking the vow of celibacy, poverty, and service is not for every good-intended soul. I have instructed you for several months in scripture and rules of piety, now is your chance to see if you can live a monk's mission on your way to London. I've sent a missive to the good Friar Thomas to expect you. Contact him directly if you wish to continue your training when you get to the monastery."

He patted John's shoulder. "I pray the solitary time will be healing to your soul as you travel with minimal necessities and the fine staff your sister made. Forsaking material possessions, comfort, the royal status, and the respect with which you've been born and raised may be harder than you expect." He stared John in the eyes, his voice lower and grew serious. "I've found that being a good priest has often been far harder in practice than being a good soldier when conflict arises. On the occasion, when dealing with unreasonable folk, our former training dictates a volatile situation can be more easily settled at the point of a sharp blade, than with a soft word and patience."

He raised his face toward heaven and loosed a deep breath. "However, prayer and the sword of God's Holy Word can be far more effective at bringing true and lasting peace." He paused and his tone lightened. "I do admit, on more trying occasions, of having used a combination of the two—a sharp blade and the Holy Word."

Smiling, he tugged the sleeve of John's finely woven linen tunic, then from the ground beside him, he picked up and handed him a worn leather bag, the type carried by soldiers to protect their few earthly belongings. "Trading your fine garments for the plain robe and sandals of a monk, which are inside my old kit, should help you remember your mission and—"

Before he could finish, an old woman on a donkey led by a young woman, came toward them.

"Sister Olthea!" Father Alvin rushed forward to greet them.

"You should be in bed. I planned to come and see you before the evening meal."

"Oh, Father, I tried to tell 'er." The young woman dropped the donkey's lead rope and tugged a shawl up around the old woman's hunched shoulders. "Just as I thought she'd drawn 'er last breath, she sat straight up and insisted the Lord told 'er to go at once to the castle to meet Lady Evangeline's stubborn son."

"Wait." Before John could voice his protest for being called stubborn, the old woman waved her hand at the girl hovering beside her.

"Don't fuss, Bethie." She glanced up at Father Alvin. "Just as I heard the angels sing and glimpsed the pearly gates of heaven, God woke me and told me I must do this last thing before I go home to live with Him forever." Olthea tapped the donkey on the left shoulder, and the animal obediently knelt down. The old woman turned to Father Alvin. "Give me a hand, priest."

"Gladly." Father Alvin smiled and gently helped the frail woman off the beast. He remained close by her side with a hand on her back for support. "Even though you are a devout Protestant, I still consider you part of my flock."

"Aye, you're a good man, Alvin, but I 'aven't come to debate the differences in our beliefs." She motioned to John. "You, young man, come here."

Like the donkey, John too obeyed and took a knee before her out of respect and to look her in the eyes. As frail as her body appeared, her eyes were clear and dark as a deep well, which sent a chill down his spine. Infirmed or not, this woman exuded power and authority.

"I've been sent to you with a twofold purpose." She leaned closer. "Hand me the rope." Bethie quickly handed Olthea the donkey's lead. "I was told to give you my most valuable possession." She clutched the woven hemp, as if reluctant to release it. "My husband, Wallis, found her orphaned beside the road and gave her to me less than a month before he passed away." With a gentle touch, she brushed her hand over the donkey's long ear. "She was such a wee thing. A few days old and alone after the wolves killed her mother. For the past thirteen years, this sweet donkey has been my closest and most devoted companion."

The donkey stood from its kneeling position and edged closer to Olthea until it was nearly leaning on the fragile woman. John feared the beast would knock her over. She put a shaky arm over the donkey's neck and ruffled the short mane, causing the animal to close its eyes, as if content with her mistress's gentle touch.

"Look closely, young man." She traced the line of black hair across and down each shoulder, then pointed down the animal's back. "Jesus rode on a borrowed donkey not long before His crucifixion. Since then, God blessed each of these animals with the mark of the cross."

John leaned in until he saw the pattern. A narrow stripe of dark hair ran down its back and a line crossed horizontally at the shoulders, something he'd never noticed before.

"Here." She pressed the rope into John's hand. "Her name is Precious." She squinted and pointed a crooked finger at him. "Say it."

John stared at the rope and then the beast, speechless until the priest bumped John's shoulder.

"Ah-h. The donkey's name is Precious." Though his little sister, Hanna, often used the word to describe many things from puppies to piglets, he had never had an occasion to use it, especially regarding anything like the long-eared, raggedy beast before him. "I thank you, Sister Olthea, but I can't take her. I'm about to leave on a trip, and I don't know when I'll return."

The old woman sighed and looked up to heaven. "Oh, Lord, are you sure?" She closed her eyes, then opened them. "You are to take Precious with you on your journey, for the Lord says you'll have need of her along the way." She frowned and took a deep breath that looked like it might have toppled her, if not for the donkey and Father Alvin's support. "You will be sorely tempted, but you must not give her away, abandon her, or treat her unkindly."

She rubbed the donkey's head and leaned over to speak into its long ear. "This is your new master, Precious." The donkey shook its head and gave a little bray that sounded like the donkey version of John's protest. Olthea glanced up at John. "This is a sacred trust. Do you agree to do as instructed?"

"Yes, Sister." The words were out of his mouth before he could stop them. He had been praying for God's leading, but taking a scruffy-looking, contrary donkey with him to London? Was this another hasty vow of which the priest had warned? The tug in his spirit suggested there was something bigger than his own plans taking place here.

"Fine." She gave him her first smile, warming him deep inside, as if the ice that had settled around his heart since the war had begun to thaw. "One more thing." She was visibly weakening before his eyes, and he suddenly feared she would expire before she had her final say.

John motioned to a hovering servant. "Quickly, bring a chair." To another, "Get the open carriage brought around to take Sister Olthea home. Make sure Cook sends some fresh broth and whatever supplies Bethie thinks they will need."

After the servant sent a messenger to the stable to fulfill John's other request, the man escorted the younger woman into the castle. John waited with Olthea while a chair was brought for her to use as preparations were being made for her trip home.

"Thank you, Lord. I finally get to ride in a fancy carriage before I die." Her giggle of delight turned into a hacking cough that turned her lips blue. Bethie came rushing toward them from the castle's kitchen, holding a steaming cup.

"Here, breathe in the vapors." She held it in front of the old woman until color returned to her lips. "It's a mixture of herbs, peppermint, and…"

"Enough prattle. I must finish my message." Olthea pushed the cup away and glanced up at John. "I was told to tell you, don't be stubborn with your opinion of what God expects of you in His service. He has a plan for your life which is quite different from what you might imagine."

She drew the cup closer and took another deep breath. "Like your friend protected you, you are to protect Precious and the charges God is sending your way. It will take every skill you've learned to keep them safe. I am to remind you of God's Holy Word, Romans 8:28. Look it up or have the priest find it for you." Spent, the old woman leaned more heavily against the donkey that remained by her side.

John searched his memory for the scripture she quoted. *We know that all things work together for good to them that love God, to them who are the called according to His purpose.* Was it meant as a warning or a promise?

"Be forewarned, Lord Stanton. Precious won't budge unless ye use 'er name. Sister Olthea trained her that way so no one could steal 'er." Bethie smiled as she offered the dangling rope to John. "The beast has a mind of 'er own and will take every advantage of yur distractions."

"I shall purpose to do my best." He glanced down at the rope, surprised that he had missed its removal from his grasp. With a scowl at the donkey, he again took possession of the lead.

The carriage pulled up and Father Alvin carried Olthea to it and helped settle her against the plush seats.

"I feel like Enoch in the Bible when the Lord sent down His own chariot to gather him home." Her words were barely above a whisper.

Bethie secured the supplies from the kitchen on the floor, by their feet, and covered the old woman with a fine wool blanket, left in the carriage for such a purpose. The anticipation of riding in the large roofless conveyance obviously brought great joy to the old woman, one who had probably worked hard all her life without knowing such pampering.

A heavy knot of guilt pressed against his chest for the many privileges and luxuries he'd taken for granted his whole life.

"Brother John...don't forget..." Her breath was coming in short gasps between words. "Talk to God...He will hear you." She smiled. "Like you...Precious has secrets."

"Thank you. I won't forget." He sent a quick glance around and hoped no one saw his surprise when she'd called him Brother John, the name he would use on his journey. No one but Father Alvin knew of his plans to walk to London or travel as a monk.

The old woman closed her eyes and relaxed against the seat. Father Alvin climbed up onto the carriage next to the driver to escort the women home. After his wave good-bye, the carriage departed.

The donkey tried to follow, and by her braying, she was not at all amused that her mistress had left her behind.

This time, John kept a firm grip on the rope. When the carriage was out of sight, John tugged on the lead, but the donkey wouldn't move.

"Come on, you lop-eared beast." John tried to shove the donkey forward, but her stiff-legged stance made it impossible. Against his will, he submitted to Bethie's instruction. "Precious, come along." The reluctant animal allowed John to lead her into the barn where he made sure she was well fed and watered.

He too needed nourishment, so he went to one of his favorite places in the castle, a cozy table in an alcove closest to the kitchen where the family chose to sit for less formal meals. He partook of a satisfying amount of lamb stew and warm bread smeared with freshly churned butter. This might be his last hearty feast for a long while, so he took his time and savored every bite.

An uneasy feeling, as when he went off to serve in the king's army, washed over him. He recognized the familiar flutter of excitement and anticipation of a new adventure, but this time it was overshadowed by the heaviness of responsibility and a holy commitment to fulfill his vow.

As John finished his second serving, William came into the dining alcove.

"I'm starved." He wiped his freshly washed hands with a towel handed to him by a servant before he flopped down across from John. "I've been up since before dawn, but me and my men found and dealt with the pack of wolves attacking sheep in the north pasture." He leaned back as the cook's assistant placed a large bowl of lamb stew before him and refilled the plate of bread and butter. "Thank you, Mildred." He waited until the woman left before he said a quick prayer and dug into the feast with the zeal of a person who hadn't eaten in a week.

"Sorry I missed the hunt. I take it you got them all?"

William nodded, unable to speak with his mouth full. "There were only three wolves in this pack, but they were some of the biggest and most vicious I've ever encountered." He spoke between bites. "Seeing those huge beasts up close reminded me of the stories old man Barton used to tell when we were kids. You know the ones about the giant wolf-like beasts that roamed the land in ancient days that were big enough to swallow a boy whole." He laughed. "Glad these wolves weren't quite that big."

"I remember the nightmares those stories gave me as a child." John smiled. "Sounds like you need to increase patrols to make sure no more of them appear."

"I thought the same and have already doubled the patrol for the next few weeks to make sure we got them all." Waving his buttered bread in the air, he regaled John with the high points of the hunt.

All John could think of was what would have happened if

those beasts had cornered little Hanna in the forest, instead of that half-grown wolf cub he ran off when he found her. "Do what you must to end this danger before a child is hurt."

William glanced up and nodded, then went back to his story. "You should have been there. We had our hands full."

As William continued the exciting tale, John could easily imagine the adventure in vivid detail. He always enjoyed the camaraderie of the hunt, and this one proved to be more exciting than usual. But he'd lost his appetite for killing since he'd come home critically wounded from his last battle.

William dug into his second helping at a more modest pace. "With the hunt completed, you are free to leave on your holy pilgrimage whenever you choose." With his spoon paused over the bowl, William waited for John's reaction.

"Aye. I'll leave today." John raised his chin and frowned, sending his closest friend a silent, but clear signal that there would be no further discussion on the subject of his trip.

William had barely finished his last bite when one of his huntsmen hurried into the room.

"Lord Stanton, a villager says he spotted a dead deer at the edge of the forest. Two strangers had passed by his hut early this morn. Could be poachers." He glanced from John to William, waiting for instructions.

"Gamekeeper, this is your business." John rose from the table and waited as his friend wiped his mouth and stood. "I'll say my good-bye now so you can be on your way."

William grabbed his jacket from the hook by the door.

"Aye. We've no time to lose if 'tis poachers. We need to stop them before they've taken anymore of the castle's game. I'd like to catch the thieves red-handed to see if it's the hungry wanting meat to fill their empty bellies, or rebels who have chosen to test our laws." William paused and smiled. "I pray God's guidance and safety be with you on your trip, m'Lord." When there were witnesses around he fell back to addressing John and his family by their proper titles. The chasm between servants and nobles, low-born and high-born was not to be ignored, at least in front of those who hadn't earned their trust and friendship.

"And the same for you and your huntsmen." John watched William from the doorway as he swung up onto his horse. He placed his peg leg in a specially made sling Elise had designed to give him balance and support while riding.

Regret burned John's conscience that his friend's sacrifice to save John's life had cost him his leg, which made the sling necessary.

William left at a gallop, headed in the direction of the village. Six huntsmen followed, all armed with swords, bows, and spears.

It was getting late in the afternoon when John and the donkey finally left on his quest, but he was determined to leave, lest something urgent came up needing his immediate attention. The castle had competent staff to handle most any crisis, but they would come to him first if he remained.

Strapping his supplies on the donkey would allow him to wait and change into his monk's robe and sandals after he was well away from the village. He would shave his beard and cut his hair then, too. Shaving the top of his head to complete the tonsure would happen after he had finished his officiates training and took his vows.

Leaving his sword behind was, to him, a symbol of walking away from his old life. A sense of relief lightened his steps.

He chose a secondary road less likely to be used by carriages and wagons because of its narrow winding passage before it too met up with the main road. Because of its infrequent use, he should make it a good distance away from the castle before he chanced an encounter of anyone who knew him. Overgrown brush and trees threatened to reclaim the trail in places. After a couple of hours, they passed by a particularly dense section of forest. A loud rustle from the underbrush made the donkey sidestep, bumping into John.

"Don't worry, donkey, you're too ornery and tough for a lion or a wolf to bother with you for its next meal. Besides, I promised your mistress I'd protect you." Yet the thought of fending off vicious wolves or other predators with only a staff had him second-guessing his decision to leave his sword behind.

The wooden staff Elise had made him fit his palm perfectly and the weight well balanced. He tested it with a few practice jabs into the air, satisfied that if need be, it could be used to fend off man or beast.

He had hesitated accepting her gift only after she insisted the *mechanics* came to her in a dream. She'd refused to explain. Instead, she grinned and said she couldn't wait for him to find out its secrets. What kind of mechanics was needed for a walking staff?

He touched the intricate carving of leaves and vines that decorated the rod the first ten inches down from the top, leaving the remaining length unadorned. Rubbing his hand down the smooth finish, he found nothing that indicated anything mechanical.

A tug on the rope turned his attention to Precious. She had stopped to graze beside the road, taking advantage of his wandering thoughts. He hadn't realized how far they'd traveled, but the sun was waning, forcing him to make camp and get changed before dark.

He led the donkey to a small stream for her to drink, then tied her to a tree, leaving a length of rope long enough for her to graze. With her secured, he searched through his supplies for his monk's robe and sandals and slipped them on. He had packed everything into his own kit and sent a servant to return Father Alvin's to him. Not to return it empty, he filled it full of wine, vegetables, and grain, and added a portion of mutton as a thank you gift for all he'd done for John.

The coarseness of the habit's fabric would take getting used to, along with the other changes required for his transformation. He pulled his dagger from his gear and hesitated only a few moments before he shaved his beard high on each side above the ear, then spent several minutes cutting his hair short enough to conform to a novice monk.

An odd sensation of loss surprised him when he touched his bare face and neck. How would he feel when the top of his head was shaved? He'd never given his hair much thought except when it needed washed, tended, or tied out of his way with a thin strip of leather.

He tossed away the cut hair and tucked the unneeded piece of leather into the bag, along with his former clothing. Inside he found his flask of water and the linen bag containing a small pouch of parched grains and dried fruit he'd packed before he left.

He ran his hand down the staff again, but found no indentation or lever that Elise implied she had included in her creation.

Thinking of mysteries, he couldn't help but wonder about the charges the old prophetess insisted he was to protect along the way. How would he know them?

CHAPTER 4

"Princess Roseanna, the earl has ordered yur meals be brought to yur room and requests ye and yur aunt remain 'ere until morrow's eve." Hilda's tone came across more as a gloat than a request. "'E says it's for yur safety since 'is grace has important business to take care of and can't squire ye about."

Julianna watched the buxom servant girl put down the heavy tray and flit about with the actions of one in charge.

"Where's yur aunt?" Hilda gazed about the room, then crossed over to the large wardrobe and peered inside, as if finding her there would not be out of the ordinary. "Ye need to keep better charge of the old lady. She's got 'erself lost at least a dozen times since ye got 'ere." Tugging out a fine silk robe, she held it against her heavier frame before hanging it back in the closet. "I'll send someone to find 'er."

"That won't be necessary, Hilda. She can't have wandered far. I've familiarized myself with the manor and can navigate quite well. If my Aunt Lois doesn't return presently, I'll go and find her myself."

"No!" Her voice rose, and her arrogance changed to fear. "His lordship insists ye both remain in yur room so as not to disturb 'is plans for the evening." Hilda smoothed her apron, allowing her expression to return to smug authority. "Stay where yur at. I'll send a body to find and fetch 'er back 'ere…again."

She lit the fireplace and the two candlesticks nearest the door, leaving the rest of the room in shadows, for the sightless princess would not have need of light. Hesitating before putting her hand on the door handle, she turned back toward Julianna. "I'll not be able to attend ye this evening, for I'm needed to serve 'is lordship's new guests." She frowned as if trying to discern the princess's willingness to obey the earl's orders. "Lydia will come later to aid ye getting ready for bed."

Without waiting for a reply, she slipped through the door and closed it with a click. The echo of heavy footsteps revealed her path as she left the guest's wing.

"Hilda, you have no idea with whom you are really dealing." Julianna whispered as she stood and stretched. Now that she was alone, she roamed around the room freely, able to drop her blind pretense, hopefully for the last time.

The armchair where she'd been sitting faced the door, and gave her the advantage when anyone entered, as well as a view of the whole room. The nearby window afforded her a spacious view of the courtyard and could provide a way of escape in an emergency, though she prayed that would not be necessary. It was a long way down to the ground, and because of the heavy covering of moss growing on the north wall, the limestone would be extremely slippery.

She couldn't wait to be gone from this place. Being in the presence of the loathsome Augustine Grimmer, Earl of Arnsberg, and pretending to be awed by his home and person irked her beyond measure. The earl's raspy voice was as repulsive as his sweaty touch. She had used every skill she'd mastered over the years to remain in character.

A delectable aroma drew her to the tray Hilda had delivered. She raised the silver cover to check the food.

"Really?" She flicked a spindly brown spider off the platter's edge, no doubt the wench's doing. As the earl made his intentions to court Princess Rosanna known to the servants, Hilda's ill-disguised jealousy had become more and more annoying. The title, Earl of Arnsberg, was merely an honorary title bestowed upon him for services rendered to the Crown. What exactly he did to earn it she hadn't been able to uncover, but the title came with this small estate and modest funds to run it.

Now he wanted an heir, which required a new wife, preferably with royal blood, since he had none, though he fabricated a kinship to a distant cousin of the king. Because of the research given her, she knew him to be the illegitimate son of a disgraced knight and a serving wench.

The servant girl's dreams of being the next bride of the manor would never happen and could endanger her life if the earl found out about her meddling in his affairs. If the rumors were correct, the earl's last two wives had met with suspicious deaths when they failed to give him an heir, so getting rid of a mere servant would not even raise brows.

She felt sorry for the girl, but putting up with her childish pranks had grown tiresome. The Grandfork Institute for Higher Learning excelled in teaching its students far more effective ways when dealing with nuisances, as the serving girl would soon discover.

Over their morning tea, Lois confessed to Julianna of making a covert visit to the spiteful girl's quarters two days ago, when all of the servants were busy about their early morning chores. Her retribution was inspired by an especially noxious vine Lois had found on one of her walks in the garden. She'd used gloves to harvest the leaves, then dried them.

With a sardonic smile and a gleam of satisfaction in her eyes, she casually mentioned sprinkling a generous amount of the powdered plant over the girl's blankets and bed linens. The result of the weed's residue on bare skin would cause relentless itching and a rash. After one night in her bed, the wench would be too occupied with her own discomfort to cause them any trouble for days. With her lack of a rash, she apparently hadn't spent the last two nights in her own bed, thwarting Lois's efforts to remove the nosy wench from snooping.

Julianna was glad Lois had restrained her retribution to less lethal means, for as much as she disliked Hilda, she didn't warrant a death sentence, unlike her traitorous master.

The very thought of the earl's evil deeds set Julianna's nerves on edge. She drew her dagger, checked the edge for sharpness then replaced it inside the hidden pocket in another of her specially designed dresses. The king gave Julianna and Lois strict orders not to dispatch the earl, only bring back the evidence against him and his followers. The king wanted the pleasure of sending all of the Black Guards to the gallows as a public warning to others who might be tempted to rebel against the Crown.

The aroma of garlic and chicken filled the room and reminded her she was hungry. Checking to make sure there were no other nasty surprises, she picked up one of the chicken pasties from the tray and broke it in half. The crust flaked beneath her fingers, allowing the steam to escape and fill the air with the delectable scents of sage, garlic, and other herbs. One nibble of the creamy, well-seasoned filling and she was assured there were no foul additions to the cook's recipe. After finishing one, she ate another, and then wrapped the remaining four in one of the linen napkins from the tray. She was tempted to eat one more, but Steven and Everett were always hungry and would appreciate the snack.

No doubt Lois had eaten by now and hopefully secured more food for their trip, while she snooped for more evidence against the earl and his contacts. Julianna, Lois, Steven, and Everett would need to travel as fast as the carriage horses could safely be driven, stopping only long enough to water and rest the team before resuming their trip. There would be no time to stop at inns along the way. Napping in the carriage would have to do until they arrived in London and delivered their findings. She didn't look forward to the bone-jarring trip, but their mission was too important to delay.

Lois had discussed dividing the team and sending the men to take the carriage on to London, while she and Lois traveled by boat, which would be the faster route. The dread of not knowing who to trust, with so many traitors with ill intent toward the king, had her second guessing every decision.

Julianna drew a deep breath to calm her nerves. Lois would know what to do. Still, a shiver of apprehension chilled her spine with the many dangers that could hinder them--too many for her peace of mind.

Until time for their departure, she had to wait—her least favorite part of any assignment.

During their visit, to assure her that his home was fit for a princess of her royal lineage, the earl had escorted her around the manor, visiting each of the downstairs rooms. Lois had followed in pretended disinterest, waiting for her opportunity to disappear unnoticed from the tour to check out his office more thoroughly.

During her third search, she located a hidden wall safe behind an oil painting depicting the king's palace. Fortunately, Lois had skills that made opening the safe an easy task. She snatched a stack of papers and returned to their room. The documents proved the earl's duplicity as one of the leaders in the Black Guard.

"Oh, no." Lois had handed Julianna several sheets of papers. The memory of her mentor's grim expression still stirred a ripple of fear in Julianna.

Julianna's heart sped up as she had read through the content. Lois had stolen a signed directive for the assassination of the King of England, by a dozen high-ranking officials. Another document included an order to send a network of hired assassins throughout the kingdom to kill all who could claim the monarchy after the king's death. The murders could count in the hundreds if they sought every person with a bloodline tracing to the throne. One of the papers listed several names, even the real Princess Roseanna's father. Her name must have been left off the list as bride for the earl, giving him legal right to claim the throne.

Julianna ran a hand over the leather pouch containing the documents, which was tied around her waist and hidden by the many layers of her dress. It would have been nice to identify all of the Black Guard's followers, but her team's goal was to live long enough to deliver their evidence. The king's soldiers would be sent to arrest the earl, and the king's chief jailer would be expected to glean from the earl each Black Guard member's name with whatever means necessary, even torture.

A chill passed over her with the knowledge that the same fate that awaited the earl would happen to her and Lois, if their ruse was discovered before their mission was complete.

Impersonating the real Princess Roseanna Kent had been more difficult than she could have imagined. Unlike the princess, Julianna was neither blind, nor a legitimate member of the royal family.

Julianna's father had made sure she would never use his name or title when he abandoned her to the Grandfork Institute for Higher Learning. She rubbed the distinctive scar just below her right elbow, which stirred a familiar ache whenever she thought of her father's betrayal.

She cleared her throat. There were more important things to do than whine about the injustices of life that she could do nothing about…for now.

Julianna busied herself lighting more candles to displace the gloom.

In her previous assignments, she had been many things including a beggar, a stable hand, and a servant. One time only, she had pretended to be a prostitute. Thankfully, she never had to go so far as to give herself to the mark to achieve her goal, but she would never forget having the same heart-pounding fear of failure that stirred in her now. Her mistake then could have cost her everything.

She rubbed her arms to erase the memory of the horrid man's hands on her. The wine decanter on the table only served to remind her of how even a small error could cost them their lives. The drugged wine she'd fed the mark had eventually sent him into a deep sleep, but not before he'd grabbed for her and torn her gown. She should have used more sleeping potion because of the man's large girth. The terror of his sudden attack had been followed by weak-kneed relief when he finally collapsed unconscious. Not trusting how long he would remain asleep, she'd hurried her search of his quarters.

The stolen jewels and love letters she had been sent to recover were the bounty of a trusting liaison between the old chancellor's young wife and the charming thief posing as a scholar in need of a benefactor. To save embarrassment, Julianna had been hired independently, which was allowed on occasion, and sent to retrieve the stolen items in question.

What she found was something of far more value. Sensitive documents taken from the office of the king's chancellor were hidden in a cleverly designed leather pouch around the thief's waist. After examining and memorizing the materials, she later turned over everything to the chancellor's wife, but kept the soft leather pouch as a reminder of how easily one could be deceived by a liar with a handsome face. And...the consequences of what could go wrong on an assignment no matter how well she'd prepared.

The horrified woman had promised to return the documents to their hidden cabinet, hoping her husband would never be the wiser. If knowledge of the document's theft had reached the king, the chancellor and his wife would have been hung for treason. The emotional woman had rewarded Julianna with a modest amount of silver—far less than either her or her lover's miserable lives were worth, for Julianna's silence. She also promised to be of help if Julianna ever had need.

Julianna seriously doubted the adulteress could be trusted to keep her word—any more than Augustine Grimmer, the Earl of Arnsberg had honored his vow of allegiance to the King of England and the realm when Prince John took the throne.

Julianna's failure to inform the king about those stolen papers could still result in the same fate as the earl faced if the matter were found out. Fortunately, the stolen documents were only impending treaties, which would be negotiated and changed many times before being signed. Therefore not of significant importance to bother the king when he had far more urgent matters pending...like finding the leaders of the Black Guard before they carried out their death threats against him.

Julianna rubbed her arms to ward off the icy fear that the warmth of the fire couldn't displace. Had she played her part well enough this time to avoid suspicion?

The very atmosphere of the manor over the last two days had changed from pompous gaiety to hushed whispers and tense, short-tempered servants. The change had alerted her and Lois that something big was about to happen.

Unable to remain still, Julianna again went to the door,

hoping to hear her mentor's footsteps. Only silence, except for the loud ticking of the clock in their quarters. The feeling of imminent danger seemed to get stronger with every passing minute.

Since the documents were safely in their possession, Lois had agreed they needed to flee tonight. After the noon meal, she had alerted Everett to have the carriage waiting near the side servant's entrance at the eighth hour when there would be a changing of the guards. The darkness would allow for a safer departure. With the added confusion of guests coming and going there should be far less scrutiny.

"Lois, where are you?" She glanced at the clock again. Her mentor had left their room over two hours ago, dressed as a servant in hopes of seeing the earl's guests arriving. Had one of the servants recognized her?

Julianna paced to the door, but withdrew her hand from the knob. "Don't panic. She's fine." If she kept saying that maybe it would be true.

Lois couldn't have been discovered, or someone would have brought her to their room. Disguised as a serving wench, Lois was cunning enough to blend into the staff, and since guests often brought their own servants with them, there would be many strangers helping serve. Lois had an amazing ability to recall any event she saw or conversation she'd overheard, and she was fluent in seven languages and skilled with most weapons, including poison. Still, there was always the element of unpredictability to factor into the danger of being discovered.

When the chime of the clock sounded out the seventh hour, Julianna turned from the fire.

She couldn't wait any longer for Lois's return. It was time to finish preparation for their departure. Their plan was to meet at the carriage if either was delayed.

From deep within the wardrobe, she pulled out a small

leather valise. She removed her necklace, which held the key needed to unlock the case. The valise contained the jewelry borrowed for this assignment, items far more valuable than those retrieved for the chancellor's wife. The headmaster of the institution, Sir Alistair Craven, didn't know the identities of the agents the king would use for the assignment, but he voiced his strong opposition, because of the great risks involved. However, he obeyed the king's order to take charge of providing the expensive items needed for their ruse. The headmaster, above all else, expected the emeralds, rubies, sapphires, and diamonds to be returned, even if they, the lowly spies didn't survive.

From a secret compartment within the case, she used the same key to open and withdraw the letter she had forged before the trip calling them back to London and a second letter scripted by Lois to explain their sudden departure. She rubbed a finger over the official insignia on the missive, authenticating it as from the royal house. It was as good a forgery as she'd ever made. A certain amount of pride warmed her. The second note was more crudely written, as if penned by the shaky hand-writing of a doddering old woman, to the earl on the blind Princess Roseanna's behalf.

In place of the letters, she secured the jewelry, which she wrapped in a soft cloth, and relocked the compartment.

She gave a quick glance around for the best place to leave the letters where they could be easily spotted. After securing them beneath a heavy candlestick on the mantle, so they wouldn't fall into the fire, she stepped back to make sure they could be seen from the door.

With all of the guests arriving and the disruption of the household, she hoped the earl would believe she had received an emergency missive from her guardian to come home imme-diately, for her father was gravely ill and requesting her pres-ence. The real Princess Roseanna had been abandoned by her father to the institute when she lost her sight, so Julianna knew her well. After helping Julianna prepare for the assignment, the princess was sent into hiding to a distant abbey, under another name. Her father was locked away in a remote monastery far from London until the assignment was completed. She hoped he remained there until they were all safely home.

To the small valise, she added a change of clothes for herself and Lois. For each of them, she chose a simple unlined linen shift with a loose fitting tunic as a covering, which could be folded tight enough to fit into the narrow space. Hopefully, the boys had protected the supplies they had left hidden in the carriage knowing their need for a quick departure.

Lois had taught her students to always have a secondary stash of money, a change of clothes, food, a flask of clean water, and weapons to access for emergencies while on assignment.

With the emergency supplies in the carriage as their primary source, this small case became their secondary stash. As she closed and locked the valise, her hand brushed the hem of her favorite gown hanging in the closet. The blue silk shimmered in the candlelight, changing from the light blue of a morning sky to a dark stormy sapphire. Lois said the shade of sapphire matched Julianna's eyes when she was angry. Having worn it once, only long enough for the seamstress to declare it finished, she hated leaving it behind the most. Besides the color, she had loved the way the fabric flowed like liquid around her hips and legs as she moved.

She ran her hand over the silks, fine wools, and satins. She'd never owned such expensive finery, all of which were designed specifically for her by the queen's own seamstress. Leaving the beautiful gowns for Hilda to fawn over was only tolerable when she remembered the powdered weed in the girl's bed. Once the wench was covered in a rash, it would be a long while before she would have thoughts of wearing anything that touched her irritated skin, no matter how fine the weave of the cloth. Of course, the girl would recover eventually with no lasting after-effects.

Leaving a closet full of expensive garments was intended to confirm the other note written by Lois about not wanting to disturb the earl and his guests with their hasty departure. The words assured him of the princess's plans to return to the manor once the crisis was over. If the clothing's presence in the wardrobe diverted suspicion and gave them time to get away, the sacrifice of the garments would be well worth it.

She pulled on her traveling cloak. No time to mourn the silly loss of gowns. Her sole focus needed to be on the mission. With a leather strap, she attached the small cylinder case around her waist and settled it in the small of her back, hidden beneath her cloak to leave both hands free. She tried to open the door. It was locked.

Julianna tightened her jaw.

"You little rat. Were you afraid I would show up and take attention away from you? Or perhaps you feared your master's wrath if we dismissed his orders and refused to be kept prisoners in our room for the night?" The lock must be well oiled, for she never heard it engage. Good! Then it would work to her advantage too.

Julianna tugged an ornate hairpin from her coiffeur. The long, slender spike worked equally well as a weapon. She retrieved one of the notes from the mantle and slid it halfway under the door. With a slight poke in the keyhole with the hairpin, the key on the outside of the door dropped onto the paper, and she pulled it inside the room. A giggle of delight bubbled from within her. It was such a simple task to escape if one knew what to do. When the servant, Lydia, came later tonight, she would find the door locked but no key. The fault would fall on the devious Hilda. With so many guests needing attention, it could take a while to find the master key and investigate Julianna's silence. She returned the note to its place under the candlestick and left the room, locking the door and pocketing the key.

Hopefully, she would see Lois from the top of the servants' stairway. She listened until there were no sounds of footsteps from the foyer below, then slipped into the hidden alcove.

After days roaming around the manor, she'd found the perfect hiding place to view the banquet room. The dark corner allowed her to remain hidden from the view of the ten or so men below. Uncovering the plans and identities of the traitors could be worth the added danger if they weren't discovered in the process.

She made a mental note of every feature of each stranger. The earl sat at the head of the long banquet table, his demeanor deceptively jovial. However, the humor did not reach his eyes, which were narrowed with concentration. His gaze scanned the room, as if expecting trouble.

Surprise sucked the breath from her when she spotted Lois. She was flitting around the room filling mugs of ale and wine, her girth padded to make her look fat, dressed as a servant with a floppy lace head covering, which hid a good portion of her artificially aged features. Old servants were usually ignored, and her disguise kept her virtually invisible to the men she served and to the other servants, who never questioned an extra pair of hands to help with the work. Every movement was fluid, with care given not to spill a drop or do anything to draw attention.

Lois stilled. Julianna knew her mentor's every mood and her current stiff stance conveyed fear. What had she seen? As Julianna searched the room, the feeling of evil seemed to hover in every shadow as conversation stopped, then resumed in more subdued tones.

A new guest had arrived. He faced away to speak to a servant. When he turned toward the banquet room, she saw his face.

Julianna gasped.

Frederick Compton! The king's chief advisor…and the only man who would recognize both Julianna and Lois as spies. He must be the reason the other spies had lost their lives.

Lois must have realized Julianna was watching, for she brushed her hand over her left cheek, the signal to flee, before she strode out of the room.

They were to meet at the carriage. The clock in the great hall chimed eight—the changing of the guards. There was no time to lose.

Julianna hurried down the stairway, hoping to avoid running into another soul. She reached the servants' entrance that led to the kitchen and controlled her pace, not to raise suspicion. The exit was mere steps away.

Fear pounded in her chest when she smelled the distinctive scent of tobacco laced with mint. She knew of only one man who used that blend.

"Girl, can you direct me to the wine cellar?" Lord Compton's voice was unmistakable.

Julianna froze. She clutched a dagger hidden beneath her cloak. Rather than turn and risk him seeing her face, she pointed the way with her left hand.

"That way, yo'r lor'ship." Her voice mimicked the cook's uneducated droll with an accent of low country. The sleeve of her cloak slipped up and exposed the "J" shaped scar above her wrist. She dropped her arm to her side, hoping he hadn't noticed the mark or the fine cloak she was wearing. She held her breath, ready to attack if necessary.

"Your Lordship. Please allow me to personally escort you to the wine cellar. I've been instructed to allow you to pick any bottle from the earl's fine collection." The wine steward's voice was enough to distract Lord Compton.

Julianna made her exit and hurried to the carriage waiting in the shadows. Lois leaned out and motioned for her to hurry. Once Julianna stepped inside, Everett set the carriage in motion, keeping to the servant's paths until they reached the road, then whipped the horses into a gallop equal to their desperate need to escape. They had a long way to go and very little time to get there.

Julianna couldn't shake the feeling that the most dangerous part of their journey had just begun.

"But for my vow, vile donkey, I would let you rot in this stinkin' briar patch without a second thought." John wiped the sweat off his brow and continued to disentangle the beast from its prison of sharp barbs. The scratches on his hands, exposed arms and legs bled and burned from the thorns. He cut away the last of the hindering vines with the dagger he carried for skinning small game and cutting food for his dinner.

According to his growling stomach, his last meal had been too many hours ago. His sword would have made short work of this nightmare, but he might have been tempted to do more than dispose of the torturous mess.

"If you escape again, I am of a mind to repent of my vow and leave you to whatever predicament in which you next find yourself." With the beast finally freed, he tugged on her lead, but she refused to move.

He loosed a string of less savory words more suited to low-born soldier's vocabulary than a monk's, then succumbed to the animal's stubbornness. "Come, Precious." The words tasted like bile in his mouth every time he was forced to address the beast. She wouldn't move or obey without being properly entreated.

Still grumbling, he led her to a nearby stream where he doctored her wounds before he tended to his own. After cleansing them with water, he applied one of his mother's herbal salves he'd brought with him for such an occasion, though he never expected to have to share it with the mean-tempered, long-eared bane of his existence. Though at the present, she stood amazingly still and suspiciously contrite while he ministered to her. At least she hadn't bitten or kicked him in the process, but he refused to let his guard down.

It was hard not to blast the beast with contempt, since she was the reason for most of their miseries. But with the many aches and pains he'd suffered because of her exploits, once started, his rants might escalate into more yelling and cursing. Hardly the conduct of someone who claimed to serve the Church, so it was better to keep his mouth closed.

She was a master at untying knots, no matter how compli-cated. But he found tying the end of her lead higher than she could reach, even standing on her hind legs, worked best for keeping her secured when unattended.

The old wound in his side ached from sleeping on the hard ground, and climbing up a tree took more effort than he could manage last night. He'd remembered a technique used on the horses while in the king's army to keep them from wandering away, yet allowed them to graze when not needed. Using the same type of hobble on the donkey's front fetlocks hadn't worked though. The beast had managed to untie his interpreta-tion of a triple-over-and-under-knot with the end woven inside. He'd have been impressed if he wasn't so angry.

Chasing down the determined beast had hindered his progress by days. Instead of helping folks along the way as was his intent, he spent his time asking for their help tracking her down. It was humiliating.

So far, his prayers had gone unanswered about the donkey, his trip, or his future. The only surprise was that he hadn't had a nightmare about the war since he had begun this trip, only about chasing the fool beast into dark phantom places he'd never been, nor hoped to ever visit.

While at the stream, he washed away his grime and put on his monk's robe, which he'd discarded before he entered the briars, lest the garment be ruined. He still had his former clothing tucked away in his kit in case of emergency, but if he wore that, he would be treated as one of privilege and might be recognized. He had no intention of giving up his quest because of briar-torn and ruined clothing.

He returned his soap and salve to the bag and tied the kit on the donkey's back, careful not to touch any of her cuts. For once, she didn't pull at her load or bare her teeth at him.

"Good. I'm glad you finally realized I'm the master in this venture."

Watered, rested, and doctored, they resumed their journey.

After an hour or so, John noticed that the donkey had walked meekly beside him and hadn't once tried to tug the lead out of his grasp when there was slack. This was highly unusual.

A twinge of guilt made him brush a hand over her nose, but there was no sign of fever, and she didn't try to bite him. Hopefully she hadn't made herself ill by eating those briars while waiting to be rescued. For a split second, he pondered her death as a way of fulfilling his obligation to the contrary beast. But he'd promised to protect her, as his friend had protected him.

"When you save my life, I'll treat you with the same respect I treat William." His rant was justified after all he'd gone through since he'd met this beast.

They rounded a bend that merged the secondary road with the more traveled main road. The donkey suddenly broke into a gallop, dragging John in her wake. It took a moment before he heard the sound of women's screams.

Blood pounded through his chest, gathering fear. The

screams reminded him of his last battle and the hostages he'd sought to rescue. His breath came faster, making him light-headed, but he refused to turn loose of the donkey's lead. The crudely made sandals were comfortable enough for walking, but not for running. The bottoms slapped against his feet with every stride, threatening to topple him onto his face in the dirt.

They came upon the sight of a fine carriage stopped in the middle of the road. Two men lay prone on the driver's seat with spears sticking out of them, dead or wounded he couldn't tell, but they were unmoving.

Two well-dressed women stood outside the carriage with their backs to him, as a couple of angry brigands stood before them, waving swords.

"Don't make trouble and maybe we'll let you live!" A red-haired brigand yelled and inched closer to them.

Precious lurched forward, jerking the rope out of John's grasp. He managed to keep hold of his staff and charged after her. Precious bared her teeth and brayed loud enough to draw everyone's attention.

The women took advantage of the distraction, by rushing the men in unison. By the time John neared them, the women had stolen the swords from the brigands and taken up a stance back-to-back. The women wielded the heavy steel blades with both hands, as if they knew how to use them.

He stumbled to a stop and his breath caught in his throat. The younger of the two women was the most beautiful female he had ever encountered. She could have been a Viking maiden by her stature and fair features, fierce with intent as she focused on one of their attackers. Her pale hair had loosed in the battle, and brushed her shoulders with every move.

John closed the gap between him and the nearest brigand.

Bleeding from a stab wound to his arm, the red-haired man swung his fist at the older woman. She ducked in time to save her face, but the punch caught her shoulder with sufficient force to knock her to the ground. The brigand kicked her in the side and twisted the sword from her grasp.

"Stop!" John swung his staff and struck the red-haired man with a hard jab to his gut. The sword fell from his hand, as the man doubled over. He stumbled backward, stepping on the old woman's ankle before falling to the ground.

Her scream of pain was followed by her very unladylike threats of retribution, which struck John as humorous from such a small woman of her advanced years.

Precious squealed as a third man, wearing a dirty green coat, leapt out of the carriage with a dagger in his hand, swiping it at John. The donkey turned and kicked the man in the side. As he hit the ground, the dagger flew from the brigand's grasp. Then the beast wheeled around and pounced on his chest with her sharp front hooves, leaving the man gasping for air.

While Precious stood over the man with teeth bared, John turned his focus again on the younger woman. Her attacker had a jagged scar across his face and a droopy eye, his expression pinched and angry.

There was something familiar about the man. Could it be?

"Get 'er Angus!" The red-headed man managed between groans as he tried to get to his feet.

The scar-faced Angus charged forward, threatening to over-power the Viking maiden.

The young woman leapt to the side with the grace of a doe avoiding a predator, and swung the captured sword with the skill of a trained warrior. Scar-face Angus jumped back, getting nicked for his effort.

The only female John had ever known with such skill was his mother, who rivaled his father in cunning and enthusiasm for battle when sparring, especially with a dull-edged practice sword.

John ran forward, swinging his staff in an arc to distract her opponent.

"Behind you!" The old woman screamed, but the warning came too late. The red-haired brigand was again on his feet. Though the man was smaller in stature than John, he still managed to swing and hit John with surprising force. His old war wound burned with intensity that threatened to bring him to his knees.

John drew a cleansing breath and used his staff to regain his footing then pointed it at his attacker. The man cursed and grabbed its end.

"You're going to die, monk. This is none of yur business!" The red-haired brigand loosed another string of curses and tried to twist the staff from John's grip.

Click.

"Aarrgh!" The man screamed in pain. His hand was impaled on a steel blade released from the end of the staff.

John stumbled backward as his opponent jerked free. Apparently a hidden blade was the surprise Elise had spoken of when she gave him the staff.

The red-haired man was bleeding profusely, as he escaped toward the carriage.

John, once again, turned to face the young woman's battle, this time armed with hardened steel.

"Look, yur ladyship all we want is for you to come with us. Please, I don't want to have to hurt you." The scar-faced attacker's high-pitched plea deepened into a threat. Focused on the woman, the man failed to notice John's approach.

The woman's glance met John's. She gave him a quick nod to convey her intent.

John tightened his grip around his staff and stood ready to aid her in her next move against the enemy.

She dropped to a knee, sword angled upward, ready to use

her position to her advantage. "Behind, you brigand." She smiled at her opponent.

The man turned toward John, swinging his dagger at him. He froze, mid-swipe, his eyes widening in recognition.

"You!" As soon as the scar-faced brigand focused on John, the Viking maiden swung her sword at her attacker's legs, hitting his right calf and cutting it deep.

Wham!

John felt a sharp pain on the back of his head. He pitched forward, landing on the Viking maiden. The world went dark.

~

Hot air blowing in his face threatened to suffocate him. John waved a hand to ward off the assault, stopping at large nostrils, then big lips opened. A hot wet tongue swiped across his hand, then his face.

"Stop! I can't breathe." He opened his eyes and found himself face to face with Precious, who was drooling over him. "What do you think you're doing, donkey?" He pushed her away.

The back of his head pounded. He brushed a hand over the area and felt a large knot. Rubbing the tender spot did not erase the pain. When he tried to sit up, the ground beneath him swayed until he stilled.

"I think she's worried about you." A voice as musical and soothing as a bubbling brook teased his hearing, while his eyes tried to focus on the source.

His breath caught as he made eye contact with the Viking maiden smiling down at him. Her hair was as flaxen as ripe wheat ready for harvest, and her eyes were as blue as a summer's morn. His pulse quickened with appreciation, until he shoved down those thoughts with a frown. His life as a monk did not allow for flights of fancy or vain imaginations about beautiful women.

"The donkey may seem happy with me at the moment, but she's usually more inclined to bite than lick me." He propped himself up to a sitting position and attempted to stand, but his legs were still too wobbly. He rested against the tree trunk nearest him. "I'm Brother John." He reached out a hand and the beautiful woman grasped it in a surprisingly firm handshake for a woman.

"I'm…" A disapproving grunt came from behind her.

"She is Princess Roseanna Kent of the royal household, and niece of His Royal Highness, King…"

"Oh, please, Aunt Lois, surely we can dispense with the titles in such dire circumstances." She turned to John and smiled. "You, kind sir, may call me Roseanna."

"And how should I address you?" John turned his attention toward the older woman, who also reclined against a tree—in considerable pain by the grimace on her face.

"Lady Kent will do nicely." The princess frowned as the old woman mumbled something in a language he didn't recognize, though his mother made sure he and his sisters were well versed in French, Latin, and Italian.

"What happened to the brigands?" He glanced around and noticed the carriage was gone, as were their attackers. His eyesight had fully cleared and strength was returning to his limbs. Using the tree for support, he stood, but had to use the oak to remain steady.

"After being toppled by a rock, you fell on me, pinning me to the ground. The brigand, who the donkey knocked down, was able to help the scar-face one escape when she went to check on you. I suspect because of the severity of their wounds, they chose to escape rather than risk further confrontation. They did so by taking our carriage." She rubbed her arm. "None would have gotten away had I been free to stop them."

"I'm terribly sorry. Next time I'm attacked from behind I'll try my best to avoid falling on you." He motioned to her arm. "Did I hurt you?"

"Nothing serious." She held up his staff and studied its intricate carvings. With a twist of her wrist the blade disappeared into the solid oak casing as if it didn't exist.

She had discovered its secrets within minutes, where he had carried the thing for almost a week and had no idea of its workings. In his defense, he had been focused on a contrary donkey he couldn't let out of his sight. At the moment, that donkey seemed content to graze on the lush grass beside the road.

"Such fine craftsmanship." The princess ran her hand down the staff's smooth surface. "Where did you have it commissioned?"

"I'd rather not say." He reached over and took possession of his property. "Tell me, how bad is your aunt injured?"

"I am not deaf, monk. I can answer for myself." Lady Kent tried to stand, tugging against a low limb. He handed the staff back to the princess and picked up the woman to set her on a fallen log. "Unhand me, young man. I am more than capable of standing on my own." Her haughty tone wavered with pain.

"I am sure of it, m'lady, but why forsake strong arms and help when offered?" John grinned and knelt in front of her to examine her swollen ankle. His headache grew more intense when he bent over, but the accompanying blurriness passed.

She gasped and slapped his hands away when he probed the injury.

"I don't think it's broken, but it is badly bruised and swollen." He leaned back and smiled.

"I am fully aware of the extent of the injury, monk. However, my niece and I have an urgent matter to attend, so if you will be so kind as to sell me your donkey, we'll be on our way." She sucked in a breath when she adjusted her position.

"As much as I would like to do as you ask, the donkey isn't for sale." He glanced over at Precious. She raised her head as if to listen to their discussion, then resumed her grazing. He was sure the beast smiled when he declined the offer to be rid of her. "She is my solemn responsibility. I promised her old master."

"You have my word, we will return her to you unharmed." The princess seemed determined to make a deal. "With the loss of our guards and carriage, we must find a way to reach London."

John was certain she rarely heard the word *no* when she wanted something, but this time he would not waver. However, if she persisted and her pleading turned into tears, he might be just as easily swayed as the next man. To avoid the temptation of ridding himself of the donkey and bask in the princess' smile of approval, he chose to ignore her and turned his attention on the older woman.

"My mother taught me and my siblings about herbs and poultices. I can help ease your discomfort and speed up the healing if you will allow me to help you." He stood, ignoring the sudden spike of pain in the back of his head.

"Fine." The old woman waved her hand like a royal used to having her needs met.

"I need to gather some wet moss to cover your foot and ease the swelling. I heard a brook nearby. Its banks should have plenty of it. I'll also bring back water." Putting a hand to the tree, he steadied his stance before he walked over to the donkey and removed his bag of supplies.

He pulled out a small clay bottle and shook it. "This still has a few sips of water. I have a mixture of herbs to use for the pain." Removing the leather stopper, he took a pinch of dried herbs from a folded linen cloth, dropped it inside the bottle and shook it. "It will taste bitter, but trust me, it will help."

The princess reached for it, sniffed the contents, then took it to her reluctant aunt. She stood over her until the older woman finished the draught.

"Thank you." The princess returned the empty bottle to

John. Her smile sent a ripple down his spine and strengthened his still wobbly limbs. He'd never had this kind of reaction to any woman, and was not about to question those feelings at the moment.

He walked into the forest, headed toward the stream, then remembered he had left his kit opened. Precious was nosey enough to destroy its contents, so he retraced his steps. When he neared the road, the serious tone of the women's voices made him pause. He stood in the shadow of an ancient oak and watched as the princess rummaged through his belongings, then hand the leather bag over to her aunt who did the same.

"He's hiding something." The aunt pulled one item at a time from the bag to examine.

"I agree. He's tall, well-muscled, and ran into the fight like a trained soldier. His teeth are good and his speech is that of an educated man." The princess spread out the items as her aunt handed them to her.

"Perhaps he is escaping a commission in the King's Army, disguised as a monk. It's been done before." The aunt stopped when she took out the pouches of herbs. If she poured out even one of those valuable aids… But she sniffed the contents of each before carefully refolding the linen. His relief temporarily edged out the anger growing within him at their invasion into his belongings.

"He fought with honor in our defense. That is not the way of a coward. I find it hard to believe he's running away from service to the Crown." The princess waited as her aunt completed her investigation of his belongings.

"When was the last time you knew a monk who owned such expensive clothing? This cloak alone would cost a knight at least a couple of year's wages, as would the fine linen tunic." The aunt fingered the weighted hem of his cloak and rubbed the cloth against her cheek, as if assessing its monetary value.

"The items could have been a gift from a generous benefactor." The princess turned toward the opening between the trees, as if sensing his presence. He couldn't be seen from where she stood, but he pressed closer to the tree just in case. "We need his help."

"I agree. We have no other choice with Everett and Steven dead." The old woman crossed herself and mumbled a prayer for their souls. "They were good men who didn't deserve to die so young, nor without a proper burial."

A faraway look came into her eyes. "Those who give their lives for the Crown and Church have earned a place in the institute's cemetery, where people can remember and mourn them properly. Not just a hasty scribbled name in the king's dusty ledger, with the word deceased marked by it." Anger laced the old woman's tone, and determination etched a scowl across her brow.

"Once we've completed our assignment, we'll send someone from the institute to search for them and see to their return and burial. But for now we need to keep going." The princess gathered the items and replaced them neatly into the bag. "It won't be long before others will come to hunt us down. If we are to escape the earl's gang of cutthroats, we must trust this handsome monk to get us safely to London."

John backed away. The women would make sure the donkey didn't destroy his belongings, but a feeling of betrayal soured his stomach. He found the stream, gathered the moss, and filled the clay pot with water. The sooner he was rid of these women the better his life would be. He had no desire to be drawn into further battles that were none of his concern.

The words of the prophetess came to mind. *Like your friend protected you, you are to protect Precious and the charges God is sending your way. It will take every skill you've learned to keep them safe.*

Were these women the charges he was to help? He groaned with despair. All he'd wanted since he came home from war was to live in peace. Instead, he was pledged to protect a donkey and two women who seem more than capable of protecting themselves.

Would their secrets get them all killed?

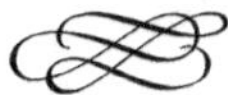

CHAPTER 6

"Did you recognize the brigand with the droopy eye and scarred face?" Julianna hated to think that the handsome monk might have connections to thieves and assassins, but there'd been a look of recognition when they first spotted each other.

"Aye. At least I think it was a lad that grew up in our village, but it's been several years since he left home to seek his fortune." Brother John frowned. "He was a good lad when I knew him. It's hard to imagine what could have happened to cause him to take up with the likes of those brigands."

"When you've lived as long as I, you'll see how situations can change even good people into monsters." Lois's voice was raspy from the pain in her leg and ankle.

"How soon will we reach a village where we can hire adequate transportation?" Julianna sent another glance toward her mentor. Brother John's moss and bandage had helped at first, but her foot and ankle had swollen again, probably from the jostling of riding the donkey. She needed to keep her leg raised, which riding in a carriage or a wagon would allow.

"I don't know how long it will take to get to a village or an inn." By the clipped tone of his voice and the set of his jaw he was unhappy answering her questions. Had she'd done something else to cause his sour attitude? Maybe his head still hurt.

"The safety of the princess is of the utmost urgency. I fear others will try to kidnap her." Lois shifted her weight, as if hunting for a more comfortable position on the well-rounded donkey. "Can't we go any faster?"

"This animal goes at her own pace, and trying to make her hurry only results in her stopping in defiance." He led the donkey with a firm grip on her lead rope, as if she might suddenly bolt or runaway. With his staff balanced in his right hand, he appeared focused on their path.

But then he stopped.

"What's the matter?" Julianna searched the road in front and behind them for potential danger, but nothing seemed out of the ordinary.

"Hide! Get into the trees." Worry etched his face. "Come, Precious." He clicked his tongue to hurry the donkey. He led the way off the road and far enough inside the forest so they couldn't be seen and stopped.

"What is…?" Julianna followed them into the hiding place and waited beside the monk.

"I can't see the road." Lois craned her neck, but the tall oaks and boxwoods were a dense barrier.

"Shhh. Don't make a sound." The monk gripped his staff as if ready for battle.

A farm wagon crept down the road, hauling firewood stacked higher than the sides. The team of horses pulled the heavy load with drooped heads, as though they'd come a long distance with little rest.

A righteous man regardeth the life of his beast. She's heard Lois repeat that proverb often during the years she'd known her. *If you want to discern the character of a man, watch how he treats chil-*

dren, animals, and those less fortunate. Actions always speak louder than words.

Maybe the appearance of the team proved the driver wasn't a good person, but they still might make a deal with him to take them to the nearest inn. He was headed in the same direction they were going.

Julianna touched Brother John's arm, but he shook his head. She could compensate the wagon driver to remove enough of his load to allow them to ride. It would be a more practical conveyance than the stubbornly slow donkey.

"But Lois needs to ride."

"Wait," he whispered.

Within seconds, a lone rider and his lathered mount raced up to the wagon, but the driver continued on his way.

The rider slowed, then rode next to the wagon, close enough to question the driver and scan the load of firewood he was hauling. "Have you seen a carriage or anyone pass by you on this road?"

"Besides you? No, and I ain't got time to chat about the weather neither." The unfriendly driver spat on the road, barely missing the stranger's horse.

The rider threw back his heavy cloak and put his hand on a black-handled dagger at his waist and paused. He cursed, then whipped his mount into a gallop again, stirring up a cloud of dust in his wake. She could hear the driver cursing the man until the wagon moved out of sight.

The silver triangle imprinted on the rider's dagger hilt had been easily visible—the emblem of the royal weapons maker favored by the king and the institute. Only those authorized by the king could commission that craftsman, and every weapon he made was marked by the silver triangle. His swords and daggers were prized especially by assassins for their balance, hardness of the steel, and how well they kept their sharp edge.

She fingered the dagger at her side. It also bore the silver triangle.

What did it mean? Was the rider a friend or foe?

A chill teased her neck. She edged closer to the monk and tightened her grip on the brigand's sword.

If they had asked for a ride with the farmer, as she'd wanted, they would have been caught by the rider.

If the earl suspected them as spies, he would have placed a bounty on their heads. Besides the Black Guard, every freelance assassin would be hunting them by now, the kind of man-hunters who kept on a target until they overtook it. She knew such men from the institute and had trained beside many of them over the years.

Their best chance to complete the mission would be to avoid any threat or future confrontation, if possible. Maybe if they changed their appearance… Julianna turned to Lois and saw her pinched features from the pain. With her injury their journey would be severely hindered, making their chances of discovery too great. She whispered a prayer for God's help.

After several minutes of silence, the monk relaxed his stance. "There's an old footpath hidden by the dense foliage. See?" He pointed to a faint path not far from where they had taken cover. He led the donkey onto the old trail. "Perhaps it will be safer to travel on that path until we come to a village or inn."

"How did you know the rider was a brigand?" Julianna studied him.

"By the sound of a horse being ridden hard. Wisdom dictated caution." By the tight grip on his staff and furrowed brow, something was bothering him. Perhaps the fear of running into more assassins, or maybe it was the added responsibility of helping her and Lois that made him less approachable.

She couldn't afford to worry about him, but they needed his help. The urgency to get to London with their information grew more desperate with Lois's injury.

In the earl's dining hall, Lois had overheard that the plot to assassinate King John was to take place soon. The attack against those with the royal bloodline would also take place during the same time, so none could be warned and escape. The exact date and time were never revealed, but with her and Lois's disappearance and the subsequent attack by the brigands, someone must have suspected them as spies. Or perhaps the earl had missed the papers Lois had stolen. Either of those could cause the Black Guard to put their assassination plans in motion sooner than planned.

The silence that had settled over them as they walked didn't help or improve the heaviness of her thoughts. She had to say something to lighten the tension.

"Precious was equal to her name today the way she protected us during the fight. Did you train her to do that?" Julianna cringed at such a frivolous sounding comment. *Even a fool appears wise with his mouth shut*—another favorite proverb of Lois.

"No. She does what she wants when she wants," Brother John grumbled.

"I agree, m'lady. Precious is very smart and a blessing indeed." Lois patted the little donkey and praised her.

Brother John remained silent and sullen. Still, she refused to be angry with his short temper. He'd padded the donkey's back with the fine cloak they'd found in his kit, and had torn the linen tunic in strips for bandages to wrap Lois's ankle to hold the moss securely in place. He'd done a good job with his doctoring skills, and those acts of kindness had helped ease her pain. Though it may not sound like it to untrained ears, Julianna recognized the respect Lois had in her voice when she addressed the mysterious monk.

They had been walking an hour when Precious stopped and pawed the ground, causing Julianna to nearly bump into John.

Raised voices sounded from the trail ahead. She peered around him, but trees concealed their source.

"Wait here and be quiet. I'll see what's going on." He handed Julianna the lead rope and hurried ahead. For a big man, he could move surprisingly quiet when he wanted.

Julianna turned to her mentor, who was focused on the path ahead. "Do you need to get off and stretch?"

"Shhh." Lois leaned down and rubbed the donkey's neck. "Let's get a bit closer, Precious. Be as quiet as you can, my little friend."

The donkey seemed to understand her words, for she started forward and followed the monk's path. She nimbly avoided sticks or rocks that could reveal their movement.

Within minutes, they found John, who stood concealed behind a large willow tree, watching the three men who were conversing with raised voices.

John turned, frowned, and motioned for them to stay hidden.

"You were bested by a crazy old lady and a blind woman?" The same rider who had questioned the wagon driver on the road stood in front of two of the brigands who had attacked them and stole their carriage. That the rider knew them answered her question of whether the man was a friend or foe.

The rider wore a long coat with a sword strapped to his side. He was shorter than the monk but stockier, and had long black hair and bushy eyebrows. But it was his dark eyes as he glared at the red-headed brigand with the wounded hand, which caught Julianna's attention. Even from this distance, she could read his murderous intent by his stiff posture and clenched fists.

She strained to hear, for there was something familiar about the dark stranger's voice. Julianna stepped aside and edged closer to get a better look.

"Theroux!" Lois gasped.

John glared at them, his anger apparent by his scowl and pinched lips.

Julianna glanced at her mentor. Lois's eyes were wide with shock. Her face had paled to a deathly white. When she made eye contact with Julianna, she blinked, then shook her head, a signal that they would speak later.

Julianna returned her focus to the men. Who was this mysterious Theroux and how well did Lois know him?

"We weren't bested by the crazy old lady and the princess." The red-headed brigand glanced at the ground.

"If you've hurt them…" Theroux's threat hung in the air like an unseen apparition, ready to wreak vengeance.

"No, no." Red-headed brigand raised his hand to defend his statement. "We just roughed them up a bit. Besides, they had help. At least four or five strangers happened on the road. We barely escaped with our lives." He waved a bandaged hand toward the inn in the clearing behind them. "Angus is back at the inn resting. His leg is still grievin' him mightily from the wound he received in the fight."

"Let me remind you of your assignment." Theroux's words were low, and his scowl darkened his eyes to black orbs. "You weren't hired to hurt the women, nor *'rough them up a bit'*. All you had to do was capture the carriage and bring them back to the earl's manor." The stranger's voice grew colder and more menacing with each word.

"After we all got injured, we had to escape." The red-haired brigand took a step back. "We'll rest a few hours to doctor our wounds then be off." His injured hand shook at his side. "We captured them once, we can do it again. You can trust us."

The taller of the two brigands wore a green coat and hung back, obviously intimidated by the stranger. He'd remained silent, but now nodded in agreement. This was the second of the three attackers, the one who had killed Everett and Steven and who Precious had kicked to the ground. He was also the one who struck Brother John with the rock, which knocked him out.

Theroux's fingers flexed, as he took a step closer. "Were you followed by the hoard of rescuers who wounded you?"

"We…ah…they had no horses, only one scraggly, old donkey." The red-haired man swiped the sweat off his brow, his gaze dropping to the ground with his lie.

The green-coat brigand grinned, revealing his missing front teeth, which Lois had knocked out with a surprise punch to his face when the brigands attacked their carriage.

"What did you do with the carriage? Did you search it?" Theroux focused on the brigand nearest him.

"Aye. We stripped it to the frame. Only found a bag of clothes and some food hidden under the seat." The red-haired man straightened his posture with his declaration.

Julianna knew that there had been several gold coins in their stash. There was apparently no truth or honor among the earl's hirelings.

"No worries. We removed the team before we pushed the carriage and the drivers' bodies off the road into a deep gully a few miles back. It broke into a hundred pieces," the green-coat brigand boasted.

"Imbecile! How did you plan to bring the women back without the carriage?" Theroux's voice had risen again.

"We didn't think about that." Green-coat looked down at the ground and wrung his hands. "We'll just steal some horses for them to ride."

"What did you do with the carriage horses?" Theroux glanced to his left, toward the green-coat brigand. His action revealed a nasty scar on his neck before he again faced the red-haired man.

"We sold 'em. They were some very fine animals. No reason not to make a little extra coin for our suffering." His grin turned to fear when Theroux reached to his waist.

Quicker than she would have imagined possible, he drew a dagger and plunged the blade into the man's chest. The second man reached for his own weapon, but Theroux was too fast. He produced a second dagger and threw it, hitting Green-coat in the chest hard enough to stagger him back before his body hit the ground.

"You were ordered not to harm the women! The Black Guard does not tolerate failure." Still raging, he cursed the dead men as he dragged first one body and then the other to a familiar wagon with the two tired horses tied to a tree. The driver was lying on the pile of firewood in the back.

Theroux patted each brigand down until he found their gold, then hoisted his victims up beside the driver's body and covered them with an old grey tarp. "Now, to finish off your cohort."

Julianna gripped the sword she'd taken from the green-coated brigand. Fear and anger warred within her. She had never witnessed such blatant disregard for human life. The assassin walked toward the inn with purpose in his stride. Another life was about to be forfeited to satisfy Theroux's rage.

John eased away from his hiding place and made his way back to them. Glaring at her like an angry father at a naughty child, he took possession of the lead rope. "Come, Precious." He led their little group away from the inn.

When they were far enough away not to be heard, he stopped. His normally meadow-green eyes darkened with his anger to a deep emerald and focused on her. "Can you not follow a simple command?" A muscle along his jaw twitched with barely-restrained anger. "You could have gotten us all killed."

Ire rose within her. He had no reason to be angry with her, nor did he have the authority to command her to do or not do anything. "But we weren't, so what do we do now?"

"God willing, we survive." He closed his eyes and bowed his head, as if in prayer.

She and Lois kept quiet until he glanced up. By the light in his eyes and a slight smile he must have received his answer.

"Of course!" Without further explanation, he led them across the main road and took a path leading away from London and their destination. "Come. I know where we are to go for help."

"Wait." Julianna reached out and clutched his arm. A spark, like lightning striking a tall tree in a thunderstorm, tingled up her arm. She sucked in a breath and released him as if she'd been burned.

He rubbed the spot she had touched, but continued on without speaking. At least she had the satisfaction of knowing he'd felt it too.

"It is imperative we reach London as soon as possible...for our safety." She couldn't disguise her breathlessness from their contact.

"So you've said...multiple times." He pushed a hand through his short-cropped hair and drew a deep breath. "I understand you have an urgent need to reach London, but to do so, you must change your appearance to avoid those sent to stop you. There is only one place I know where you can do that without drawing undo attention to our little group." He smiled, the kind of smile that conveyed hope to the one looking on.

Hope stirred up a longing in her. She wanted more. His confidence and peace made her long for home, someplace other than the institute—a real home, husband, and family of her own.

Dangerous thoughts for someone indentured to the Crown.

John led his charges to the abbey where his parents were avid benefactors. His family visited at least two or three times a year to bring clothing and hard-to-obtain supplies. He and his siblings had learned many life lessons there. By serving the less fortunate they were able to become thankful for their many blessings. His parents believed their royal heritage was a responsibility from God, Who reminded His disciples that to whom much was given, much was required.

The nuns there would welcome them, but he would need to speak to the abbess to explain his appearance and warn her not to speak of his family. His biggest concern was that by going there, they might also draw the assassins to the abbey. He didn't want to be the cause of such danger coming into their midst.

"Where are you taking us?" The princess stepped closer to him until he could smell the lavender from her clothing.

"The only place I know you'll be safe." John deliberately gave a vague answer, and her eyes fairly sparked with irritation. He shouldn't provoke her, but he couldn't seem to help himself. The connection he felt with this woman both confused and thrilled him. Not something he should explore if he wanted to fulfill his vow to be monk.

Maybe this was a test. If so, it was proving to be a very difficult one.

"We need to know more details." She huffed, and her scowl deepened.

"It's a small abbey near here. The sisters have an orphanage there, where they also care for the elderly and infirmed." He watched as she waited for him to continue. When he didn't explain further, her expression of annoyance made him smile.

"Must you be *so* madding?" She frowned and her blue eyes darkened to sapphire. "You do that on purpose, don't you?"

"Of course, he does." Lois murmured from her place on the donkey. "He probably has sisters that he tormented in his youth with the same tactic. Am I correct, young monk?"

"Perhaps." He couldn't resist the dangerous game he'd started.

"See? He's doing it again." She hurried ahead of him, turned and pointed her sword at him. "Enough, Monk! Tell us your plan or risk the consequences." Taking the impressive stance of a Viking princess prepared for battle, she stood before him, eyes flashing.

"I confess I'm tempted to inquire of the details of those consequences." He smiled, then sobered as she stepped toward him, obviously not amused. "I'm sorry. You remind me of one of my sisters." The lie stuck in his throat until he coughed to dislodge the untruth.

She was nothing like any of his three sisters. The princess was totally unique, having never met her equal. Her beauty, bravery, and spunk took his breath and stirred his heart to pounding like he'd run up a steep hill.

"You try my patience." She pointed the sword at his chest.

"Fine." He shoved the blade away with his staff. He could have easily disarmed her, but he restrained the impulse. "I believe your best chance of getting to London unharmed is to travel disguised as nuns."

He waited until she relaxed her stance before he continued. "I don't think anyone would bother members of the Church going to London on a pilgrimage to speak with His Holiness, the Pope, who is scheduled to arrive to visit the Cardinal within the month." He glanced over at Lois. "Also, the nuns at the Sisters of the Holy Heart are excellent healers and will take good care of you until you are well enough to travel again."

"I will not be left behind." Lois straightened her posture, her tone hardened with determination.

"Then perhaps we can borrow a horse and wagon from a local farmer. Or at the very least, find a donkey cart for you to ride in that will make you more comfortable."

The princess turned her attention to Lois. "Who was that man you called Theroux? How do you know him?" The tone of her voice conveyed more accusation than question.

Lois's brow furrowed. "I think going to the coast would cut our travel time by more than half. Going by sea makes more sense than traveling overland, which will take too long by wagon or donkey cart."

He started to turn away, but from the corner of his gaze, he saw the old woman frown and shake her head once, a signal the princess must understand but disliked, by her scowl and pinched lips.

Lois continued as if undeterred by the interruption. "We can take a ship to the nearest port and get transportation to our destination once we dock."

John raised his brows. "Don't you think the people who are chasing you will have those docks covered with spies? They'll be looking for two women with your distinct descriptions."

"We can easily change our appearance to make us harder to identify." The princess spoke the words with confidence. How often had they used that art of deception to fool others?

He glanced from the princess to her aunt. Were they disguised now, or had her royal status forced them to use methods to change their looks in the past for their safety, and to move around freely without being accosted?

His conscience stirred. The simple monk's robe and sandals that he wore had also felt like a disguise since he'd begun this journey. Perhaps once he took his vows, he'd feel more at ease. He had no plans to share his secrets with his companions, so what gave him the right to question them about theirs?

Still, the prophetess's word kept ringing in his ears. He was responsible for keeping these two charges safe.

"Altering your appearances might work, but only if you travel separately. Milady, your injured ankle will limit your ability to go anywhere unaided." John didn't want to imagine what would happen if either of the women were caught by the dark-eyed stranger who could kill without blinking.

"You have a point. However, we are not going to be separated, so for now we'll go along with your plan, Brother John." The aunt grimaced as she shifted positions. Her swollen ankle looked painful, but until they reached the abbey there was little more he could do for her.

"Fine. We need to keep moving. The abbess closes the gates at dusk and won't open them again for any reason until the morning's light." He glanced down at the donkey. She had not tugged on the rope, and had remained suspiciously docile this whole time. Maybe the diminutive aunt reminded her of her old master. A good thing, since it meant less grief for him.

He didn't remember a carriage at the abbey, but they did have an old plow horse used for farming their gardens. He couldn't borrow old Brownie, though, and leave them without a means to tend the fields.

Was the beast beside him trained to pull a cart? That would help. But if not, she would be safe left with the nuns until he could return for her. He needed to find more comfortable transportation for the injured woman.

His conscience burned at the thought of going against his plan to travel alone, but he couldn't ignore his need to see the women safely to London. Though unspoken, he could feel the tension between the two. Whatever they had that the brigands wanted, they were willing to risk their lives to get it to their destination.

~

They arrived at the Abbey of the Sisters of the Holy Heart just as the sun edged its way down to the horizon. His thoughts warmed with the sounds of children's laughter stirring memories of his many childhood visits. The acres of gardens surrounding the abbey were full of fruit trees and vegetables planted in straight, tidy rows. A small, well-tended vineyard had been planted beyond the gardens. It had been too long since his last visit, a regret this trip helped to remedy.

He spotted the abbess, who stood holding a bell at the entrance. She rang it twice, giving notice that the gates were about to close. The children playing in the branches of the shade trees on either side of the entrance dropped down like ripe fruit from an apple tree, then raced inside. He lost count after ten, for they all wore the same tan-colored tunic and shorts and blended into one large group, disappearing inside the compound.

"Sister Agnes, have you room for some very weary travelers?" John shouted and waved his staff to gain her attention.

"John!" The woman stopped and pushed open the gate wide enough to admit him and his companions. "You are always a most welcome sight. And you've brought company."

Once inside, John took charge of closing the tall wooden

gate and securing the three steel latches. Once a rich man's castle, the man had donated it and the sixty acres surrounding to the nuns before his death. The large compound had towering stonewalls which were thick enough for two men to walk side by side along the top—a fortress that secured the safety and privacy of the sisters and their charges.

John had spent many summers scaling those walls, helping with the garden, and with his father's help, mending what needed fixed. He'd learned many useful skills wielding a hammer, ax, and hoe.

"Thank you for closing..." The abbess gasped, her eyes wide with surprise. "Lois!" She brushed past John and rushed to the donkey's side. As she embraced Lois, the abbess nearly toppled her off the beast.

"Josephine!" As Lois hugged the nun, emotion clouded her words and tears filled her eyes. "I thought you were dead."

"Josephine Westerfield is dead." She straightened. "I am Sister Agnes and the Abbess of this convent." She lowered her voice. "We'll speak later." With a wave, she motioned for a young boy, about twelve years old, who was hovering nearby, to come forward. "Alfred, would you please take this fine donkey to the barn and care for it?" She turned toward two younger nuns. "Sisters, please make up the guests quarters and add three places at our table. I'm sure our friends are hungry."

Scents of the sisters' delicious bread and hearty venison stew wafted out of the open door, and John's stomach growled loud enough to be heard by those standing close by.

"Hungry as always, I hear." Sister Agnes hugged him as he passed by and touched his short hair, then motioned to the monk's robe and sandals. "I suspect you have a story behind your attire?"

"Yes." He glanced at his companions and lowered his voice. "And it is private, so please don't mention my family or their names. I'll tell you all about it after dinner when we can speak alone."

"I can't wait." She smiled and turned her attention to the gathering crowd of children in the courtyard. "Go! Clean up and get ready to eat. Show our visitors what angels you are." She clapped her hands and the children scattered, laughing along the way. "I will inspect your efforts, so make sure you clean your hands and faces. Don't forget the one who does the best job will get a special treat." That seemed to light a fire in them as they scrambled inside, each declaring they would be the one to win this time.

He smiled, remembering his own efforts to win the hard candy, a buttery treat the abbess made for special occasions. His boyish efforts had lacked the diligence of his siblings, so he'd rarely won the prize.

He turned his attention to Lois and gathered her off the donkey. Ignoring her half-hearted protest that she could manage on her own, he kept her in his arms. She must be in more pain than she let on not to criticize his efforts.

The princess gathered his kit and cloak from the donkey as the boy tried to lead the stubborn beast away. She stood stiff-legged, ears back, refusing to budge.

"Precious, go with him." John watched as the donkey shook her head but allowed the boy to lead her to the barn.

"Lois, let's get you inside and check out your injury." Sister Agnes chuckled and motioned for them to follow. "Your adventures have never failed to entertain me."

CHAPTER 8

Dinner was like nothing Julianna had ever encountered. The children weren't reprimanded to strict silence during the meal, as they were at the institute. Every little face around the long table was clean and smiling. The children's joy reflected the obvious affection the nuns held for them. Though noisy with children's chatter, peace filled the room with warmth and something else she couldn't identify. Was it love?

Even a stern reprimand from a young nun, Sister Calley, issued to a freckled-face boy, she called Thomas, was met with repentance. He sheepishly apologized to the girl next to him for poking her with his spoon when she refused to share the last of her bread pudding with him.

Julianna closed her eyes and visualized a home of her own filled with such happiness. The boisterous symphony of children's voices rose and ebbed while they related their morning's lessons and playtime adventures.

A young, dark-eyed girl of perhaps Italian descent won the prize for doing the best job washing her face and hands, and was praised for helping others. Little Gina stood, and her grin revealed two missing front teeth and deep dimples on each cheek. She giggled when she accepted the candy, praise, and a hug from Sister Agnes. When she returned to her chair, Julianna noticed an ugly raised scar running down the length of the backside of her left arm, the evidence of a terrible burn.

Memories Julianna thought she'd banished rushed back to her. She was nine-years-old again, hiding away in the kitchen to escape her stepmother's screams and insults. This day, Julianna was cleaning carrots and potatoes for a soup the cook was preparing.

Once loosed, the rampaging thoughts were merciless. The suffocating stench of burning flesh enveloped her, along with excruciating pain and, far worse, her father's betrayal.

The old scar on her arm throbbed with fresh intensity.

Tears clogged her throat, her breath came in shallow gasps.

She stood and escaped as quietly as she could, her heartbeat pounding in her ears. The stairs to the upper exterior balcony were steep, but would provide a private place to grieve. Halfway up, eyes blurry with unshed tears, she stumbled and reached out, but missed the railing. Arms flailing, she fell backward.

"I've got you." John caught her and pulled her close to his chest.

"I…" She couldn't make the words come out. A deep sob cut off her breath.

He carried her to a room where the children were schooled and lowered her to a bench. Once settled, he closed the door, then sat beside her. "What's wrong?"

"I…" She swept a hand in the air, her throat still clogged with grief. The loose sleeve of her dress slid up, revealing the source of her pain. With a swift motion she tugged the fabric back in place to hide the ugly scar.

With compassion in his eyes, he caught her arm. His touch sent warmth up to her shoulder as he inched up the fabric and traced the scar in a slow motion.

"I have a scar too." He took her hand and rested it on his side. She could feel a large raised furrow beneath the fabric. "I was badly injured in battle while in the service of the king." He paused, then replaced her hand on the table. "My friend, William saved my life, but it cost him his leg."

"I had no friend to save me." She could no longer hold back the hurt and injustice. "I was not much older than Gina when my father remarried. His second wife decided she didn't want another woman's child to care for once she was with child with my father's *legitimate heir*."

She risked a glance, but John's eyes were unwavering and filled with compassion. "One day, she decided I needed to curtsey and address her as Your Ladyship, not by her name, Dorothy, as my father had instructed." The scene played out in her mind, as it had often since that time. If only she had done as Dorothy had demanded, maybe things would have been different.

"I told her my father said I didn't have to, and then I continued cleaning the vegetables. Dorothy became enraged and came at me with a hot poker from the fireplace." Julianna slid the sleeve higher on her arm to expose the fullness of the scar. The hook of the poker made a *J*. "I raised my arm in defense and was badly burned." Julianna closed her eyes and put her hand to her mouth to still the anger burning her throat. John placed a hand on her shoulder, warming her with his touch.

"The crazed woman laughed when I shoved her away. She dropped the poker then stumbled back onto it. The hot iron set her dress on fire. Dorothy stood screaming at me while the flames grew larger. The servants had scattered, so I took the pail of water I'd been washing the vegetables in and poured it on her to put out the fire." Julianna grimaced at the ugly mark on her arm. "Dorothy wasn't burned, only her garments, but she told my father it was me who attacked her and I had tried to burn her alive. The servants were so frightened of the woman that they refused to tell the truth no matter how much I begged them."

Tugging her sleeve down, she smoothed the fabric. "He was furious and refused to listen to me. Within the hour, he had one of the gardeners take me away to a large stone building. The gardener gave a note to the man at the door and left me there without even a good-bye." She glanced around the school room. "It was not nearly as nice a place as this."

She stood, needing to pace. "The Grandfork Institute for Higher Learning is where I grew up." She brushed the tears from her eyes. "Four months later, the cook came to ask for my forgiveness. Cook said that Dorothy lost the baby and became more unstable, setting several fires. The last one nearly burned down the stables. My father put her away in the asylum, where she died soon after. As soon as the woman was removed from the manor, the cook confessed to my father the truth that I was not to blame, yet he never visited me or repented of my unjust banishment."

"So I take it you are not Princess Rosanna Kent and Lois isn't your aunt." His voice was soft, but the tone had hardened.

"No." A moment of fear stirred within her for having revealed the truth, but the sense of clarity it brought made it worth the risk. "Since my arrival at the institute at age nine, my name has been Julianna Westerfield. Lois has been my teacher, friend, and mentor." Unburdening on this attentive monk lifted her spirit and gave her a glimmer of freedom. The secrets imposed on her by the institute had kept her weighted down for as long as she could remember. "We are agents of the Crown and the Church." She drew a deep breath before she continued. "Lois and I have been on a secret assignment to uncover the identities of the Black Guard."

"Julianna!"

They turned and saw Lois just inside the doorway, sitting in a chair with wheels, aided by Sister Agnes.

"This is an interesting turn of events, but not totally unexpected." Sister Agnes smiled, shut the door, and maneuvered the chair on wheels to the table closest to John.

"We must trust him and warn him of the dire consequences of our assignment—for his own safety." Julianna moved to sit beside her mentor.

Lois remained silent, glaring at her as if she had revealed a monstrous truth too deadly to expose. Julianna returned the glare, refusing to be intimidated. She was tired of all the secrets and had questions that needed answers. "While the room is filled with truth, would you like to tell us about your connection to the Sister Agnes?"

Lois crossed her arms. Her lips pinched in a firm line and a scowl etched a deep furrow across her brow.

Sister Agnes's voice broke through the tension. "We grew up together in the Grandfork Institute for Higher Learning over twenty years ago." The abbess allowed that information to sink in a minute before she continued, ignoring Lois's scowling disapproval. "We became best friends, since we were the only girls to be admitted at that time. It wasn't until years later that those in charge found out how useful girls could be for their purpose of spying."

She glanced over to Julianna. "I believe, after us, you were the only female accepted until they increased the number to almost thirty percent about eight years ago." She frowned. "I hate to think of all of the other abandoned little girls that ended up as indentured slaves or prostitutes because their rich and entitled fathers decided they weren't wanted." She smiled and spread her arms wide. "I wanted this place to be a sanctuary of love and care for all of those little children who have been rejected and forgotten, no matter what their family crest revealed."

"How did you get free to do this?" Julianna leaned forward. "I was led to believe only death or a written release issued by the King himself could free us from our indentured service to the institute."

"I died." She offered a sad smile. "Along with the lies of the old life. The institute stole any hope of a family with their daily reminders of my debt to them. Their cruel method of keeping those in their charge dependent on them, both physically and mentally, was to deceive us into believing we were special. That we were chosen to belong to the institution, and therefore destined to live and die doing the King and the Church's bidding."

She closed her eyes and paused before she opened them again. "They tried their best to declare their status as the All Mighty, so they could eliminate all hope of a future other than the one they gave us. I believed them until I fell in love with a fellow student." She glanced over at Lois. "But he loved another."

Lois bent her head down and a groan escaped. Sister Agnes patted her friend's shoulder. "I have no anger or hard feelings against you, dear friend. Since I left the past behind, I've found true peace and purpose, which is to care for the less fortunate and share God's love. The seclusion of the abbey has provided a fulfilling life here with no regrets."

"Was the man's name, Theroux?" John spoke the words burning in Julianna's thoughts.

"Yes! But how did you know?" Sister Agnes' surprise was clear, then she turned to Lois.

"Like you, he disappeared only a month after you were declared dead. I was told he had died, too." Lois's tone was soft with regret.

The pain in her mentor's eyes had nothing to do with the woman's injured ankle. Julianna was familiar with that kind of pain. The same deep hurt she saw in the mirror, the eyes of someone betrayed.

Julianna turned to the abbess. "We came upon Theroux before we arrived here and watched as he murdered those brigands who had attacked us, killed our drivers, and stole our carriage." Julianna's gut clenched with the thought of either of these fine women having loved such an undeserving blackheart.

"After two months, when you didn't return from your last assignment, Josephine, the headmaster declared you dead. No grave or even a marker. Your name was crossed through as if it had never existed." Lois dabbed at the tears coursing down her face. "I was heartbroken that we had words before you left. Words I couldn't take back."

Her voice lowered until Julianna had to strain to hear. "I found comfort in Theroux's arms, and yes, in spite of my denial to you, we had fallen in love. He had promised to find a way for us to disappear from the institute, never to be found. Our first act of rebellion was to get married." She drew a deep breath and released it. "He came to me late one evening with grand plans. He wanted me to leave that very night, sail away with him to a villa he'd purchased in Portugal, and assume new identities."

"His voice sounded familiar. Why?" Julianna rubbed her forehead, trying to place where she had heard it. Ever since the incident when he rode up to the wagon and spoke to the driver, a memory had pricked like a splinter under her skin. It refused to be ignored, yet remained foggy and unreachable.

"You had only been with the institute a few weeks, and I had been assigned to be your teacher. That evening I met Theroux in the stables, you followed." A blush tinted her cheeks. "You saw us kissing and overheard our plans to escape. You came out from your hiding place behind the stall door and demanded we take you with us. Theroux was furious and threatened to slit your throat."

"Now I remember." She rubbed her neck. "You pushed me behind you and told him he had to go without you." Tears burned Julianna's eyes. "You could have escaped and had freedom and a family, but for me."

Lois reached out and patted Julianna's hand. "Today proved I made the right choice. Theroux had always been a bit of a hothead. He was ruthless when going after a target, making him a favorite with the headmaster. Even the king used him to eliminate his br..." She coughed and rubbed her hand over her mouth. "Not something any of you need to know, for your own safety. Enough to say Theroux enjoyed the art of spying, tracking his prey, and killing, far too much."

She dabbed the last of her tears away. "I can't imagine ever having had a happy life with such a man." Anger lit her eyes and furrowed her brow. "He was said to have perished in a ship wreck while tracking a traitor of the Crown—or so it was written on the official report. And though a ship was found sunk near the coast, his body was never recovered. He was hailed a hero and his name was used as an inspiration to the rest of us." Lois slammed her hand down on the table. "Lies! All lies."

Julianna had suspected for years the institute manipulated facts to motivate the students. A clear realization washed through her—if she were ever to be free, she too would have to stage a fatal accident to escape their evil clutches. With the carriage smashed and the drivers dead, maybe this was that opportunity.

Yet, could she risk abandoning their current mission, for her selfish desire of freedom?

She glanced at John. By his scowl and tense posture, the hard facts, as revealed in this room might have been too difficult for him to accept.

Restless, he shifted on the bench several times, then stood. Having been severely wounded in the King's service, he understood the responsibility of fulfilling one's obligation to the Crown. Did he think them horrible to question their duty?

It was not their choice to be sent to the institute to be taught such things as spying and worse, nor were they unredeemable because of the unusual subjects of their education. They could still love and be loved, couldn't they?

At last, he spoke. "Your former friend, Theroux, must be a good tracker if what you said is accurate. Not many assassins live long once they freelance their services. They hold no allegiance to country or kin, and none is afforded them. We should make plans to leave here tomorrow, or the day after, at the latest."

John turned toward the elder nun. "Sister Agnes could we talk? We need to plan for the worst. Hopefully, he won't figure out we've been here, but if he should find his way to the abbey…" He raised his hands in surrender.

"I agree. Come to my office." Sister Agnes turned and opened the door.

A little boy scrambled up from a kneeling position, the imprint of the keyhole remained on his ear.

"Thomas! Why are you not in bed?"

"I…I has to tell you somethin', sister." He backed away with a guilty expression. If he had heard half of what was said in this room, he could put them all in grave danger. It could even cost him his life if the wrong people thought he knew too much to live.

"Come with me, young man. We will talk and I'll explain the bad things that can happen when you disobey and break the rules." She put a hand on the troublemaker's shoulder and turned toward John. "Give me about twenty minutes, then meet me in my office." Leading the way, she steered the eight-year-old with a firm hand. "You get four extra scriptures about obedience to memorize and…" The rest of her admonition was lost when she disappeared down a corridor leading to her office.

John turned to them. "I need to check on the donkey lest she finds a way out of her stall. Even though she can't escape the compound, she can cause trouble." He seemed in a hurry to leave, but then he hesitated. "Can I help you find the guest's quarters?"

Julianna stepped behind her mentor. "Sister Calley showed me how to get there. With this rolling chair I think I can manage to get Lois to her room without help." She pushed the chair to the open door.

"The abbess said your sister, Elise, designed this rolling chair for an elderly monk named Brother Knobben, who had lost his legs." Lois frowned. "I hope you are as clever as your sister in finding ways to get us safely to London, young monk." Lois's stern tone softened when she glanced up at John.

"With God all things are possible." He smiled. "Get a good-night's rest. We'll speak in the morning." He turned and went the opposite direction.

"I can tell you like this monk." Lois reached up behind her and patted Julianna's hand resting on the handle at the top of the chair.

"I...am grateful to him." Julianna's thoughts of the handsome monk threatened to stray into deeper emotions than gratitude, which she planned to ignore.

"Sister Agnes told me John's from a very good family and is an honorable man who we can rely on and trust." When they arrived at Lois's room, she allowed Julianna to help her into the bedclothes loaned to her by the nuns.

Once her friend was settled in bed, Julianna walked to the door. The day's excitement had left her exhausted. What the future held, she had no idea, but for now, she felt safe within this fortress.

"Julianna, as much as the institute has failed us with their lies, the importance of our assignment has only grown graver with the lives at stake. This is no time for romantic notions of disappearing or of marriage until this evil has been dealt with."

"I know, Lois, but it's hard not to dream of a happier future when I'm in this special place." Julianna closed the door and retreated to the privacy of her own room. She couldn't shake the feeling that traveling to London would be the most dangerous part of their journey.

The flutter of something deep in her heart whenever she thought of John stirred up a different kind of danger.

God please save us all.

CHAPTER 9

John awoke with a gasp. The room was dark but for a small candle that had melted halfway down, marking the middle of the night. Sweat soaked his nightshirt, and his heart pounded with the fears stirred up by the familiar dream.

His past transgressions haunted him over and over in the nightmares. Why had he foolishly disobeyed his superior's orders to wait for reinforcements? He had charged into the battle, willing to risk all to free the faceless female hostages. The echoes of their screams for help lingered in his mind like a harbinger of impending doom.

In reality, the women had been part of the enemy's plot to lure the king's forces into a trap. Their screams were as real as their motive was evil. In his desperation to save those women, he was struck down in battle, and would have died at the enemy's hand, had William not intervened. That intervention cost William his leg. Eighteen others under his command were also seriously injured, and five of those later died from their wounds.

The reinforcements had finally arrived and vanquished their

weakened opponents. The battle had been declared a victory, and he had been discharged as a wounded hero, but he would forever know the truth. He still felt the shame of the suffering he'd caused the brave men who followed him into battle because he believed a lie.

He must have fallen back to sleep, for the dream changed. The hostages were now Julianna dressed as a princess, along with Lois and the donkey. Why the donkey kept creeping into his dreams was maddening. What did it mean?

The last nightmare had awakened him before dawn. He couldn't shake the fear of having been captured and unable to save Julianna from the madman wielding a black sword. The blade and the hilt were black as night, but for a small silver triangle emblazed on the handle.

He got up and paced around the small space. The castle's turret room had been deemed his domain whenever he came to visit since he was a child. It worked well for him now, since it was far enough away that if he cried out in the night, no one heard.

Its remoteness afforded him privacy for his prayers. Father Alvin had encouraged him to tell God everything that troubled his mind and heart. He also deemed confession a very beneficial way to deal with any of the guilt and shame that held him captive since the battle.

Bending his knee to the Lord, he poured out his grief and prayed for forgiveness that would free him from the tormenting nightmares and the heaviness of his shame. He quoted a familiar scripture that Father Alvin had quoted many times.

1 John 1:9 If we confess our sins, he is faithful to forgive us our sins, and to cleanse us from all unrighteousness.

No penance required as payment, one must simply accept His forgiveness.

Perhaps he didn't deserve God's absolution.

Last evening, Sister Agnes had listened to him as he babbled on about everything. She waited until he finished his story of the battle, speaking of his guilt and of his vow to become a monk. She gave him almost the same admonition as that of Father Alvin. God's plans for his life may not be the same as he thought.

Lord, give me wisdom and protect our journey.

With those final words, he stood.

The sound of bells calling the nuns to prayer at dawn always woke him as a child, though the guests were allowed to sleep longer if they chose. His mother insisted that they all rise at the same time. She wanted them to learn good habits, and by her standards, prayer was the best foundation of every day.

He stretched and headed for the bucket of water to wash and shave his face. The nuns had provided a clean robe for him, so he could wash the one he had on when he arrived. Perhaps it was their polite way of telling him he reeked.

By the short length, that exposed his shins up to his knees, he'd wager a guess this garment had belonged to the late Brother Knobben. Having lost his legs in an accident, the nuns must have shortened his robe for his convenience. He must have also been a good deal rounder than John, for the bulk of it required a sash to be tied around his middle to keep from being swallowed by the tent-worthy excess. He pulled on his pants to cover his legs, allowing the short robe to serve more as a tunic.

Urgency grew within him to get on with their journey. Somewhere out there, a ruthless killer was tracking the women. Perhaps they would listen to his offer to take the evidence to the king so they could remain safely at the abbey.

First, he needed to wash his dirty robe. He would speak to them while it was drying. He turned to gather the dirty garment from the only chair in the room. It wasn't there. The room was barren of any other furniture, so where could the robe be?

Moving over to the window, he spotted it on the clothesline waving in the wind. Apparently, he'd slept through the intruder's visit. He couldn't let it happen again. He had to be alert during the night in case of an assassin's attack.

Movement near the laundry caught his attention. Being up so high in the tower gave him a good view of the people below. The woman with pale hair had to be Julianna. She dried her hands after hanging more of the wash and her laughter rose on the breeze when a ball, made of tightly woven grass, rolled at her feet. A small girl raced up to retrieve it and won a hug from Julianna.

He smiled. The vision surrounded him with warmth. The Viking princess would make a good mother if given the chance. The thought that her bondage to the Crown may prevent her from ever enjoying such a life, caused an ache of regret in his chest.

He watched as she helped the nuns corral the children to do their chores, until his stomach growled loud enough not to be ignored. There was much to do to get ready for travel, and no time left for idle thoughts.

He made his way down the steep stairs heading to the dining hall, Sister Agnes's advice repeating in his mind.

John, you must allow the Lord to take the mistakes of the past and accept His forgiveness. You'll have a hard time hearing Him or trusting Him to lead you in safety if you try and rely solely on your own power and understanding. You're on a reckless journey of your own making, a self-fulfilling punishment which you've chosen to atone for your misdeeds. His Word says He forgives you and His Word doesn't lie, does it?

No. But... He'd started to defend himself.

He trusts you enough, dear boy, to escort Julianna and Lois to London. The Black Guard must be stopped no matter what you think of the king or the lies told by the institute that we revealed last night. Accept God's love and trust Him to protect you and your charges along the way. She'd prayed with him, then waved him away to his hideaway in the tower.

The aroma of roasted meat and hot bread drifted up to him, bringing him back to the present. As he arrived in the large dining hall, he could still taste the fresh butter, honey, and creamy porridge from his visits here as a child. He was late, but the room was suspiciously empty.

Children's laughter drifted through the open door leading to the kitchen, so he went to investigate. Voices led him toward the kitchen. He saw through the open exterior door, the scene just outside.

"She won't budge." Alfred, the young boy Sister Agnes had entrusted with Precious last night, stood in the yard with his hands on his hips and a frustrated pinch of his lips.

"Maybe, if you give her a carrot you can lead her back to the barnyard. I'll go get one." Sister Calley sounded as vexed as Alfred. She turned and rushed into the kitchen, followed by the donkey hot on her heels. "No! No, donkey. You can't come inside."

The donkey wasn't listening and pushed passed the nun, dragging Alfred behind. Halfway through the kitchen, Precious spotted John, but was stopped from reaching him, by the addition of Sister Calley pulling against the lead. With a series of brays that rattled the windows and echoed against the tall ceilings of the kitchen, the donkey pawed the stone floor and tugged against her captors. John hurried forward and brushed a hand over her head.

"Hush, now Precious. See? I haven't left you." John spoke in soft tones to calm the donkey until she quieted.

"Wow, she really likes you, Brother John." Alfred smiled and slapped John on the back, then glanced down and motioned to John's habit. "Did you grow a bunch last night? Sister Agnes says nighttime is when we grow the most, and why we need to get a good night's sleep."

John laughed at the puzzled look on the twelve-year-old's face. "Sister Agnes is probably right, but this time I haven't outgrown my robe. The sisters allowed me to borrow Brother Knobben's old robe while mine dries." He pointed through the window to the laundry hanging on the line. "See?"

"Oh-h." Satisfied that the mystery was solved to his satisfaction, he turned his attention to the donkey. "I fed and watered her this morning, but when I went to leave her stall, she pushed past me and headed to the abbey." He bent down to pet the long-eared beast. "Guess you found what you were looking for, huh, girl?" He chuckled and took her halter as if to lead her outside again, but she refused to move.

"Precious, go with Alfred. I promise we won't leave without you." John patted the donkey and ran his hand down her back to check for sores or hot spots from carrying Lois the day before. Everything appeared fine.

The donkey followed the boy, and John walked with them to the barn. He wanted to make sure she ate a good meal of oats and barley. "Thank you for taking such good care of my... donkey." He almost said, *my friend.*

She had been an annoying hindrance since they'd started out on this journey, but somehow they'd arrived at the right place at the right time to help Julianna and Lois. With Precious settled, he left her eating her grain. His stomach grumbled, reminding him he needed to eat, too.

As he left the barnyard, he spotted a small rig in the weeds and went to inspect it. With Alfred's help, they rolled the surprisingly well-built cart into the open, and found it sound with the exception of a couple of rotted floorboards. Alfred took him to a pile of discarded lumber, where John measured and picked two that would work as replacements. After mending the cart, he wiped the sweat from his face.

"Do you know if the abbey has any harness small enough for a donkey?"

"I think I saw some in the tool shed." The boy led him to a small wood outbuilding.

The door hinges were well oiled, showing a lot of use. Rakes, shovels, axes, and all manner of gardening tools hung in tidy rows along the wall, each item clean and ready for use.

"I think I saw something…" Alfred moved a stack of harvest buckets. "Here."

"Good find, Alfred. This is just what I needed." John patted the boy on the shoulder and gathered the bits and pieces that made up the harness. "By its size, it could fit a donkey."

Once outside, John spread the harness pieces out across the ground to check its condition in the sunlight.

"It's not too bad." He rubbed his thumb across the traces that would connect the donkey to the cart. "See this crack?" Alfred bent down for a closer look and nodded. "As long as it doesn't tear when I pull it, it should be strong enough." The leather held fast. "While in the shed, I found this to condition the leather." He held up a dusty jar of tallow that had been rendered down and filtered to remove impurities so it wouldn't spoil. "What I need for you to do is rub this over the leather, careful not to miss any spots." He glanced up at the boy. "Will you do that for me?" He handed him a large rag to use for the chore.

"Sure." The boy's eagerness to help warmed John's heart. "Can I watch you harness the donkey?"

"You think she's going to throw a fit, don't you?" John laughed at his nod. "One step at a time, my young friend. Oil the harness, then we'll see what happens." His stomach growled loud enough Alfred's eyes widened.

"I skipped breakfast. Guess I'd better eat something or risk scaring the little children." He left Alfred sitting on the ground, oiling the harness and checking it for damage. He stopped by the kitchen door to wash his hands and face before going inside.

Sister Calley met him with a frown, but handed him a bowl of porridge with plenty of butter melting on a sea of cream. "We have too much to do to stop and feed stragglers who come late and expect servants to wait on them." When he sat at the table, she brought him a plate with a large chunk of roasted venison and two slices of bread, butter, and honey.

"Thank you, Sister. I'm sorry I'm late." He smiled. "I forgot how well you eat around here."

"We all work hard, and God blesses our efforts so we can feed *wayward travelers*, as well as the children in our charge." The curt tone of the nun's voice and previous comments made him wonder if she knew about his connection to Lord and Lady Stanton. Perhaps she found offense in his privileged upbringing, as well as his tardiness.

As she turned and left the room, her stiff posture left no doubt of her displeasure. He hadn't met Sister Calley until yesterday, since she had come to the convent after his last visit. What had driven her to such a remote place of service? Maybe because of Sister Agnes's new outlook on life, she had also extended mercy to others with troubled pasts.

His stomach rumbled. Time to eat. He gave thanks, then dug into the feast.

"There you are." Julianna stopped at the table as he finished, his clean robe hanging over her arm. "It's finally dry, and I thought you'd be ready to change back into it." She smiled, and his stomach fluttered against his ribs, rendering him speechless for a moment as he drew in a deep breath to steady his wandering thoughts.

"Yes, thank you." He stood and took the robe from her. Good thing he'd finished his meal before she arrived, for he doubted if he could have eaten another bite while she remained.

"Sister Agnes asked if you'd meet her in her office. The village elder has arrived, and she wanted you to speak with him and his council about the impending danger."

"I'll change at once and be right there." He ducked into a storage room and put on the longer, better fitting robe, and left Brother Knobben's garment hanging on a hook. Last night, Sister Agnes had listened patiently of his plans to fortify the abbey's defense. Using villagers, if needed, would allow them to post a sentry both day and night for a week or so.

Because he had much to do before they left today, he purposely kept the meeting with the villagers short. Hopefully, he'd instilled in them the potential danger to the convent and their village if the assassin tracked them to this place.

The elders pledged to protect the convent and their village. Peaceful villagers had little chance of success against such a man as Theroux. Before the men left, John prayed over them for God's protection, then Sister Agnes prayed a blessing over each of them.

John trailed behind as she walked the villagers out of the abbey and ushered them through the gates with lighter talk of crops and expectations of a fine harvest.

With the others gone, she turned back to John, her gaze penetrating. "John, it is God who protects us. All of the skills I learned at the institute will not keep us safe. We must trust in God."

He nodded. Her words struck deep within him, but did he truly believe them?

Harnessing Precious to the cart was thankfully uneventful. She stood quietly as John put on the harness first to see if she would allow it. She shook her head, sending the metal hooks clinking, but she didn't throw a fit. To his great relief, she remained calm, since he had a growing audience of children and nuns watching his every move.

Once the harness was secured, he walked behind and drove Precious around the courtyard a couple of times without incident. He held his breath as he attached the cart to the harness's traces then released his breath with a silent prayer when she pawed the ground at the extra weight. When he clicked his tongue, the cue to go forward, she shook her head, but responded to his command.

John walked beside the cart. "Good girl, Precious."

The children giggled as he continued his words of encouragement and praise to the beast while she pulled the cart in a straight line.

"Whoa." She stopped when John tugged the reins. He waved at the children, and they ran forward. He allowed five at a time to climb aboard the cart. John guided Precious around the courtyard without a problem.

"Excellent." Sister Agnes clapped her hands, once every child had a chance to ride. "Enough, children. Our friends must prepare for their departure." She smiled. "What do you say?"

"Thank you, Brother John." The chorus of children's voices rose in one accord.

"It's time we pack for our journey." John found Alfred standing nearby, no doubt a bit disappointed that there hadn't been the excitement he'd expected. "The cart's empty of all passengers and ready for that straw to fill the back. Make sure it's thick enough to cushion Miss Lois and hide our supplies from passersby."

Alfred nodded and took off at a jog toward the barn.

"Bring our guests their things, children." Sister Agnes waved her hand toward the abbey and three of the older children hurried off to obey. "I've packed a mixture of oats and barley for the donkey, and for you, I've included dried fruit and roasted grain, and a large portion of cured meat for you to eat on your trip."

"Thank you for your generous hospitality, Sister Agnes." John's gratitude went far deeper than mere words. God had provided for the next part of their journey, certainly the answer to prayer.

John spread a thick blanket over the straw for Lois to sit and rest her ankle. He hid the supplies and his kit under the thick layer of straw. There was less chance of having to defend their goods, if they were thought to have little worth risking the wrath of God for attacking His servants.

He slipped the sword Julianna had captured from the brigand beneath the edge of the blanket, for easy access. The cold metal brought up images of the prior day's battle. His meeting with Julianna and Lois seemed more like weeks ago because of all that had transpired. Since their first encounter, it was as if he had been swept into a rushing river, fighting for life at every turn.

At the sound of women's voices, he glanced up, his breath catching in his throat. Julianna and Lois wore nun's habits, yet Julianna's beauty could not be hidden beneath the dark veil or long robes.

"Do you think this is enough of a disguise to confuse our pursuers?" Julianna grasped her hands together and bowed her head. She was his vision of the Holy Madonna, but for the handle of the dagger sticking out of a slit in her robe.

"Y-yes, that should do." He cleared his throat. "You need to cover your dagger." He pointed to the weapon, then turned his attention toward Lois, as Sister Agnes wheeled her toward the cart. "I've padded the floor, but see if it needs more to be comfortable. We have a long way to go before we reach…" He paused as his gaze caught Thomas and two other children standing nearby, listening to every word. It would be best if they didn't know their every move. "…our next destination."

He helped Lois to stand and gave her a crutch he had fashioned from a limb with a fork at one end, which he padded with lamb's wool. "See if this is the right length." Their audience circled them and watched Lois test the crutch. "Put the padded V under your arm."

"It's fine and should help me get around on my own." Lois tucked the crutch under her arm and attempted to walk, but caught the tapered end on a patch of grass and tripped. John caught her and carried her to the side of the cart. "The length seems fine. I'm sure it will be a great help once I get used to it."

She smiled and clung to John as he leaned over the side to position her on top of the blanket.

"Hey!" A small voice yelped. "You ne'r squashed me."

John jerked Lois back to protect her from the body squirming out from beneath the blanket.

"Thomas!" Sister Agnes reached over from the other side and pulled the boy out of the cart. "What were you doing in there, child?"

John settled Lois onto the blanket, this time without the intruder.

"I wants to go to London, too." Thomas's face rose in defiance. He stood with fists curled at his side. "I's told you m' gran'da is there and he needs me."

Just as John had feared. The little boy had heard far too much when he listened in on their conversation last night.

Sister Agnes put a protective arm across the child's shoulders. "Remember, Thomas, I asked farmer Dilbert to inquire about your grandfather at the church while he was in London. He promised he would ask everyone he met if anyone knew your grandfather."

"But..." Thomas scowled, his hands still fisted.

"You like farmer Dilbert and know he is a good and honorable man. Right?"

Thomas nodded.

"He told me after he returned last week, that no one he met knew of a fisherman named Useph Browne." She knelt down to face him. "I would never lie to you, Thomas." She waited until he relaxed his stance, but then tears gathered in his eyes. "I will not give up. We'll send more inquiries until we find him. But you must stay here, so when we do locate him, he can find you."

"Don't give up hope, Thomas." Julianna knelt beside Sister Agnes. "I know many people in London and I'll ask them to help find your grandfather, too. I'll do this, but only if you stay here and do as Sister Agnes asks." She tilted the boy's head up until she could see into his eyes. "Do we have a deal?"

He dropped his glance and gave a quick nod. With a sob, he wiggled out of Sister Agnes' grasp and ran to the barn, disappearing inside.

Sister Agnes shook her head. "He's determined to find his mother's father, for she promised him before her death that his grandfather, Useph, would take care of him and teach him to fish. Hopefully, he'll listen to reason." She turned her attention to the travelers. "I pray for God's traveling mercies to keep you and protect your mission."

She hugged Julianna, then helped her onto the driver's seat of the cart, for the heavy habit made it awkward to climb aboard. Once Julianna was settled on the padded seat, the abbess went to John. "After you deliver your charges safely, then find your parents and tell them everything you know about this trouble. They'll need to be warned. I shall pray for God's help against what is to come, for I fear the situation is far more dangerous than we know." She gave John a quick hug, then, with the help of the other nuns, she herded the children away from the open gate.

John checked the cart once more before he accepted his staff from Alfred. "Keep a sharp lookout, not only for the man I described with the bushy eyebrows, but for any stranger who comes inquiring after us." He patted him on the shoulder. "Thank you for your help. You're a fine young man, Alfred."

Alfred grinned and stood a little straighter with the compliment. He waited while John led the donkey and cart out of the compound, then closed the main gates, leaving only the smaller walkthrough gate open.

If everything went well, their little group could cover about twenty-five miles a day. They would have to limit their stops only long enough to rest the donkey and the women. Traveling with his mother and sisters had always required far more rest stops than when he journeyed with his father alone.

With that in mind, he chose Scarborough as their destination. There on the coast, he had good friends who owned a fishing boat. Hopefully, the brothers would agree to abandon their fishing long enough to take their little group to London for a price.

If all went well, they would reach Scarborough and the coast in two days, then another two or three days' sail to London, where he would part company with these women.

An odd sensation of guilt and sadness washed over him at the thought of never seeing Julianna again. He should be looking forward to continue on to the monastery to fulfill his vow. Why did that thought suddenly leave him feeling hollow?

Ignoring those thoughts, John walked beside Precious, praising her for the good job of pulling the cart. That is, until Julianna chuckled. He'd forgotten he had an audience.

"You sound like a father encouraging a child." Julianna's voice held humor, which tugged a smile from him.

"She reminds me of a child at times, always wanting her way, and not cooperating if she doesn't get it." He stroked the donkey's back to make sure the harness, nor the load, had rubbed a sore, which would need tending.

"I think she's tricked you with her current obedience, so you'll forget her former bouts of rebellion." Julianna grinned when John glanced up at her comment.

"You might be right, but we have a long way to go, so I'll do what's necessary to keep her happy."

There was a distinctive rumble coming up behind them— horses being ridden hard on the dirt road. He stopped the cart to listen. Precious shook her head. She sensed them too.

"What is it?" Julianna's eyes widened.

"Riders." John kept his voice calm.

Pounding hooves were definitely heading toward them. He

led Precious and the cart to the side of the road, but kept them moving. It was now or never to test their disguises.

"Get ready to assume your roles, Sister Margaret and Sister Sarah." He tugged the hood up on his robe. Keeping his head bowed to avoid being recognized, he clutched his staff tightly in his right hand. He would be ready if the need should arise.

CHAPTER 10

Julianna glanced over her shoulder into the bed of the cart. Lois sat straighter, her hand buried in the straw. A glint of metal confirmed that the sword lay beneath.

From behind them, two men rode hard and fast, ignoring them as they raced past the cart. The men were armed with short swords and wore dirty tunics and pants. One man, with a badly sewn patch on his right leg, rode a bay and the other man rode a dappled grey. By the animals' sweaty condition, they'd been ridden hard for some time.

At least they were not the assassin, Theroux.

"They won't make it wherever they're going if they don't rest those horses soon." John rubbed a hand down the donkey's neck. "We'll stop within the hour at a stream I know." He glanced up at Julianna. "Do you need to stop before then?"

"No, we're fine." She glanced back at Lois for her nod of conformation, then at John. "How long will it take to get to Scarborough at the pace we're going now?"

"Another day, at least." He paused long enough to shake a stone from his sandal.

"Can't you ride, too?"

"No. I fear the cart will be too heavy with my added weight for her to pull."

"Then let me walk a while." She scooted to the edge and waited for him to stop the cart. "I could use a bit of exercise."

"No. It would look very suspicious for the nun to walk and the monk to ride." He smiled.

It was more likely that his male pride would not allow it, than the worry about what others might think.

The bleating of sheep and goats came toward them from around the bend ahead. A large flock soon filled the road, surrounding them in a sea of unshorn beasts as the animals pushed past the cart, headed in the opposite direction. Precious stomped her hoof and shook her head with displeasure.

"He-e-e ha-aw." Her low bray of warning was followed by a short choppy, "Heh, he, heh," as if not worthy of a full bray. The goats and sheep took heed and gave her more space, but pressed into John in their haste to avoid the donkey's wrath.

John used his staff to keep the animals from tramping on his sandaled feet.

"G'day." An older herdsman followed behind, as a younger man and two boys scurried ahead to keep the flock from wandering off the road.

"Bless you on your journey, sir." John raised his hand with the blessing.

"Thank ye." The old herdsman took a copper coin out of a small leather bag hanging from his waist and flipped it at John. "For the Church, Yur Worship."

"May the Lord bless you a hundred fold for your kindness." John smiled and caught the coin in midair, then tucked it into his pocket.

Warmth stirred within her as she watched the handsome monk interact with the herdsman. There was no sign of the commander of men, as he spoke to the lowborn man with respect.

"Might take care ahead. Ther' be a couple of bad lookin' blokes." The herdsman spit on the ground. "They's waterin' their horses, but their poor beasts look spent."

"Thank you for the warning. We'll be cautious." John waved goodbye and kept the cart moving.

The noise from the herd behind them quieted, as the sheep and goats traveled further away.

Julianna felt the tension as John scanned the road ahead. "I take it there was more to the herdsman's warning than to point out those two men that passed us some time ago. What did he mean?"

"Sometimes brigands wait at the only place fit to water stock on a long section of road, hoping for someone to come by to rob." He rolled his shoulders and raised his staff, giving it a swing. "Keep your weapons close at hand, just in case."

During the next half hour, Julianna jumped at every sound. By the time they reached the stream, there were several other travelers watering their horses and stock. The two brigands had moved on or were in hiding. They couldn't win against the six or seven armed men that had gathered, even if a couple of the men appeared aged by their white beards.

There was one wagon with a woman and a couple of boys in the back.

The people made room at a place where a gentle slope allowed the donkey and cart to reach the water.

John helped Julianna get down, then handed her the donkey's lead.

"Keep a tight hand on her so she doesn't get into trouble." He smiled and glanced at a small flock of sheep nearby. "I need to fill our water jugs upstream away from the animals."

"Don't take long, in case she decides she doesn't want to be civil." Julianna clutched the rope.

"I'll return as soon as I can." He smiled, then disappeared up a path that led upstream.

"You be nice, Precious." Julianna stood patiently while the donkey pawed the water, splashing Julianna in the process, before she settled down and drank her fill.

"Sisters." A man wearing a simple linen tunic and pants smiled and tipped his wide brim straw hat in greeting. His other hand remained on the reins of a team of horses as they drank.

"Da. Hurry! We needs to go." The children in the wagon were hopping up and down, anxious to get out. Their mother kept them waiting until the horses had been watered.

The man with the team turned his attention to the wagon and waved at the children, giving them permission to leap out of the wagon. They ran behind nearby bushes to relieve them-selves. The father led his team up to the crest of the hill where his wagon waited.

Julianna watched him help his wife climb out of the wagon. It was then she saw the woman was great with child as she waddled down to the stream to wash her face and soak her swollen ankles. Their business taken care of, the boys ran down to join their mother at the water's edge.

Julianna smiled and nodded at the woman when she stopped nearby. "You have a fine-looking family."

The woman glanced back at her husband harnessing the horses to the wagon and smiled.

"Aye. 'Tis true." She stretched and frowned. "Now, if only this young'un will come soon and be healthy." The woman motioned for her sons to come out of the water. With one on each side of her for support, they helped her up the slope. Taking a pause after each step, they made it to the wagon, where her husband met her with a pinched brow of worry.

To have a family and a good husband's concern. That woman may not have a lot of material wealth, but she was far richer than many of the people Julianna knew—those who had more than enough money but were lacking in love and happiness.

Julianna shoved down the jealousy that washed over her.

When Precious finished drinking, the animal tugged at the lead and drew Julianna's attention. She led the donkey and cart up the hill to a patch of grass. While the animal grazed, Julianna walked to the back of the cart to check on Lois. "How are you doing? Would you like me to help you out so you can stretch your legs?"

"Yes, please." Lois grinned. "I need to move a bit and find a private place to take care of other business." She scooted to the back of the cart and tugged the crutch down beside her.

John returned and stored the container of water inside the cart. He helped Lois stand and offered his hand to steady her, while she adjusted the crutch beneath her arm.

"I found a good place that will give you privacy in that direction." John pointed in the direction he had just come. "It's fairly level ground and not far. Do you want me to show you?"

"No, we'll find it." Julianna moved to Lois's side.

"Take your weapons," John whispered, then glanced around. "I met a man upstream who said he remembered those two riders that passed us. He said they didn't stay but long enough to water their horses, then moved on once they saw the amount of armed folks watering their stock. I didn't see any signs of them hiding nearby, but that doesn't mean they're not around."

"We can take care of ourselves." Julianna patted her side, and Lois did the same. She helped Lois navigate a patch of uneven ground. "How is the pain?"

"Much improved, but it still hurts a bit. I'm sure I'll be glad to get back to the cart and rest after our little outing." They followed the path until they found the place John had mentioned. Julianna stood guard first, then Lois took her turn to watch out for intruders. Afterward, they headed back toward John and the cart.

Raised voices ahead made Julianna and Lois pull their daggers from their hidden pockets as they approached the clearing.

"Oh, thank God. Sisters you're back." The husband of the pregnant woman hurried over to them, wringing his hands. "Me wife…"

"Calvin, it's time!" The wife's tone was desperate.

"Coming!" He turned to Julianna and Lois, his expression wide-eyed with fear. "Please, can you help her? I helped deliver the boys, but she's lost two babes since during the birthin'. She's desperate to save this one. I don't know what to do."

Julianna and Lois hid their weapons and followed the man to a canvas-covered shelter John was erecting to give the woman some privacy. The woman made her way inside with a blanket. Her husband carried a small trunk into the shelter next, and then hurried back out.

The couple's two young sons were standing back, quiet, but eyes wide with fear.

"Have you ever delivered a baby?" Julianna whispered to Lois as they made their way over to the shelter.

"Yes, several in fact. This will be a good lesson for you to experience." She smiled. "You never know when such knowledge might come in handy."

As Julianna prepared to duck under the flap of the shelter, she noticed John's lips moving in silent prayer. Her heart stirred also, with a plea for God's mercy and grace to help this woman and her unborn child.

"Brother John." Lois paused, about to follow Julianna inside. "See if the husband has a large pan. Fill it with water and start a fire. Bring the water to a rolling boil for several minutes then take it off the fire. Once the liquid has cooled, bring it to me." She saw his stunned expression. "Hurry! We haven't much time, if her cries are any indication."

CHAPTER 11

*J*ohn thought the cries of the woman would never cease. He shoved down the memories of the battle they invoked.

While John filled a bucket with water, the woman's husband started a fire. He placed an iron grill over the blaze to hold the heavy iron pot filled with water. It seemed to take forever, but finally the liquid came to a rolling boil. After several minutes, they took the pot off the fire to cool as instructed.

The husband poured the water into a large dishpan that had been rinsed with boiling water. He said his wife used it to mix bread dough, but it was the largest one he'd found. When the water cooled enough to touch, the husband carried it inside the tent.

The several travelers present congregated around the glen, tending their stock and waiting for the news of the birth. The story of the mother having lost the last two babes had been overheard and spread by whispers. More travelers arrived, and were told of the birthing as they watered their stock. They remained, too.

John waited outside the canvas tent. The husband stood with

him until he was summoned inside the shelter. He hurried out and went to the wagon. After the man delivered the bundle he retrieved, he returned to stand beside John.

John glanced at him. "How's she doing?"

"She's always loud when birthing the babes. I'm comforted knowing that the nuns are helping her this time." The man took out a pipe and packed it with tobacco, then lit it. "The older nun said everything was going fine."

John wasn't sure he could remain as calm as this man if his wife were having a baby. The image of Julianna came to mind. A rush of panic clenched his gut at the thought of her going through such pain.

Suddenly, a baby's cry filled the air.

A wide grin spread across the father's face. "It be over. Praise be to God." He went over to his two little sons and did a little jig, sending them into a fit of giggles.

After a few minutes, the flap of the tent was thrown back.

"It's a girl!" Julianna stepped out of the shelter with a huge smile, cradling a red-faced newborn, as if she held a grand treasure.

The crowd cheered.

The husband and two boys rushed over to see the crying infant, who had a thatch of dark hair. The crowd of spectators also moved in close enough to see the child. *Oohs* and *aahs* filled the air. Laughter and smiles spread around the glen as the strangers rejoiced with the happy family.

Several of the men slapped the husband on the back with congratulations before returning to their wagons and families. Three men carried bags of flour and grain forward, placing their gifts inside the husband's wagon. One had a linen bag with a cured ham inside. A couple of women who had arrived with their husbands just before the birth hurried over with fabric for the mother and slipped inside the tent to deliver their gifts.

"I knowed Mattie wanted a girl to help her around the

house, but another son would have been grand, too. A farm never has enough help." The man hovered over the babe and kissed her cheek then stepped inside the shelter to check on his wife.

When John gazed upon Julianna happily holding the babe as proud as any mum cuddling her newborn infant, his breath stalled in his chest. She would make a fine wife and mother one day.

A revelation washed over him so strong, he staggered back. He wanted to be her husband and the father of her children, a dangerous feeling coming from someone who claimed to want to live the celibate life of a monk.

"Isn't she precious?" Julianna moved to stand beside him, rocking the fussy infant who was shoving a tiny fist into her mouth.

The donkey brayed at hearing her name. John and Julianna chuckled.

"I need to take this hungry girl back to her mum." Julianna glanced up at John and smiled, sending his heart to pounding and flutters dancing in his gut. "We won't be long and can resume our journey."

"Yes, well. I'll go check on our girl and get her ready to go." He turned and made his way back to the cart. He needed to gather his wits.

When the harness was once again tightened for travel, he untied the animal and brought the cart nearer the tent so Lois wouldn't have so far to walk. They had a lot of miles yet to go before they made camp for the night. Several of the travelers, including the farmer, appeared to be making camp to wait until morning before traveling on. There was safety in numbers, and by the looks of those armed with bows, axes, pitch forks, and staffs, the rumors of the two brigands had already made its way around the glen.

Good-byes were exchanged with the family and other

strangers they'd met. A few asked for John to bless their journey, and afterward, insisted he take a few coins for the Church.

He was glad to be on their way, even hours behind schedule. Giving counsel and words of comfort were part of a monk's life, but he felt like a fraud. Hopefully, after he completed his training and was officially ordained by the Church, the ministry would come easier.

As they started out, John pointed to the bag that had been added to the cart. "Calvin insisted on giving us some roasted grain to take with us." John had tried to refuse, but it was important to the man to give a thanksgiving offering for his healthy child and happy wife.

"Mattie gave us both a silver coin, and refused to take no for an answer." Julianna held up the coin, worth a half-day's wages, for him to see as he walked beside the cart.

"I know. The travelers have all been more than generous with their offerings to the Church." John held up a leather pouch one of the men gave him and jiggled the hefty amount.

"It does my heart good to know there are still kind and honorable people in the realm. I pray God blesses them many times over." Lois sounded tired but her words were soft and lacked the usual sharp edge. She began to hum an old song of thanksgiving John had heard once when his family worshiped in the cathedral in London. He'd been about twelve at the time.

He'd seen so much selfishness and wickedness during his service in the King's army. The kindness and genuine concern he'd witnessed today was healing to his soul.

"Stop!" A brigand stepped out into the road with a short sword pointed at them. "The Church don't need those coins like I does."

Anger surged through John at the threat, his grip tightened on his staff. He recognized the brigand as the rider with the patch on his right pant leg.

"He-e-e ha-a-aw." Precious brayed and stomped her front hoof.

When the man glanced at the donkey, John swung his staff and knocked the sword from the brigand's hand. Before the man could react, John swung the rod low and took out the man's feet from beneath him, sending him sprawling to the dirt in a heap.

"Aarraugh!" Out of the trees rode the second robber on a dappled grey horse. He raised a short sword and waved it at John.

Before John could react, a dagger whizzed by him, hitting the rider in the shoulder. With a quick glance toward the cart, John saw a grim-faced Julianna standing, with her arm still extended from the throw. *Very impressive. But was it skill or luck that helped her hit the mark?* He turned his attention back to the wounded man.

With a screamed curse, the bleeding brigand dropped his sword, then fumbled to rid himself of the blade sticking out of his shoulder.

"Time to give up, brigands. You're outnumbered." Lois rose to her knees and leaned against the side ready to aid with the sword in her hand.

With both men disarmed, John hoped they would surrender without further bloodshed. One glance at the rider's angry face, and John twisted the top of the staff, released the steel hidden within, and took a warrior's battle stance. "If you take your friend and leave now, I and the good sisters will allow you to live." He swung the steel-topped staff down and pointed it at the chest of the would-be robber on the ground. "If not, we'll gladly pray for your sinful souls when we bury you."

"No! Don't kill us." The man on the ground begged, then scrambled up and turned his plea to the man on the horse. "We'll leave." The rider leaned over and caught his partner's raised arm, then swung him onto the back of his horse.

"Let this be a warning to you. If you don't stop stealing and find honest work, you'll die a horrible death and go to hell, where the scalding hot flames will lick your blackened souls for eternity." John's voice boomed with authority.

"Oh, God, no! I promise we'll do better." The man on the back flicked a hand full of coins into the cart as they raced away. "Pray for us, monk."

"Very impressive, Brother John." Lois laughed and slipped back into a sitting position in the cart. She busied herself with gathering the coins. "At this rate, we'll have more than enough money to pay our passage to London."

He bent over and picked up Julianna's dagger that the brigand had pulled from his shoulder, as well as the two short swords the robbers had dropped. His insides quivered from the altercation. He had reacted as a warrior, not as a peace-seeking monk…again. Would he ever learn?

"I think your little sermon probably saved many lives in the future, besides their own, if those two will only heed it." Julianna's expression was serious, not mocking, which gave him comfort. Perhaps their mission would succeed after all.

~

A gentle rain fell all through the night. John and the donkey had found shelter under the thick branches of a large fir tree, while the women slept in the cart with a tarp pulled over them to keep them, their supplies, and the straw dry.

His dreams were filled with swordplay and chasing the donkey into a dark cavern, but he must have rested, for it was daylight when he opened his eyes. The donkey snorted and blew hot breath in his face.

"Go away." The rain had stopped, but his cloak was wet and his side ached from sleeping on the damp, hard ground.

"John!" Julianna's voice raised in alarm.

He struggled out of his tangled cloak and jumped to his feet, staff in hand. Precious had already vacated the fir and stood stiff-legged, ears back as she faced a stranger who stood with his back to John. Lois and Julianna stood side by side with swords raised.

"Listen, Sisters. I don't mean you any harm. You can put down your weapons. All I want to know is a man named John here?" A familiar voice sounded weary and gruff.

"William?" John hurried up to his friend and clasped his shoulder, first in relief, then concern. His friend would never leave the keep, which he had been left in charge, unless dire circumstances made it necessary.

"John? Thank God!" William turned and clasped John's extended hand. "I feared the worst."

"What is it?" Fear clamped onto John's gut with an iron fist.

William turned and glanced back at Julianna and Lois, then returned his focus on John with a question in his gaze.

"You can speak freely in front of them." John motioned to the cart. "Come sit here and rest. You look as if you've been traveling hard and fast." John had tied the shafts of the cart to the tree to make it level, so the women could sleep more comfortably.

"Here, let me tend to your horse." Julianna took the reins of the black horse slick with sweat, standing with head down and breathing heavy from a hard ride. She frowned. Her murmurs of disapproval for the horse's poor condition were low and threatening.

"Actually, this is my horse, which you've almost ridden into the ground." Anger hardened John's voice. He turned to William, who remained standing. "Why?"

"I had to reach you before you got to London." William's voice lowered. His hand shook as he took hold of John's robe. "They're going to kill them, John. All of them! We have to—"

William's hand slacked and fell to his side. His eyelids fluttered closed.

Unconscious, he fell back into the cart, which jarred it loose from the tree. It tipped, threatening to dump him on the ground.

"Julianna!" John caught the edge to keep it level. Julianna tied the horse to a low branch and hurried back. She quickly harnessed Precious to secure the cart.

John dragged his friend up onto the straw where he would be more comfortable. Lois climbed up beside him and checked him for a heartbeat with her ear against his chest.

"Is he…?" He couldn't bear the thought of William's death.

"He's alive but exhausted. No telling how long he's been on the road." Lois ran a hand over William's face. "No fever."

John reached forward and put a hand to William's shoulder to shake him awake, but she stopped him, brushing his hand away.

"Let him sleep for a while. We'll get the information from him when he's able. Help me loosen his clothing." Lois opened William's cloak, exposing a bloodstained tunic.

"He's been injured." John's gut clenched with dread. He leaned closer to get a better view. "How bad is it?" What danger had befallen his good friend? And what did he mean by *they're going to kill them all?*

She tugged up the unconscious man's tunic and found a blood-soaked bandage, which she pulled off to assess the wound. "His side is badly bruised and scratched. He's lost some blood, too, but I don't believe it's serious." She leaned back so John could examine the wound.

He had seen all manner of wounds as a soldier and doctored his share of them after a battle, but that hadn't made it easier to see his friend injured and bleeding. With a light touch, he studied the area. "The cut's too jagged, and by the puncture marks, it's unlikely to have been caused by a knife or sword. It's been doctored and bandaged, but his hard riding must have opened the wounds again."

"I'll doctor him with that salve of yours, and put on a fresh bandage to keep the wound clean and dry. After I'm finished I'll cover him with the blanket to keep him warm until he awakens. Until then, we must assume by his urgency that others are also tracking him." She reached into the box of supplies and brought out some dried lamb and an apple, and handed them to John. "Eat. You need to keep up your strength, too. This young man did not risk his life, your horse's health…or your wrath, without cause."

"I agree. We'll go as soon as the stallion's breathing is back to normal." John swallowed the fury boiling inside at William's careless treatment of Shadow, but also knew his friend would have never willingly mistreated any animal. He went to check on his horse.

Julianna was with the stallion. "I found old scars but no visible wounds, so he should be fine after some rest. I gave him some water and a portion of oats and barley." She rubbed a hand down the black's neck. "He's magnificent."

"He is. Shadow must be tired, for he usually won't allow anyone to touch him but William or me." John ran his hand over the stallion's muzzle and the horse quickened to his touch. Shadow pressed his head into John's chest and waited for him to rub his hand over his head and neck, as was their practice. "I raised him from a foal after his mother died birthing him."

As a warhorse, Shadow had been wounded several times protecting him. The stallion had carried him through several battles and, in the end, brought him home where they both recovered. He was as fine a friend as William.

Loose and dragging her rope, Precious brayed and pulled the cart over to John, pressing against his side.

"She's jealous." Julianna took the donkey's halter and pulled her back. "It's dangerous for her to be this close to the stallion, in case he should strike out in defense of his master."

"I've seen horses bully donkeys when left in the same pasture." John checked to make sure the stallion remained tied to the nearby oak, then he led Precious to green grass next to the road to feed and water her. They could wait only long enough to rest the stallion for an hour, but then they had to resume their journey if they wanted to make it to the coast before nightfall. Hopefully, William would wake up before long and explain his dire message.

CHAPTER 12

Julianna kept the many questions burning within her to herself for the moment. John had silenced her with an angry glance when she asked about how he knew the injured man.

Growing up in the institution, she'd learned to read people and situations. The man with the peg leg and John seemed to know each other well enough for the stranger to be entrusted with John's prized horse.

As she walked beside the cart, it suddenly struck her that she knew very little about the handsome man calling himself, Brother John. She couldn't envision him as a monk, no matter how hard she tried. Even though he wore a monk's robe, he spoke as an educated man of privilege and carried himself more as a warrior than a holy man.

She glanced over at him as he walked on the opposite side of the cart, his face was pinched in a frown. Yesterday, during their stay at the river, her mind and heart had wandered, until she imagined him as a devoted husband and loving father. He would teach his family to honor and worship God, and be a fierce protector of those he loved.

She rubbed her face, hoping to dislodge such idle thoughts. Belonging to the institute did not allow for hopes of a family or a home. Besides, he seemed determined to go to London and join the monastery to complete his training.

She glanced back at the stallion tied to the end of the cart. He plodded along, more like a weary plow horse than the warhorse she knew him to be. She'd seen the scars on his shoulders and hips where the protective armor would have had gaps. By John's confession at the convent, he'd been a soldier for King John's army. His skills with weapons certainly confirmed it. The man in the back of the cart must be the William he'd spoken of who had saved his life.

Movement in the bed of the cart drew her attention. Speaking of the newcomer, he was finally waking up.

"Where am I?" William groaned.

"You're safe, young man." Lois brushed a hand over his forehead.

"William." John led the cart off the road and stopped. He stepped to the back and leaned over to take his friend's upraised hand.

"John! Is that really you wearing a monk's robe and shorn hair?" When John nodded, William sighed with relief. "I was afraid I had only dreamed I heard your voice." His words were barely above a whisper. "How did you find me?"

"You found us, my friend." John smiled and pulled his hand back to rest it on the side of the cart.

"How's Shadow? I rode him hard, but we had to reach you."

"He's recovering." John glanced back at the stallion, which stood placid after the cart stopped.

"How long have I slept?" William rubbed his wounded side and groaned, then made two attempts before he could sit upright using the side of the cart for support.

"For several hours. It's almost midday and a good time to rest the animals again. We should eat some food to keep up everyone's strength." John touched his hand to William's forehead to assess his friend's condition.

"First I have to tell you…" William brushed John's hand away, then swayed, closed his eyes, and drew a deep breath.

"Young man, I'm sure that your news is very important, but you need something to eat and drink first, if you want to stay awake long enough to share it." Lois wiggled down to the end of the cart and used her crutch to stand. Then she hobbled toward what looked like an old campsite surrounded by a circle of blackened stones. Julianna gathered firewood and started a small fire. A ring of smaller stones inside the circle made a stable place to hold the pot of water she filled from one of the water crocks.

Lois threw in some herbs and cut up vegetables they were given back at the glen, and added a chunk of cured venison. The water boiled quickly and the smell of the food soon filled the clearing.

John helped William down from the cart and led him to a log other campers had dragged next to the fire. William drank half a crock of water before his thirst was quenched.

A cove of trees provided them a respite from the sun.

After praying a blessing over the meal, Lois stirred the soup and ladled out the first cup, which she handed to William. He hesitated, but after the women and John insisted he go first, he devoured the contents in short order.

"How long has it been since you've eaten?" Julianna had only felt that kind of hunger once. About a week after she was sent to the institution, she'd made the mistake of criticizing one of her teachers' methods of teaching, which left several slower students confused. Her stubborn refusal to apologize had cost her three strikes of the rod and three days without food and water. By the third day, she realized her suffering would not change the teacher's mind. From then on, she kept her opinions to herself—at least when she could be overheard. Eventually, she'd found ways to help those who needed it when the teacher wasn't watching.

"What day is it?" William held his mug out and Lois refilled it.

"It's Sunday, I believe." John sipped his soup and waited for William to continue.

"Then it's been three days since I left Brighton. I had dried beef with me, but only enough for one day. I hadn't expected to be gone so long when I rode out to exercise Shadow and check the north pasture."

"Start from the beginning." John leaned his elbows on his knees and clasped his hands. By the way he tensed and leaned forward, he seemed barely restrained from jumping up and pacing.

Julianna felt the same.

"Last Thursday I was patrolling the northeast corner to make sure no strays had been left behind after the flocks were brought to pastures closer to the keep. I saw a horse standing alone, so I rode up to it and found his rider lying in a heap on the ground. His hand still grasped the reins, which was why the horse hadn't wandered off. If it had, I wouldn't have seen the man lying in the tall grass." William's voice grew stronger after his third helping.

He glanced over at John. "It was our old friend, Angus." William stretched out his leg with the peg and rubbed his knee. "He was still alive, but in bad shape with a leg wound. I picked him up and shoved him onto his horse, then took him to Father Alvin." He took a sip of water. "As I helped the good Father, doctor the wound, Angus came to. When he saw the priest, he cried out for mercy. He went on and on, repenting for the many misdeeds he'd done since he'd left home. He was especially grieved over nearly killing a princess and her aunt." He paused when he noticed their attention.

"That was the droopy-eyed brigand who tried to kill me?" Julianna's anger laced every word as she turned to John.

"I told you he grew up in our village." John turned to William and motioned to Julianna and Lois with a grim look. "These are the women he and two others attacked. We know that much of the story. He must have escaped the assassin who killed his fellow brigands." John rubbed his hand over his face. "That still doesn't explain your presence."

"Angus recognized me and thanked me for bringing him to the priest, then insisted I get a message to Lord and Lady Stanton. I think he feared he would die before he delivered the warning." He turned to John. "He said he had joined a secret society called the Black Guard and had been commissioned by one of the leaders to find the princess and her aunt."

"So you've said." Lois stirred the pot and filled William's cup with the last of the soup.

"He also had a list of others they were to assassinate within the next ten days." He put the mug down and wiped his mouth. "You and your family are on that list, John." His voice rose and he started to stand, but John put a hand on his shoulder to stop him. "Elise is on that list. We have to save them."

"Who are your parents?" Julianna stared at John. The realization of her suspicions regarding his privileged upbringing were true.

"Lord Henry and Lady Evangeline Stanton. I have three sisters..."

Realization flashed through her. The names on the stolen papers came to mind.

"Sarah, Elise, and Hanna?" Julianna's words were automatic, as if read from a page.

"Yes, how do you know that?" John sprang to his feet and stalked toward Julianna.

"Here, read this for yourself." She unbound the leather pouch from around her waist that contained the stolen papers and thrust it at John. Fear uncoiled within her. The names suddenly became personal, with their connection to him. "These are the documents we took from the earl. They're why we must do whatever is necessary to get them and our report of the other traitor's identities to the king. He must have time to plan his defense."

"Every person with noble bloodline that links them to the throne is on this list." John scanned the papers, then waved them at Julianna. "The Black Guard is planning to assassinate the king of England and everyone who could legally step into the throne. They plan to overthrow the monarchy and take control of the entire kingdom." His tone rose with the accusation. "You've had this all along and you didn't tell me?"

"We were ordered to go directly to London and give this information only to the King." Lois raised her hand to stop him. "We didn't know who to trust with this crucial information. And you've hardly been forthcoming with your true identity, or your parentage." Her voice was low and scolding. "Now you know why we're being pursued and why we must finish our mission."

"My parents, Elise, and Hanna are at my sister Sarah's home in the country, thirty miles outside London. Sarah's due to have her baby soon." He stopped and faced William. "We need to warn them and those at Brighton Castle. Also, the village must be told to expect assassins who will commit any atrocity to gain the information needed to fulfill their assignment."

"Father Alvin promised to spread the warning." William shifted on the log. "He has more experience in warfare than the two of us combined." William stood, and this time his stance was steady and his expression stern with determination. "He will know how to prepare those at the castle against intruders and warn the village to seek shelter at the castle, if necessary."

"Good! Then you should go with us as far as London. I'll make sure these women make it to the king unhindered to deliver their report. Once in London, you must take Shadow and ride on to Sarah's home to warn her husband and my parents." John stood with hands clenched at his side, stilling the need for action until they could leave. "Assure them I'll arrive there as soon as I can. Tell my mother not to worry."

While the men discussed their plans, Julianna and Lois cleaned up their camp and utensils, then repacked the items in the crate. Telling a mother not to worry about her child in danger was as fruitless as trying to hold back the ocean's tide. She wished she had gotten to know her own mother, for the servants told her she was a kind and beautiful woman.

"Shadow's doing better, but not yet fully recovered. You could use more rest, too. Ride in the cart for a while longer." John and William gathered the repacked supplies and walked to the cart to hide the items beneath the straw. By then, William had paled. He was too exhausted to protest and allowed John to help him climb into the back of the cart. He reclined on the straw, his body relaxed, and his eyes closed almost instantly. Lois joined him, but sat in her usual spot near the sword and supplies.

John smiled at Julianna as they walked up to the front and stood by the freshly harnessed donkey. "You get to continue walking, after all." He tugged the lead rope. "Let's go, Precious."

There would be little time to rest if they were to reach the coast before dark. After night fell, it would be harder to spot an enemy. Julianna had retied the leather pouch around her middle and hid it beneath the folds of the habit. With every noise she glanced behind and touched the dagger at her side. They couldn't afford any more delays...too many lives depended on them.

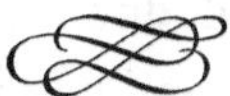

John wanted nothing more than to leap upon Shadow and race ahead to get everything ready for their departure aboard ship. But his horse wasn't ready for another hard ride just yet. The beautiful stallion had drunk more water while they were stopped at midday, but made no effort to graze the tender green grass.

The donkey maintained a steady, unhurried gait that allowed her to pull the cart and not tire. The slower pace provided time for the warhorse to regain his strength. William awoke rested enough to grumble about their snail's pace, and Shadow, too, became impatient. He pawed the ground and pranced from side to side, ignoring even William's attempt to calm him.

John handed the donkey's lead to Julianna and slipped to the back of the cart to put a hand on Shadow, while Julianna kept Precious going in the right direction.

With John's touch, the horse settled, though an occasional stomp of his foot showed his displeasure at being tied behind when he was used to being in the lead.

As John walked within arm's length of the cart, he caught snatches of conversation as Lois questioned William about the war and how he lost his leg. John winced at the topic. Though he couldn't remember much about the battle after he was struck down, he was responsible for his friend's suffering and loss. He would have escaped to the front of the cart, but the big horse fussed every time he removed his hand from him. The warhorse had also been wounded, but recovered enough to carry John home to die. For the field doctors hadn't expected him or William to live. Thankfully, God had other plans.

William's explanation of the battle was brief and a far kinder version than John would have told. No resentment tainted his voice for losing his leg, and no mention of his injuries being caused by saving John's life.

"How did you get your most current wounds?" Lois waved a hand at William's side.

"I arrived at the abbey of the Sisters of the Holy Heart hoping John might have stopped there on his journey." He rubbed his side. "Before I could dismount, some kid swung out of the tree nearest the gate and smacked me off the horse with a broken limb. The thing had been trimmed and the stubs sharpened." He grinned. "It made a very effective weapon to surprise an enemy."

"Was his name Alfred?" Lois chuckled. "He was a very clever young man."

"That was his name." He looked up at John. "Sister Agnes doctored my wounds and gave me a bit of food while Shadow drank from the watering trough in the courtyard." He rubbed his side. "It seems like there was a big fuss about another stranger who had come by, and concern for a missing boy."

"Thomas?" John asked.

"Theroux?" Lois questioned, her concern etching her brow.

"Yes, Sister Agnes seemed to know the stranger and called him Theroux. She seemed quite distressed by his appearance, but he wasn't admitted into the abbey. Then the villagers arrived and ran him off. It seems like a little boy, named Thomas disappeared during the event."

"Oh, dear." Lois frowned. "The child knows who we really are and where we're going. Just not the route we've chosen to take."

"If Theroux should come upon the boy…" John stepped closer to join the conversation. "According to the abbess, Thomas is used to surviving and getting what he wants by trading information or anything of value he can find. He's smart and able to read people. He may try to bargain his way to London with details he overheard from our conversation." John glanced up to be assured Julianna had also heard the conversation. She glanced back and met his gaze. Worry etched her pretty brow, before she returned to her task of keeping the donkey moving.

The day turned into dusk by the time they heard the clamor of a busy seaport in the distance.

"If I ride Shadow into the village and find my friends, we can be assured about our passage to sail when you arrive with the cart." John started to untie the stallion.

"I suggest you change into your tunic if you want your friends to know you when you arrive." William's tone held no humor. "I didn't recognize you the first time I saw you without your beard and shorn hair." He waved at the horse. "They may think you've stolen the horse and act without asking questions."

"A good thought, but though I still wear my pants I no longer have my tunic." John glanced at Lois. "It was donated to a good cause."

"I appreciate the offering, as it made a good bandage for my ankle." Lois tugged something out of the kit. She held up a new tunic, not as finely woven as his old one, but at least it was in one piece. "I discussed the matter with Sister Agnes, and between the two of us came up with this one." Her smile hinted at conspiracy. "Just in case you might decide to shuck the robe at a later date."

"Oh?" A flush of frustration rushed through him. The two women had decided between them that he would abandon his monk's habit and vows?

But William was right about his friends, Keet and Frank, the brothers William and he had served with in the king's army. They knew Shadow as well as they knew John and would be quick to take offense at anyone they thought had stolen the horse.

Tugging off the robe and pulling on the tunic gave him an unexpected feeling of freedom and power. A troubling thought he would ponder later. The tunic was a bit snug across his shoulders and chest, but it would have to do. He shook the straw off his traveling cloak. The hood of the garment would hide his shorn hair.

"Will Precious allow the sister to tend her until we get to the village?" William nodded to Julianna and scooted to the end of the cart. He dangled his legs off as John tightened Shadow's saddle and mounted. He pushed aside William's sling used for his peg to access the stirrup. The horse sidestepped in readiness for action.

"I think she'll do fine." He leaned down to speak quietly to William. "There are a couple of swords beneath the straw. I suggest you pick one and keep it close. There are only three ways into the village, and the assassin might post men at each road to watch for three strangers." He paused and frowned. "Perhaps I should wait and come in with you. They aren't expecting four travelers entering together."

"No. I think the sooner we leave the port the better. We can't afford to risk missing our friends, as they will leave out before daylight to fish." William kept his voice level, but worry lined the furrows of his brow.

"It should take you an hour—no more—to reach the port. I'll

find Keet and Frank and arrange our passage, then meet you behind the Empty Boot Tavern as soon as I can. The last time I was there, they had a grove of trees in the back which should make good cover with night approaching."

John waited for William to nod his approval, then he rode up to Julianna. "William knows where we'll meet. Stay safe." He hesitated again. Was he making the right decision?

"Go. We'll be fine." Julianna smiled and waved him onward. Her smile warmed him and stirred a determination to keep her safe to complete her mission. He secreted the image of her as his Viking princess deep in heart.

John turned Shadow toward the port and urged him into a gallop.

A bray made him look back. Precious brayed her disapproval again, but she continued onward. *Thank you, Lord.*

~

*I*t felt right to be riding toward an important mission, the wind in his face and his warhorse beneath him. Shadow had recovered his strength and was ready to stretch his legs.

The horse delighted in the run, his long stride ate up the miles. They arrived at the port as the setting sun glistened red and gold across the ripples of the water. Boats arrived with their day's catch, and men hurried back and forth with carts to receive the bounty and take it to the merchants to sell.

John spotted Keet's fishing boat on the far slip by the large number *3* painted black and surrounded by a thick red circle on the side of the vessel. The paint was faded but still visible, marking the three brothers' boat. Their older brother had drowned during a storm at sea while the other two brothers served in the king's army. Keet had lost a hand in the same battle that Frank had lost an eye.

The brothers were shouting orders, sending their crew to the ropes and leaping to the dock to fasten lines.

John rode through people on the street watching for a man with bushy eyebrows or anyone who looked suspicious.

The problem was that there were too many men wandering about who seemed keenly interested in him and his horse. He put a hand on his dagger. Even Shadow sensed the tension, for he pranced and threw his head as warning to any who might wander too close.

Keet stopped his shouting and went to the bow of the boat, leaning against the side facing John.

"'ay, you!" The activity on the dock paused and followed Keet as he pointed at John. "Wher' ye get that horse?"

"Raised 'em from a pup." John met his gaze and shouted their old jest. He waved, receiving a holler back of recognition. Keet and Frank hurried down the gangplank the crew had secured to the dock and met John as he dismounted.

"Commander!" Both men grinned, and the oldest brother, Keet slapped John on the shoulder. The place where Keet's other hand should have been was a stump covered by a leather cuff with an iron hook protruding from it. Frank wore an eye patch.

In spite of his nightmares, John couldn't remember what had happened after he led his men into battle. It was much later, after he was home, that William told him of Frank and Keet's injuries.

A flush of guilt made their reunion bittersweet. It had been John's fault that Keet and Frank had been in that battle. He ran a hand through his hair.

Keet stepped back when the hood of John's cloak slipped down. "Never thought to see you shorn from bow to stern. What happ'n to you? Lose a wager?"

"Long story." John glanced around. "Is there someplace we can talk in private?"

"Aye." Keet looked at his brother. "You finish up here and we'll meet at the Empty Boot."

With a nod, Frank hurried back up the gangplank and continued shouting his orders to the hands on deck. The hum of activity and chatter resumed around them as Keet and John headed to the tavern. John led Shadow to a quiet place near a watering trough. After the horse quenched his thirst, John followed Keet around to the side of the building.

"Out with it. Always knew when you had a splinter in your thoughts." Keet smiled, crossed his arms, then leaned his shoulder against the building.

"I need a big favor." John watched the hesitation cross Keet's features, but plunged ahead. "Some friends and I are in desperate need of passage to London." He paused hating the thought of putting the brothers and their crew in danger. "It's a matter of utmost urgency. Many lives are at stake." He lowered his voice in case anyone listened. "We're being pursued by hired mercenaries to keep us from arriving there."

Keet straightened and frowned. "I've never known you to speak false." He stepped away from the wall. "We'll take you." By his tone, he understood the danger. "We need to put on supplies and fresh water and unload our meager catch first, but we'll be ready to sail at first light." He glanced around. "Where's yur friends?"

"They'll be here soon. Can you also accommodate my horse, a donkey, and a cart?" John hated to ask more, but bringing the animals was necessary.

"Aye." Keet raised his eyebrows, but kept the surprise out of his voice. He'd been that kind of can-do soldier, too. His word was his bond. "We just finished improvements to our hole to haul more freight when the fishing ain't so good, as now."

"I'll make sure you're well compensated for the trip." John drew out his pouch that contained the coins given to them along the way, plus he'd found more sewn in the hem of his cloak. His mother used to do that when they were children to secure funds while they were at the market or large crowds. When she'd found time to place the money in the hem before they left was a mystery but it would come in handy now.

"You saved our hides mor'n I can count, while in the king's service. Yur money ain't no good with us." Keet slapped John on the shoulder. "I'll need to catch Frank and our hands a'fore they disappear into drink, if we're to get the boat ready before morn." With that, Keet hurried toward the wharf and was swallowed up in the crowds.

As the village light keeper lit the lanterns lining the wharf and walkways of the businesses, a foreboding settled across John's shoulders. William and the women should have been here by now. Should he go look for them and chance missing them, or stay here and wait? He bowed his head and prayed for guidance.

A flash of urgency surged through his spirit. He mounted Shadow and headed in the direction they would have come. The waning light made it hard to find the cart's tracks. At the edge of town he finally caught sight of wheel marks. The right wheel had a nick in it, like their cart.

Some type of struggle had happened there. Scuff marks of Precious's hooves, and the cart had been backed over its previous grooves. More alarming were the tracks he spotted of a man, by the size and shape of the boots, and a barefoot child that led away from town.

He followed the tracks as they led off behind a half-collapsed, abandoned building not far from there. Shadow pawed the ground, then sidestepped away from the building. John trusted the stallion's sense of danger. The warnings had saved him many times, at home and in battle.

The evening was cool and calm. John heard the sound of people talking in low tones. He dismounted and withdrew his staff from where it was tied to the saddle. Following the voices, he led Shadow to the back of the building, which still remained intact. A boarded up window, with a broken slat, was the right height to see inside.

The donkey was tied up near the entrance, still harnessed to the cart. By her twisting and pawing, she wasn't happy about it. He watched as she tugged on the knot.

Careful to keep his presence unknown, he pried the board loose to get a better view. With only a single lantern lighting the space, he saw Lois and Julianna tied to support beams. Thomas was tied to the post next to Lois. So, his were the child's tracks. But where was William? How many brigands held them hostage?

With the fragile condition of the building, he had to make sure his attempt to rescue them didn't jeopardize their safety. He searched the perimeter from his limited view point, hoping to locate William. A cold chill ran through him.

The man he most feared of finding them walked in front of the lantern. *Please, God, protect and deliver us from evil.*

"Theroux, don't do this." Lois's plea seemed to agitate the assassin, for he paced back and forth, then stopped before her.

"Lois, I have been hired to bring you and those papers back to the earl. The *princess*, I assume, is another of your protégés from the institute."

"Yes, I am." Julianna squirmed and pulled against the ropes that tied her wrists together. "You don't understand..."

"Hush. Our captor isn't interested in the truth or doing what is right." Lois's face filled with anger. "You threatened a little boy's life to get us to cooperate. I knew you were ruthless, but cruel?"

"I didn't hurt him, did I?" Theroux kicked the boy's foot, making him wail in fear.

"I'm sorry, Miss Lois, for helpin' 'im, but he promised he would take me to London and find my gran'da if I told him." Thomas kicked dirt at him. "You lied." He raised his face, his expression defiant. "Sister Agnes says lying is a sin and nothing good will come of it."

"Didn't you lie, Thomas, when you said you would wait for us to find your grandfather?" Julianna leaned away from the post where she was tied, so she could see the boy.

"I…" Thomas nodded and hung his head down. Tears ran down his face and dripped from his chin.

"Leave the boy alone. He knows he done wrong, don't ya, lad?" Theroux knelt down and wiped the boy's face with a dirty rag he found on the ground. "You kind of remind me of myself at your age." His expression turned dark and moody. "I lived with a no-account uncle, mostly caring for myself, while he gambled away every coin my father left me when he died. The drunken gambler sold me to the institute when I was not much older than you."

While the assassin droned on about his hard life, John scanned the dim room for William, but couldn't see him. He moved to another broken slat and peered inside. His friend lay on the ground, unmoving, next to the doorway. John's heart skipped a beat. Surely this madman hadn't killed William. Finally, his friend groaned and moved his hand.

John's relief was short-lived, for the movement drew Theroux's attention.

"Leave him alone. The poor man can't hurt you after you hit him, then stripped him of his peg leg." Lois's words tugged Theroux's focus away from William. "We all have horror stories of how we arrived at the institution. What changed you from the man I knew?" Lois searched the man's face as if she was truly interested in his answer. "I always believed you better than you thought you were."

"Yes, well, I believed you loved me enough to run away with me." Theroux gave William a cursory nudge with his foot. When his victim didn't move, he stomped toward Lois and knelt before her.

As the ex-lovers sparred with words, spilling out their disappointments and ruined expectations of the other, John tied Shadow to a low limb and inched around to the open doorway. As the conversation grew louder and more heated, he slipped inside and hid behind what was left of a large crate. He had a clear view of everyone's position.

All but William were tied to a support beam. What were his chances of subduing Theroux, a seasoned assassin, before the man countered with deadly force? John's staff would be of little defense against this man. Even if John could retrieve a sword hidden within the cart, his chances of success were slim. Unless… A distraction could give him the element of surprise, then maybe…

"He-e-e haw-w-w!" Having untied the knot that loosed her from captivity, Precious let loose an ear-piercing bray and trotted toward Julianna, who sat a stone's throw from where John hid. From his position, he caught a glimpse of metal at the waist of her habit. A dagger?

Hands tied behind her back, she fingered the weapon until it yielded to her determined efforts. Before John could edge forward to help, she slit the rope restraining her wrists.

The donkey was almost upon them, when Julianna leapt up, dagger in hand.

With a click releasing the narrow steel blade in his staff, John rushed out from his hiding place, distracting her only momentarily.

Theroux turned and charged toward him, but Precious rammed the man with her shoulder, knocking him to the ground. His short sword dropped from his hand, sliding out of reach.

John grabbed Precious's halter and backed her up, until the thick wooden wheel of the cart pinned the right leg of the felled assassin beneath it. His anguished cry moved even John to compassion, but not enough to release him until Julianna finished tying his hands together.

As soon as Julianna made sure the assassin was unable to wiggle loose of his bonds, John moved the cart off him and she tied his ankles together.

John searched the assassin for more weapons and found five daggers of varied length and width, a vial of what John had to assume was poison, and a thin metal blade, commonly used for picking locks and more diabolical purposes. Stripped of his shoes and his shirt loosened to eliminate further weapons, also revealed many scars, some barely healed. The assassin had lived a hard life. John patted down Theroux until he had exhausted places to hide weapons on his person, as guided by Lois's suggestions.

While John took care of Theroux, Julianna had hurried over to cut Lois's restraints, then checked Precious over.

"You're fine. The bad man can't hurt you." Lois loosed Thomas and gathered him in an embrace.

John dragged the bound Theroux to the nearest support post and tied him with more ropes to the upright where Lois had been bound.

Finally confident that the assassin was secured, John went to find his friend and assess his injuries.

"William, can you hear me?" John gently rolled his friend over onto his back where he could see his face.

William blinked then offered a weary grin. Ignoring John's offer to help, he sat up and rubbed the dirt off of his hair and his face. "I was walking beside the cart when the boy stepped out in front of us, begging for our help." He turned and glared at Theroux. "That man jumped me when I went to see what was wrong."

"You're not hurt?" John's heart still pounded with fear for his friend's life.

"I'll live." He winced as he straightened. "With a few more

bruises added to the ones I already had." He searched the ground around him. "If only I had come to in time to help you. I would have rectified his misconception that a man with only one leg is helpless."

"Here." Thomas held out the undamaged wooden peg. "I's found it over by the door where he threw it."

"Thanks, boy." William examined the peg and then strapped it back onto his thigh.

John extended a hand. William hesitated, but accepted the help to stand. "What are we going to do with him?" He glanced over at Theroux.

"We'll stay here for the night, taking turns watching him. The boat will be ready at first light." John walked over to the assassin. "We can't afford for you to get loose and follow, so you're going with us. I'm sure King John will know what to do with you."

"He'll hang him." Lois's voice held sadness and regret.

"I'm not dead yet, my beautiful petite." Theroux smiled at her and leaned back, as if content to rest.

CHAPTER 14

"Cock-a-doodle-doo-o." The rooster's crow from a nearby farm warned the group that dawn was nearing. The sounds of cows lowing, ready to be milked, overrode the muted sounds of the group getting the cart and their injured prisoner ready to go.

Julianna suspected the heavy cart had possibly broken a bone or two in the man's ankle, by the swelling and purple-black discoloration of the area. The cart that did him damage would also make it possible to transport him. John had wrapped their prisoner's ankle without resistance, maybe because Julianna held a sword ready.

"Look what I found strapped to Theroux's saddle." William held up a leather valise.

"That's ours." Lois turned to Theroux. "Where did you find this?"

"I deposited my *garbage* in the same gully as they disposed of the carriage. I searched the wreckage and found the valise hidden beneath a secret floor panel." He smiled at Lois. "A favorite hiding place of yours, I believe."

Lois harrumphed. "How would you know? It's been years since we last met."

"I remember every detail about you, my love." If Theroux intended to provoke Lois into another verbal battle of the wits, he failed, for she ignored him.

"Did you find our two drivers?" Julianna hated to ask, but had to know.

"I only found one body. He had dark curly hair." Theroux didn't smile. He must have realized the man had also been sent from the institute. "I met a sheepherder on the road who said some farmer had found a young man badly wounded on the road. The farmer took him home for his wife to doctor."

He grimaced when he moved his leg. "It must have taken the young man more than a day to crawl up out of that gully to be found." Respect for the man's courage carried in his words. "That's all I know of his condition."

Turning his glance from Julianna to Lois, he frowned. "I was more concerned about finding you before any more of the earl's hirelings discovered your trail." He focused on her. "My plan, from the moment I knew it was you who I was commissioned to find, was to protect you. You have to believe me."

"You tied me and my friends up. So, no, I don't trust anything you say." Lois narrowed her gaze at him. "You are a trained liar."

"I had hoped they had somehow survived. Everett was a good and loyal operative." Julianna interrupted what could have been another loud and lengthy discussion between the two veterans of the institute. "I'll keep Steven in my prayers that he heals from his injuries."

"We'll have someone check on him once we've finished our assignment." Lois's tone was somber. She turned her attention to repositioning their supplies and hid what shouldn't be seen, then prepared a place for Theroux in the cart, away from anything he could use to free himself.

Julianna adjusted her habit to make sure her dagger didn't show. He had used Thomas to get them to stop, then attacked them by surprise, knocking William out with a single blow. Threatening Thomas' life made sure they would surrender and cooperate with him. Theroux murdered people without any sign of guilt. She had feared the worse for the poor, frightened Thomas if they had resisted.

John again donned his monk's robe over his other garments. Did he expect more trouble and hope their continued deception would divert attention away from them?

As he saddled Shadow, the donkey brayed and swished her tail. Something was off about her actions.

Perhaps it was her jealousy wanting her master's full attention. The stallion stomped his hoof with impatience, but settled down when John ran a hand down his neck.

John glanced over at William standing at his side. "You'll need to ride Shadow to leave space for our two new passengers."

Julianna checked to make sure Theroux remained firmly tied before John and William dragged him to the back of the cart, then thrust him inside next to Lois. By her mentor's frown she would not tolerate any nonsense and kept a dagger in her hand as warning.

John stepped back and turned to Julianna. "We'll take his horse to the village with us. The bay gelding will make a good saddle horse once the animal's chipped hoof has mended. I'll ask Keet if he or Frank want the horse."

Thomas climbed up on the seat of the cart and edged to the left side, next to where Julianna walked.

Julianna glanced back at their prisoner.

"I won't make any trouble." Theroux smiled at Lois. "I'm right where I've wanted to be for as long as I can remember… next to you."

"Oh, please. If you had truly wanted me, you knew where to find me." Lois's expression revealed no emotion.

"'Tis true." He smiled when he saw he held her attention. "And I came often to check on you, but you always seemed happy enough without me." He glanced down, then up at her again. "I was afraid to approach you with plans to escape again, but I had to see you."

"Impossible. The building and grounds are impenetrable fortresses." Lois's tone was harsh. She glared at him, as if he was lying.

"There are secret passages into the institute if you know where to look." He lowered his voice and switched to a language unfamiliar to Julianna, as he and Lois conversed. Left out of their private conversation, she turned her attention to John who walked on the opposite side of the cart with his left hand on the lead and his right hand holding his staff. Since Theroux refused to reveal how many other assassins had been dispatched to find them, they were all on edge, searching for anything out of the ordinary.

John took charge of their growing band of travelers with such ease. She could understand how he could have led men in battle. With quiet authority, he instilled confidence with his leadership.

Fortunately, they met no other assassins during their trip to the docks. Captain Keet gladly accepted the gift of Theroux's bay and asked a friend to care for the horse until he returned.

Julianna stood on the dock and watched the boat's crew load and stow supplies, with the captain shouting orders and everyone jumping to obey. They got the cart loaded, then turned their attention to the livestock.

Shadow didn't fuss when the straps were placed around him or when he was lifted up off the dock with a sturdy pulley system and lowered safely into the boat's hold.

"Keet had the crew build a couple of stalls to secure the animals for the trip." John stepped up beside Julianna.

"Shadow seemed almost docile during the whole process of

getting him aboard." Julianna recognized the familiar flutters in her midsection whenever he was near. She smiled with the knowledge he also felt the attraction between them, by the way he sought her out.

"He's well trained, having been transported by ship many times." The pride in John's voice matched the satisfaction in his smile.

When the crew put the straps around Precious, she twitched her tail, lowered her head, bucked, and gave a throaty bray of displeasure.

"I'd better intervene before someone gets hurt." John strode over to the donkey and put a hand on her neck. She settled under his touch and calm encouragement, even as she dangled over the water, then lowered into the hole. John hurried aboard to meet her once she landed.

How well she'd tolerate being in the hold for the remainder of the trip was anyone's guess.

Julianna walked up the gangplank, but even in her nun's habit, she drew too many lustful stares from passersby and a few of the captain's crew.

"You'll not gawk at the nuns as if you've ne'er seen one, if you want to sail with me." Captain Keet cuffed the crewmember who had been staring at Julianna as a thirsty man longed for a sip of water.

"Aye, Cap'n." The man focused on the deck. "Sorry, Sister. I forgot myself. Please forgive me." He waited until Julianna mumbled her forgiveness, then he went back to work pulling lines into the boat to set sail.

She appreciated the protection and respect the habit afforded her, for there were still many devout fishermen who depended on God's protection and generosity in finding fish each time they sailed. They would do nothing to call down the Lord's wrath upon them. Yet, she had also heard a few crew members grumble about having two females on board again and the trouble they'd brought with them. Females on board were considered bad luck, nuns or not.

A chill threaded its way down her spine. She prayed for a safe journey for the sake of the many lives depending on the success of their mission. There were too few days left to get their evidence to the king and spread the word to warn those on the list.

The captain's brother, and first mate, Frank, and their crew gave Theroux a wide berth once they knew who he was. Assassins were feared as much as they were despised. Several of the crewmembers offered to tie weights to his ankles and drop him overboard once they got underway.

Theroux wasn't amused, but he kept his comments addressed to Lois, who took on the role as his guard. For truth be known, she was the person most qualified to deal with him, should some incident occur.

"How are you doing, Thomas?" Julianna leaned against the railing beside the boy, who seemed less confident about going to London. "You said you wanted to find your grandfather and help him with his fishing boat. Well, here's your chance to find out what they do on a fishing boat."

"Aye, Sister." He glanced up at her. "But what if he's not there? What am I to do then?" For a child, he seemed to carry the weight of the world on his thin shoulders. Sister Agnes had shared how emaciated Thomas was when a farmer's wife brought him to the abbey. The poor boy had lost his mother of the flux. He never knew his father, only the stories of his granddad, whom his mother assured him, was a good man who would welcome his only grandson.

Though Thomas was only eight or nine, he had the eyes of an old man, weary of life but determined to survive.

"Don't worry about that today. We'll help you find him, but it will have to wait until after we finish our mission, which must be kept secret." She turned his face until she could look into his eyes. "Understand? You mustn't speak of it again."

"I won't tell no body." He crossed his chest. "I promise."

She released him and smiled. "For now, go and find out what you can do to help these men and ask lots of questions. You want to be able to show your grandfather you'll be a great help. Right?"

"Aye." He turned his attention to the man checking the nets stacked on either side of the bow.

She watched John come across the deck toward her. His stride was confident, as if walking on a rolling deck was easy. Whereas, she doubted she would ever truly enjoy sailing. Her efforts to move across the deck were more an exercise in determination to get from one fixed object to another without ending in a heap, as the deck moved up and down with each swell. Thankfully, the day was clear and the captain's promise of smooth sailing gave her hope.

"Keet said that if the weather stays fair, we should make London in a couple of days." John's arm brushed hers as he leaned on the railing beside her, stirring the flutters within her and flushing her skin. Hopefully he would think it the salt air that brought the sudden color to her cheeks.

"Good. I'm not convinced Theroux will continue his passive attitude once we get close to London." Julianna drew in a calming breath. Falling in love with a man determined to become a monk was not her plan. Fighting her attraction to him guaranteed many sleepless nights.

"Keet has assigned a man to keep watch when Lois needs a break. I pray there are no problems." John smiled at Julianna, sending warm ribbons of longing floating up and down her body, mocking her efforts to keep her heart safe from him.

"Capt'n says yur needed below, Commander, er-r Brother John." The crewman stepped back, his cheeks turning red.

The unmistakable bray of the donkey and the squeal of the stallion, swept up from the hole.

"What now?" He frowned and hurried away.

It had been a sweet dream to hope the trip would be uneventful. She drew a deep breath to clear the flutters.

~

Julianna didn't see John again until the next day. He looked haggard and sleep deprived when he stopped in the galley for a bite to eat.

"Hard night?" Julianna sipped her tea and stared at the hard chunk of bread the cook called a biscuit.

"I'd rather not talk about it." He pushed his hand through his cropped hair, then reached for the cup of tea the cook handed him.

"Are Precious and Shadow all right?" She'd heard the crew talking about the stallion causing a ruckus, stirred up by the donkey. According to Thomas, the captain threatened to have both animals butchered and hauled out of the hold to use as fish bait, lest the stallion kick a hole in the side of the boat and sink them. John and William had spent the night down there. Around the second watch, the men finally got both animals secured with additional hobbles, and the ale put into their water buckets helped put the anxious beasts to rest.

"Fine. Everything's just fine." John gulped down his drink and held his empty cup out for more. The cook filled it again and gave him the same hard bread as Julianna had on her plate. John picked up the biscuit and dipped it in his hot tea. After letting it soak a moment, he lifted out the bread and ate it with no problem.

"So that's how it's done." She repeated his actions and found the softer bread tasty, with a hint of sweet and spice that lingered on her tongue after she swallowed.

"I'll have what they're having." Lois hobbled into the galley, her ankle still bound, using the crutch to steady her. She sat beside Julianna, looking just as exhausted as John. "I managed to get more information from Theroux."

She paused long enough to savor the tea-soaked bread and a long sip of the hot drink. "He says the head of the institute, Lord Alistair Cravens, is also involved up to his ears in the conspiracy against the king. He's been giving money and information to the earl for months."

A new wave of shock slipped through Julianna. "That we were assigned by the king himself may be the only reason we survived without detection. It's a blessing we left the earl's manor when we did, or we would have suffered the same fate as the others sent to spy on him." She took another sip of tea to get rid of the nasty taste of betrayal. "Since Lord Cravens is also deeply involved, how many others of our fellow brethren have been compromised by his deceptive objectives?" Julianna glanced over at Lois. "Who can we trust? Even in these nun's habits, they might recognize us. I've tried, but can't think of another disguise to better escape detection."

"True, but I think I have a plan." Lois sipped her tea. "First I need to run it by Theroux."

"What? You can't do that." John stood, his voice rising in alarm. "If he should somehow escape, we wouldn't have a chance to get you safely to the king in time."

CHAPTER 15

*J*ohn was exhausted.

William had awakened him once in the night with a hard poke to the shoulder, using the blunt end of John's staff. The man knew from experience that if he came too close, he risked injury, as John usually fought his way to consciousness.

The scowl on William's face made it clear John had been in the midst of an old nightmare. The fading memory of women screaming for help now possessed the voices of Julianna and Lois. He remembered being desperate to save them, shouting orders to charge. The little sleep he'd managed afterward was filled with shadowy figures chasing them into dark tunnels, with swords and threats which did little to ease his weariness.

"Keet, I'm sorry for the trouble last night." John found the captain at the wheel, watching the horizon while keeping the boat on course.

"I would have dumped the lot of you overboard had it gone on for much longer." He smiled to soften his words. "This boat is all me and Frank own after our father and brother's deaths. I would do anything to protect it against harm, even if it meant risking your disfavor."

"If I had known the trouble that donkey would cause, I would have left her behind." That might have been a harder decision than he'd like to make, but he'd have done it.

The disturbance had left him weary with doubts about everything he had purposed to do. His vows to serve the Church and his vows to protect the contrary donkey all seemed too much to deal with at the moment. Were his growing feelings for Julianna merely a test, or a sign from God for redirection?

Once they were all safely on shore in London, he would address his fears and doubts. Until then, he had to protect Lois and Julianna and hand over a very dangerous prisoner to the king's guards. Theroux faced torture and a death sentence, a sad ending for any soul, deserved or not.

Sending William to find and warn John's family was of equal importance. He prayed Shadow was up to the long arduous ride after his stay in the hold.

"Hey, Vander, secure that line." Keet waved his hand at a crewmember, while keeping the wheel steady with a hook attached by a leather cuff around his arm. The cuff stayed on by a harness that extended across his shoulders.

John studied the cuff, realizing some similarities to the harness William wore to keep his peg in place.

"Your sister, Elise, fashioned this handy piece." Keet must have noticed his interest, for he held it in front of John for closer inspection.

"When did you meet my sister?" That bit of information was more surprising than the fine workmanship of the cuff.

"Because of our injuries, me and Frank were sent home afore you. We didn't know then if you had survived your wounds or not." He placed his hook on the wheel again and glanced out to sea, as if the mention of war stirred up old memories. "I don't think I ever told you thanks for saving me life."

He turned his attention back to John and slapped him on the shoulder. "You rode up on Shadow like an avenging angel, and knocked down the bloke who took off my hand a'fore he could finish the job." He again turned his attention to the waves. "It was then that the spear pierced your side and knocked you off the stallion. If William hadn't intervened, we'd all have been goners." He glanced over at William sitting on the deck, showing Thomas how to tie different kinds of knots. "He be a good man, and should have been knighted for his valor, though I don't think the higher-ups thought either of you would survive your wounds."

"We almost didn't, but for our determined families and lots of prayer." John had not remembered the details of what led up to his wounds in the battle, nor the reason why he hadn't deflected the spear that pierced his side. "So how did you meet Elise?"

"With our father and older brother dead, Frank and I had to get back to fishing, wounded or not, if our mother were to eat and keep a roof over her head." He rubbed the wheel with his good hand, stroking it with affection akin to something sacred. "My da built this boat by hand, and we know every splinter of her."

John tried to stem his impatience, but a sigh escaped.

"Yes, back to your sister." He laughed. "Frank and I had delivered a special order of milled cedar to a merchant in London and had stayed in port to wait for payment." He murmured a curse of pox on the merchant. "The scoundrel tried to ignore his debt until we refused to off-load the lumber. He finally paid, but we swore we'd never have dealin's with the blackheart again and let it be known far and wide..."

John cleared his throat.

"We were sitting on deck coolin' our heels waitin' for our fee, when two women ran up our gangplank and hid behind some barrels. Frank and I watched as some fancy-pants scoundrel and his three cohorts ran along the dock, lookin' behind freight and shoutin' at anyone they saw. When they noticed us, they yelled, 'We're lookin for two witches who escaped arrest. You seen 'em?'"

"Witches?" John gasped at such an accusation. He'd heard of some scientists having been accused of witchcraft when a scientific experiment went awry. But Elise?

"Aye. But we hollers back at 'em to get along or they would be digging out from under a mess of fish guts." He shook his head with a chuckle. "You should have seen those mangy curs run away."

He noticed John's lack of humor. "Turns out Lady Elise and her companion, Isabella, were the two they were searching for. I wore a large bandage around my wrist at the time, but the women didn't seem to notice. Could be because they were too upset, so I took them down to the galley and gave 'em some tea and bread. They begged for passage, but I wanted to know more a'fore I committed to taking them anywhere."

John tried to stem his impatience while Keet dealt with more orders to the crew. He alone was in charge of the boat, as Frank caught up on his sleep so he would be alert to take the night watch.

"The long and the short of it, Lady Elise had been wrongly accused of practicing witchcraft by some would-be suitor she slighted. It was his way of getting revenge. I heard later that pompous jay had the headmaster of the school for scientific studies arrested and tried on the same charges of witchcraft, putting the fear of death on every student. On a later trip to London, I found out that all charges had been dropped and every student cleared, but by then Lady Elise had returned home.

"She was adamant that she was needed at Brighton Castle, and her parents, Lord and Lady Stanton, would gladly pay for their passages. That's when I put two and two together. I told her I had served with Lord John Stanton and would help her by taking her as far as I could." He stopped to watch a crewman climb to the crow's nest to scan for any obstacles or ships ahead.

After the man successfully climbed onto his perch, Keet smiled. "We left London right after we got paid and unloaded the lumber. My crew wasn't too happy about leaving without checking out the ale houses, but I knew it wouldn't be long before those fancy-pants accusers had the law checkin' each boat for 'em." He threw out a few more orders. "It was the best and the worse trip I've ever sailed."

He lowered his voice as he continued. "We came up against a terrible storm halfway to port that almost sunk us 'fore the prayers of those sweet women reached the Almighty's throne." He turned toward John and grinned. "Somewhere between London an' Brighton Castle, I fell in love with Isabella, and she with me. After we docked, I couldn't exactly let them travel alone for the three days it would take to reach Brighton Castle. I left Frank in charge and borrowed a wagon to take the ladies home."

He rubbed a smudge off the polished leather. "We made it to the castle without further mishap, but yours and William's mums were not there. They had gone to retrieve you both from the battlefield and bring you home. Yur da had arrived from a business trip only hours before us. Everyone in the castle was upset, since no one knew how you were doing." Keet frowned. "Your da gave orders for Elise to stay home with her little sister and he left the following morning to find your mum. I had prepared to take my leave, too but your sister insisted I stay at the castle long enough for her to fashion this cuff." He held up the hook and smiled. "Isabella told me later she had wanted me to linger long enough for the travelin' priest to arrive at their village."

Keet's grin widened until his face lit up with such joy, envy stirred within John. "I went home with a bonny bride and a strong hook for a missing hand." His smile of happiness told more of the story than words. "Both have worked out better than I could 'ave ever dreamed. I 'ave a wee son now, and am as happy a man as can be." He glanced up at John. "I owe your sister more than mere thanks. You may have saved my life, but she gave me a life worth livin'. A wondrous life I never knew was possible." He sobered. "I am still awed at how God could turn somethin' bad into a blessin'."

Dark clouds that were but a faint line on the horizon minutes ago now grew and gathered to the north, ending any further idle conversation. The wind picked up stirring up white caps on the water.

"Looks like a bad one, Capt'n." The crewman in the crow's nest shouted down then pointed at the black closing in on the boat, blotting out the sun in its wake. The captain waved him down.

"Get below and keep those animals calm." Keet ordered John, as he studied the storm clouds. "And take your people with you." He made eye contact with John. "Commander, I knowed you are a man of God and will pray, but make sure those nuns get to praying, too. We're goin' to need all we can get. There is no safe harbor anywhere near here, so we'll have to ride it out." His attention turned to his crew, shouting orders to trim sails and make fast everything loose on the deck.

John found William and the boy standing nearby. They'd heard the captain's orders.

"I'll meet you below." William grabbed the boy's hand and headed down to the hold of the ship.

John followed them down and made sure the animals were given some ale in their water to ease their restlessness. Animals sensed when storms were coming, and the tension of the people around them. As much as he wanted to make sure the animals didn't cause a fuss, William had a way with animals. Even the contrary donkey had taken a liking to him. He was more than capable of tending them.

John needed to find Julianna and make sure she was safe.

"Thomas and I will watch them. You go check on our prisoner and let the nuns know what's coming." William waved John away.

"Send word if you need me." John left and, after a brief search, found Julianna in a small cabin with Lois. Theroux sat back against the wall. His tied hands were secured to a heavy iron ring beside him.

"There's a storm brewing, and by the captain's reaction, I'd say it's serious. He asked that you pray." He touched Julianna's hand. "I know you're not nuns, but he doesn't. The least we can do is plea for the wellbeing of the ship and all those aboard."

"Monk, can you hear confessions?" Theroux searched John's face, his expression serious. "I've done more than my share of evil deeds, but being around Lois again reminds me that there is hope for a better life." His gaze met Lois's. "I don't want to die with this heavy burden on my conscience."

"I...ah..." John hesitated. No doubt the man living the life of an assassin had a hefty load of ungodly deeds to shed, but John wasn't sure he wanted to hear the sordid details.

Hear him and lead him to Me. The voice of God was clear, giving John courage and the words to speak.

"Yes, I'll hear your confession and guide you to salvation, if that's what you want." John half expected the man to burst out laughing and accuse him of being a hypocrite.

A passage from the first chapter of Isaiah slipped through his mind. *When you spread forth your hands, I will hide my eyes from you; yea, when ye make many prayers, I will not hear: your hands are full of blood. Wash you, make you clean; put away the evil of your doings from before mine eyes; cease to do evil; learn to do well; seek judgment, relieve the oppressed, judge the fatherless, plead for the widow. Come now, and let us reason together, saith the Lord: though your sins be as scarlet, they shall be whiter than snow; though they be red like crimson, they shall be as wool.*

This was the same scripture that Father Alvin had prayed with him. This passage and more proclaimed him cleansed of his most foul deeds. The least he could do was help this lost soul find peace, too.

Peace.

Why had John not accepted Jesus's forgiveness and His peace when it was presented to him? The time had come to practice what he preached. A weight as heavy as a boat's anchor lifted off John's shoulders. He took his first deep breath of freedom since the war.

"Brother John." Lois touched his arm to draw his attention. "I would also like you to hear my confession. I believe in God and pray, but I fear it's not enough." Her eyes had filled with tears, and when she glanced up at him, he saw the purity of her request. These were not idle words, but an earnest plea from her heart.

Julianna hurried to the door of the cabin. "I'll check on the animals and give you privacy." Her voice clouded with emotion.

John watched her leave. Disappointment hit him like a fist slamming into his chest. By the easy way she prays, he assumed that she knew Jesus as her Savior, so why did she rush off? Had he been wrong?

With tears running down their faces unashamed, Theroux slipped to his knees, though his tied hands pulled the rope taunt to do so. Lois moved to his side and knelt. She reached up and touched his shoulder.

John turned his attention to those who wanted freedom.

"For God so loved the world that He gave His only begotten Son, that whosoever believeth in Him shall not perish but have everlasting life." He raised his face toward heaven. "Thank you, Lord, for dying on the cross for me and my friends so we may have Your life eternal."

CHAPTER 16

*J*ulianna had to have air. The cabin had closed in on her, threatening to suffocate her until she was gasping for breath. She had accepted Jesus as Savior years ago, and had wished for someone she could trust to answer her many questions, as she read the Holy Word.

Not staying and praying with them was wrong, but she couldn't help it. Her heart wasn't ready to acknowledge John as a holy man, who would best fulfill his mission as a celibate monk.

The tears she'd held back now streamed down her face. She could no longer deny her feelings for him. She loved him and saw in him the husband she'd longed for since she met him. Had she imagined the connection they had from the beginning?

The grief of her loss was as heartbreaking as if she had experienced a death. The death of a dream buried deep before he came into her life.

God forgive me for falling in love with the man you chose to serve you.

She stumbled up the stairs until she made it to the door that led out on the deck. The boat bucked, nearly flinging her from her perch on the stairs. She grabbed the latch, only to have the door jerked open, pulling her out with it.

The boat pitched up and down, then side to side. The rain slashed at her face like icy needles. The ropes attached to the main mast popped like whips cracking over lazy oxen. Loud rumbles of thunder accompanied bright clashes of lightning, revealing the scene before her. She watched in horror as the brave crew, some with ropes tied around their waists, fought the gale-force winds, shouting to be heard over the howling gusts.

God save them, save us all.

Holding onto the door with all her strength, she glimpsed clouds churning like a dark cauldron all around them, while the wind increased in strength. The boat shot forward when the sails broke free, threatening to break the mast. The huge beam creaked, but held fast.

Losing her grip on the door frame, she was being sucked out into the storm.

"Stay below!" Frank grabbed her arm in a vise-like grip and pushed her back inside. Red-faced with the effort, he managed to close and secure the hatch. "Don't try and go out on deck for any reason until this storm is o'er. It's unlikely we'll be able to save you from yur folly, sister." His gaze narrowed. "What did you need on deck?"

"Just some air." Her voice quivered from her close call, and the bruise forming where he clutched her arm stung. She knew her answer sounded daft, but it was the truth.

"Aye, sister, I've had my share of dark moments when the walls and ceilings seemed to close in. The evil forces stirring the storm can do that." He smiled and nudged her to the stairs that led below. "Let's see if any of the crew could use some extra hands. Keeping busy helps those dangerous notions pass."

With every step down, the feeling of impending doom grew stronger. *Oh, Lord please save us.* When she had been at the institute for some months, she had found a holy book in the library and taken it to her room. It was a rare Bible handwritten and translated into English by the monks at the Monastery of Wearmouth Jarrow in the seventh century. The power of the Holy Word brought her comfort, but she had longed for more instruction in the meaning of some of the passages. No holy man was available to instruct the students, even though the Church was supposed to sponsor their studies.

Hiding beneath the stairway in her favorite spot to escape tormentors, she'd once overheard the headmaster talking with the cardinal.

"You're not to fill the students' heads with religion, if you want the enemies of the Church and Crown to disappear. A man with a conscience has no place learning the art of spying or assassinations."

The cardinal gave a weak argument for souls, but from then on there were no more ardent sermons or demands they learn the Ten Commandments. She had found the Commandments in Exodus 20:3-17 and Deuteronomy 5:7-21. No wonder they didn't want the students to learn God's rules to live by, for each commandment was in direct contrast with the dictates of the Crown and Church's mission to create an army of spies and assassins. She had increased her reading of the Holy Book after that, but made sure it was hidden away when she was not in her room.

Once she returned to London and completed her assignment, she would go to her room and retrieve the book before she disappeared. It was her most valuable possession, even more than the gold and silver she had managed to save over the years.

When she made it to the last rung of the ship's ladder into the hold, she stepped down into water up to mid-shin. The stench of fish and animal waste made her gag. In the flickering lantern light, she glanced over at the men standing knee deep in the swirling froth filled with straw, manure, and more than a few dead rats.

"Are we sinking?" Her heart pounded at the thought of being trapped inside as it went down.

Three men waited until she stepped down and cleared the way, then two of them climbed higher and disappeared out of sight, and the third remained stationed halfway up the stairs.

"Nay, sister, just a wee bit of water sloshing about. Nothin' we can't bail out, hey, men?" Frank handed her a bucket. "Dippin' out the water takes many hands during a storm."

He turned, bent down, and drew his own bucket into the water to fill it, then passed it on to a crewmember who passed it on to the man balanced on the stairs. He then lifted the bucket up higher. She assumed he gave it to someone close to a port hole above the waterline, who dumped it out and sent the empty bucket back down to repeat the process.

Out of the way of the crewmen, Thomas sat cross-legged on top of a tall crate an arm's length above the waterline. He never uttered a word, but his eyes were big with fear.

Shadow and Precious stomped about, splashing anyone near them. They were not happy standing in the rising water, but seemed to sense the need to remain calm as William sat on a crate near their heads, speaking in low tones. When he started to climb down to help, Frank raised his hand.

"Stay where ye are. Yur doing more good by keeping those animals quiet than lift'n a bucket." Frank turned his attention back to his task, and William returned to stroking the donkey with one hand and the stallion in the next stall with the other.

If the animals caused any trouble, she had no doubt they would be put down to save the boat and its passengers. Frank and every crewmember wore a dagger at their waists. The death of either animal would grieve John, something she wouldn't allow if she could help it.

She focused on filling her next bucket and tried not to think of the filth she stood in.

"Liven us with a song, Mr. Flannery." Frank kept filling bucket after bucket, so Julianna did the same. "Be mindful of our company."

"Aye, sir." Flannery, slight in stature, had deep-wrinkled skin, darkened from hours working in the sun, and an infectious grin almost hidden by a scraggly white beard. He started with a loud and boisterous tune about fishermen and their many loves in life, none greater than fishing. Julianna suspected words were changed as necessary to clean up the lyrics, often sending the men into guffaws of laughter, lightening the mood and the seemingly unending, tedious task.

The hard labor and the men's humor helped to relieve her fear, too. She joined in once she learned the tune and the words, which also seemed to amuse the men as they bailed, until they finally made headway and reduced the depth to below her ankles.

The roar of the storm had diminished also, a true answer to prayer. So said those resting their aching shoulders and backs from all of the bending and lifting. Julianna refused to quit until the last man sat down his bucket.

Cheers erupted all around.

"I'd take you on any boat I be on, sister." Words repeated by others of the crew as they filed out to take on further duties above deck.

"Aye, sister. You did fine work and gained the respect of the crew in the process." Frank waved her to the stairs. Unless you plan on sleeping on wet straw, 'tis time to go up to your quarters. You earned a good rest."

"We'll sleep here to watch over the animals." William turned to Thomas to confirm his decision, and the boy nodded his approval. There were several large wooden crates that had remained dry on top, which would make a good place to spread out their pallets to sleep. Thomas yawned and stretched out on the blankets William laid out for him. William waved Julianna away as he unfolded his own bedding.

Her legs ached and she swayed, the weight of her wet habit almost toppling her backward until Frank put a hand out to restore her balance.

"There you go, sister." He opened her cabin door and waited until she entered, then closed it. The sound of his footsteps on the stairs faded before she could make her way to her bunk.

She unlaced her sodden shoes and dropped them on the floor. The wet stockings were more difficult to shed, but finally succumbed to her persistence. She took off the soaking wet habit and hung it beside her stockings over a line stretched against one end of the small cabin.

Her exhaustion hit with a vengeance, leaving her limbs weak and threatening to dump her on the floor. By the last of her strength and sheer determination, she pulled herself onto the waist-high bunk and slipped beneath the coarsely woven wool blanket. She pushed away thoughts of their mission to lose herself in the heaviness of slumber.

~

*V*oices shouting words she couldn't quite understand drew Julianna out a very lovely dream. She rubbed her eyes and stretched, still feeling the warmth of John's arms around her as they slept. Only the sounds of their children's laughter spurred them to rise. The feeling of peace and happiness wrapped her in a cocoon so vivid, she was loath to awaken fully.

"Arise, sleepyhead." A cheerful voice unlike Lois's more solemn tone startled Julianna to wakefulness. "The sun is shining and all is well with the world…at least for now."

"Lois?" Julianna pushed up to a sitting position and watched as her mentor's grin lit her face, making her appear years younger. She pointed to a clean and dry habit she must have rinsed out while Julianna slept. Even her shoes and stockings no longer reeked of the filthy water from the hold.

"Your things are finally dry and fit to wear again." She sat a pot of tea and two cups on the tiny table and flopped down in the only chair beside it. Lois had never *flopped* down, as would a person at ease, at least not around Julianna. She'd always demanded strict adherence to protocol, with stiff posture, and head and spine in a straight line.

"What happened to you?" Julianna winced. Every muscle ached.

"I am free." Her voice grew as giddy as a maiden in love. "I never knew life could be this...joyful." She stood and twirled around the tiny space, bumping into the wall and giggling when she dropped into the chair again.

"Your ankle." Julianna couldn't believe what she was witnessing.

"My ankle is healed." Lois lifted her leg and tugged the habit high enough to show off her stocking and shoe. "See?" She rotated her foot and grinned. "Here, drink your tea and I'll tell you all about the miraculous things that happened last night." She handed Julianna a cup of hot tea and returned to her seat to pour another for herself.

CHAPTER 17

"She did what?" John had managed a few minutes' sleep after spending a good portion of the night answering questions both Lois and Theroux had about their new faith and their Savior Who set them free. He'd been shocked to find out they had been secretly married years ago by a traveling priest. After checking on William, Thomas, and the livestock, he'd gone up on deck to help wherever he was needed and ran across Frank.

"The good sister bailed water right alongside the crew until the last man quit." Frank slapped John on the back. "She be a bonny lass. Too bad nuns cain't marry...or monks. You two would make a good match." He smiled. "I should know, because I've found the woman of me dreams." He pointed to Keet, who was bending over the side of the boat inspecting something. "His wife, Isabella, introduced me to Cantry."

He closed his eyes and a smile played across his face. "She's got plenty of curves, brown hair, and green eyes that flash golden when she gets angry." His eyes opened and he glanced over to John. "A man needs a wife what's got plenty of spunk if ye want a happy life."

John smiled. For a man who had sworn, during his time in the army, that he'd never marry, Frank giving marital advice was like a frog telling a turtle about the wonders of flight. Still, he was happy for his friend.

"As soon as her da, who's a wool merchant, returns from Ireland, we'll marry." As Frank continued speaking, he offered a long list of dos and don'ts to ensure a happy marriage.

John listened patiently, nodding when appropriate. Julianna stepped out on deck, looking rested and none the worse for having bailed untold number of buckets of water out of the cargo hold. He smiled when he saw her stretch, wince, roll her shoulders, and then rub her neck.

"I have a salve that might help with those aches." John's heart sped up as she turned her smile on him.

"Oh, that would be wonderful. I found aches in places I didn't know I had." Julianna chuckled, but winced as she raised her arm to tuck a loose strand of flaxen hair back into the hood of her habit.

"What's all of the excitement?" She pointed to the crew rushing to and fro, pulling on ropes and dropping a huge net over the side.

"They spotted a large school of fish." He turned to face her. "The storm pushed us at least a half day ahead of schedule. And we continue to make good time, so the captains decided they shouldn't miss this opportunity to gather the bounty the storm put in our path."

"I heard from the men how bad the fishing has been of late. They're worried about feeding their families. This is truly a blessing from God." Julianna watched the activity with interest. "These are all hardworking men who deserve a good catch." She stepped back as a crewman hurried past her carrying a long pole with a hook on the end. "Can we help or should we stay out of the way?"

"I suggest we keep out of their way unless they ask for our

help." John put a hand on her back and guided her away from the main activity. His admiration for her grew within him. Even with her sore muscles, she was still willing to do more.

It took a couple of hours to pull in the heavily laden nets, their largest haul this season according to Frank. By their excitement, the men expected to fill their coffers with coins after they sold their catch at the port in London.

Keet grinned and slapped John on the shoulder when he saw him standing on the deck.

"God has truly blessed us, Commander...er...Brother John." He did a little jig. "I can finally buy Isabella that bonny little cottage on the hill overlooking the port. She wants a house where she can watch the boats arrive each day. She says it's so she'll have me meal ready when I get home, but I thinks she likes getting prettied up for me, like I could love her any more than I do."

"Cap'n, the nets are about to burst with our catch and there's no more room in the hold. Where should we put them?" The crewman shifted from one foot to the other, waiting for instructions.

The reason there was less room in the hold for their catch was because a donkey, a warhorse, and a large cart filled the space. The barrels lining the hold were already filled with fish, so there were no more places to put this large catch.

"How about we build a crate in the middle of the deck?" John couldn't stand the thought of the crew losing even one of the fish they'd worked so hard to catch.

"Aye!" Keet turned to Frank. "Gather every spare piece of lumber we have on board and we'll build as large a container as will fit on the deck." He turned to John. "Would you lend a hand?"

"Surely." John headed to the middle of the deck and walked out the measurements, as crewmen gathered lumber and brought it to him. He instructed the men helping him as they nailed board after board.

In less than an hour, a makeshift crate large enough to accept the entire catch—net, fish, and all—was finished. They lined the bottom and sides with an old sail to keep anything from escaping and to hold water long enough to keep the fish fresh until they unloaded them at the dock.

"Well done, mateys. Now we need some water to keep them fresh." Frank circled the crate, checking the load.

"We find we need some of that water we removed last night, Sister. Would you like to help?" An older hand laughed and waved at Julianna to join them.

"I must decline your gracious invitation, kind sir. I fear I'd be more of a hindrance, since I could barely lift my teacup to my mouth this morning." She grinned. "I believe you have a song for such a task, right, Mr. Flannery?"

A spark of displeasure slid through John at the looks of admiration the men gave Julianna. Even her good-natured responses to their teasing irritated him.

The men roared with laughter and Flannery sang to the top of his lungs a song about fishermen and their love of the sea. John's irritation turned to laughter when he heard the amended lyrics, for he had heard the far brawnier version. He appreciated the kindness the crew afforded Julianna with the omissions.

"I don't know how they do this hard labor every day with such joy." Julianna leaned against the rail beside him.

"That's because it's the life they've been called to do." Would his life as a monk fill him with such joy? He had to admit that leading Theroux and Lois to the Lord gave him immense satisfaction, but according to Father Alvin, any Christian could do the same. Could it be true? Could he serve God, fulfill his vow, and still marry?

To clear his mind, he grabbed a bucket and stepped into a

second line making it equal with five men stretched from each side of the ship, passing buckets to fill the crate. It soon turned into a friendly competition to see how many water-filled buckets each side could produce. In short order the deck and the men were thoroughly soaked from their hurried efforts, but the crate was filled to capacity and no fish had escaped in the process. The boat set low in the water with their heavy load, as it sailed toward London harbor.

~

John's first glimpse of London's harbor stirred both relief and fear in his gut. Were there hired assassins waiting to ambush them the moment they disembarked? Would they make it to the palace to deliver the news in time to give warning to those on the list?

William came up beside him and leaned on the rail.

"Good to see you out of the hold. Is everything all right with the livestock?" The donkey and stallion might get anxious without he or William down there to keep them calm.

"Aye. The boy seems to have taken a liken' to the animals and they to him. He wanted to stay below, so I took my chance to breathe some clean air not tainted with the stench of fish or a barnyard." He stretched and drew in several deep breaths. "I think the boy dreads leaving the boat, lest he can't find his granddad. I don't think he knows what to do if Useph Browne is nowhere to be found."

"I understand his apprehension of not knowing what we'll find once we arrive." John raised his face to soak in the sunshine and peace. After they leave the ship, there would be no time to rest until their mission was complete.

The softer steps of a woman followed by the brush of her habit against his arm announced Julianna's presence next to him.

. . .

"*H*ow long before we dock and disembark?" She touched her middle. Delivering the valuable papers in the leather pouch she wore and completing her assignment were probably weighing heavy on her mind.

"According to the first mate, we should arrive within the hour. Are Lois and Theroux ready?" John's concern about delivering the assassin to be hung had weighed heavy on his conscience since their talk. He had prayed much about what to do, but as yet, had no clear direction except to take him with them.

The boat sailed into the harbor and found a slip to dock. Hands secured the vessel and dropped the gangplank, ready to unload their guests first, then the fish. By the time Shadow, Precious, and the cart were unloaded, merchants were lined up to bid for a share of the catch. The dock was crowded, but they managed to get the donkey harnessed to the cart and Shadow saddled.

"God speed, William. Take it slow until Shadow has his land legs under him, then race to warn my family." John rubbed a hand down Shadow's neck to bid him farewell.

"I'll find them in time. Not to worry." He saluted John, then rode the warhorse through the clutter of people and cargo lining the dock. John watched until he was out of sight.

Thomas had teared up when it was time for William to leave, but the boy wanted to find his grandfather more. It was a tough decision for one so young. John admired his determination, but he had promised to come back and check on the lad as soon as possible.

Keet had agreed to help Thomas find out what he could about Useph Browne, and now both man and boy stood on the deck to wave farewell.

John turned to the women and Theroux. "Let's go." He led

the donkey, cart, and its passengers forward. Julianna took her position walking beside the donkey opposite of John.

"Follow the street until you can turn right." Hands and ankles tied, Theroux shifted his position in the cart until he, too, faced forward, with Lois at his side.

The crowd thinned a block later, and John found the side street Theroux had spoken of. He glanced up and saw two tall spires above the shop rooftops. One belonged to the institute, just as Theroux had described. The tallest and most ornate of the two would be the cathedral.

John could feel the hairs on the back of his neck stand up. It was the third time he had spotted the man in the black cloak, his face obscured by the hood that hid his features. The man had been trailing them since they left the dock.

John led the donkey around the backside of a livery stable and let the donkey drink, to relieve any suspicions if, in truth, they were being followed. One glance affirmed the worse. The cloaked man stepped into the shadows, but not before John caught a glimpse.

"I saw him, too." Theroux had turned, glancing behind them. "By his gait, I think it could be an assassin named Gillian. He favors his left leg after an incident involving…it doesn't matter."

"We're not far from the school. Perhaps we should make it there instead of the castle." Lois glanced over at Theroux. "What do you think? Or should we continue on straight to the keep and pretend we haven't noticed him?"

That was exactly what John had been pondering.

"Monk, head for the cathedral and stop inside the stables located behind." Theroux's tone remained calm and confident. "There is also a passage from there into the tunnels which lead to the school and the castle." He paused. "I've never used that passage to reach the keep directly, so we may have to go to the school and then backtrack. There are many tunnels, and one can easily get lost down there."

John's gut clenched at the word tunnels. He hated dark, confined spaces. He glanced over at Julianna. She had one hand on her dagger and the other touched the leather pouch around her waist. Worry furrowed her brow. Whatever she was thinking, she kept to herself.

CHAPTER 18

John's neck tingled, as if many eyes were watching them. He kept glancing around to see if he could spot the man in black, but didn't catch any more glimpses of him.

They passed several people dressed in finery, also headed to the cathedral. Their manner was festive, and John heard snatches of conversation that indicated a wedding was planned at the cathedral for some dignitary he had never heard of. Their little band was engulfed in a wave of wedding guests until it would have been difficult for the assassin to keep watch over them.

Slipping away from the crowd, John led Precious into the stables at the rear of the church and stopped in the large aisle. Several stalls lining both sides held stocky carriage horses, and more refined, high-strung riding horses that paced their stalls and whinnied for attention. Searching each stall, he found only one empty.

Theroux and Lois scooted out of the cart, then she released the rope around his ankles. They stood to the side and waited while John tended the donkey.

"You're in very high-class company." John consoled Precious as he unharnessed her and led her into the stall. He dumped the last of the grain they'd brought with them into the feed trough, though the donkey looked as if she'd gained weight since their journey began. A relief, after all the miles they'd traveled. Assuring she had a bucket of clean water, John closed the stall door and latched it. For more safety, he had Julianna help him push the cart in front of the doorway to block it.

"Hopefully, that will keep you safely contained while we complete our business." He reached inside to give her a pat, and she nipped at him, not breaking the skin but letting him know she was not happy. "You be good until we come back." His command was met with a "Heh-he-haw" and a stomp of her foot. He checked the latch again. If she had an opportunity to get out, she would.

When he went to the back of the cart to collect his kit, Lois stood beside Theroux. She held the valise containing the jewels they needed to return.

Julianna waited beside them. She held the short sword she had taken from their attackers only days ago.

As he studied his charges, it seemed like he couldn't remember a time when they weren't in his life. The events since meeting these women had swept him into a current of urgency even more intense than the war. He shouldered his staff. It would have been nice to have Theroux's more substantial sword for added assurance, but he'd sent that with William.

If their enemy had noticed the unique markings on that sword, then he too might have become a target.

John whispered a prayer of safety for them all as he followed Julianna, Lois, and Theroux farther down the aisle to the last door on the right.

"If I remember right, the passage is behind a false wall in the feed room." Limping forward, Theroux stopped in front of the door etched with the word, FEED.

Locked. It had been secured with a sturdy padlock to keep out trespassers.

"Lois you've always had a knack for these things." Theroux smiled and bowed out of the way so she could examine the lock. She pushed back the hood of her habit, touched her hair, and drew out a long and lethal-looking hairpin. With a poke and twist, the lock opened and dropped to the ground. She smiled and shoved the hairpin back in place.

"Nicely done, my love. I'm glad you've been practicing what I taught you." Theroux chuckled when she frowned at him.

"You may have taught me many things, Theroux, but lock-picking wasn't one of them." Lois stepped aside and opened the door. "I'll remain out here to keep watch for any potential inter-ruptions." She tugged the dark hood of the habit up to help hide her in the shadows while she watched for intruders.

Theroux preceded John and Julianna inside.

The sweet smell of oats and barley filled the long, narrow room. The place was clean and organized, like the one at Brighton Castle where John grew up. He'd always loved the smell of fresh hay and the sounds of the animals in their stalls. Something about it usually brought peace, but not today. His shoulders ached with tension and his palm was sore from clutching the staff in readiness for battle.

Finely woven hemp bags filled with grain were stacked along three sides of the room. The remaining wall nearest the door had three large wooden bins filled with the feed, and next to them, a work bench that held empty feed bags, water buckets, miscellaneous tools, and lanterns.

Theroux walked off several steps from the back wall toward the doorway and stopped midway. "Here, help me move these." With his wrists bound he still managed to hand John a bag of feed, who handed it to Julianna, who stacked the sack in front of the pile on the back wall, out of their way. Within minutes, Theroux uncovered a three-foot section of wall, with horizontal boards that appeared to run the length of the room with no apparent doorway.

John ran his hands over the boards and found no differences that would indicate there had ever been a secret passage. He stood and glared down at his prisoner, who knelt on the floor doing his own examination.

"Where's the passage?" He should never have believed the man had changed, even if Theroux had repented of his many sins and prayed for forgiveness. Had his prayer been a lie to gain favor with John, in hopes of leniency? If so, there would be a big surprise in store for their prisoner.

"It's here, I know it." Theroux thumped his knuckles all along the slats until his knock returned a hollow echo. "I just need to…" With a grunt, he pressed his fingers along a board with a discolored knot on one end. When he pushed the knot, it receded under his touch. As he applied more pressure a second time, a section of the jagged wood slats hinged opened, exposing a hole in the wall large enough for a person to crawl through. The air that flowed out of the dark cavern was stale.

"Wait." John bent down and peeked inside to confirm the space was a tunnel. He saw nothing but inky darkness. A chill ran down his spine. "Julianna, can you light a couple of those lanterns?"

Julianna brought the lit lanterns to John. He took one, and shoved it inside the space.

"It is a tunnel, which looks high enough to stand once you're inside." John turned to Julianna. "I'll get Lois and we'll go. Julianna, you'll go first." John stood and motioned for their prisoner to back away.

"Hurry, someone is coming." Lois rushed inside the room and closed the outer door after her. She shoved the valise into Julianna's hands. "You need to keep this safe." She gave her a look that carried an unspoken message. With the men's voices getting closer, he would have to wait to question them.

Julianna went into the tunnel, then Theroux followed by Lois. John pulled a few feed sacks close enough to hide, but not block, the opening in case it led to nowhere and they needed to return. He pushed the secret door back into place and turned a lever he found inside the tunnel to secure it. Sounds drifted through the hidden door. It sounded as if two men had entered the feed room.

"I know I saw a nun go in 'ere." The man raised his voice in defense of what he claimed. "The padlock is missing. This is the only place she could 'ave gone."

"Do you see anyone, Stewart? You'd better tell the boss someone was snooping around. It could a been them." The voices grumbled and grew faint as they left and the door banged shut.

John released his breath and turned toward the tunnel. A stone's throw away, Theroux limped ahead. The lantern light made his shadow bob against the stone wall like a ghostly apparition.

Lois held one lantern high as she followed close behind him. Julianna held the other light and had hesitated, waiting on John to catch up. He could see well enough to notice the raised eyebrows and unspoken question in her expression.

"Thanks for waiting. I secured the entrance and left space to get out if we need to return here later." The likelihood of them locating this same exit was highly unlikely if Theroux was truthful about the number of these old coal mining tunnels that ran beneath the city.

He'd hated small dark spaces since he was a child. While visiting his grandfather's castle one summer, he'd accidentally gotten locked in the dungeon when exploring. He'd heard lots of stories of ghosts moaning their eternal grief for having been imprisoned unjustly, so he'd been curious. A daft decision.

Hungry and frightened, he had prayed harder than ever before and repented of every bad thing his eight-year-old heart could think of. Especially for going down there after he'd been forbidden to do so. It took a whole day for his father to find him, hours after John's lantern had gone out. Even now he shivered with the knowledge of what could have happened. Though he found out later, the groans he heard were merely currents of air coming through broken mortar around the stone exterior, circulating up the passageways into the great hall.

His father had scolded him as he carried him up to his room. John had been half frozen, so he was given a hot bath and porridge to warm him, then sent straight to bed. His punishment of cleaning stalls and weeding the garden for the next two weeks may have fit the offense, but he worked without complaining. He'd promised God he would gladly accept his punishment if He would send someone down there to find him.

A vow was a vow. Can he keep this one without question, too?

Each shallow breath was a sharp reminder of the damp, musty dungeon and the hopelessness he'd felt of never being found.

Julianna slowed until he caught up with her, then hurried on to get closer to the two ahead of them. John stayed near enough to Julianna to smell the lavender she wore, which had a calming effect on his fears. A sudden desire to pull her closer stole his attention and made him stumble. She turned and smiled, warming him to his core. He kept his hands and mind busy with one hand on his kit and the other on his staff, which he had to carry at an angle to keep from hitting the low ceiling.

Theroux limped to a stop at a fork in the tunnel.

"I can't remember if we turn left to get the castle or right." He rubbed his forehead and glanced up at Lois. "Which way do you think? You've always had a great sense of direction."

"I've never had to navigate underground before, nor in these tunnels, which I never knew existed." Lois held the lantern closer to Theroux's face. "How did you find out about them?"

"I think I was about sixteen when I first found out there were passages beneath the institute. The cook caught me adding a substantial quantity of salt and pepper to his soup." He glanced back at John. "The man never seasoned anything, so all his food tasted the same, bland and unappetizing."

Lois murmured her agreement.

"He was furious and chased me out of the kitchen. I went to the library because it was off limits to all students and I thought the cook wouldn't look for me there. When I slipped inside, I found an opening in the library wall next to the fireplace. But before I could explore, I heard someone coming out of it, so I hid. I watched from under a desk as the headmaster immerged with another man, who I now know was the earl. The earl twisted a brass lamp hanging on the wall and the opening closed." Theroux cleared his throat. "Did anyone think to bring water?"

"Here." John opened his kit and brought out a flask of water he had filled before they left the boat.

"Thank you." Theroux took a long swallow and handed it to Lois, who also took a swig and handed it to Julianna. She declined and returned it to John. He replaced the flask and secured his kit.

"And?" Lois wasn't letting the man ignore her question.

He chuckled. "With the trouble I was in this time with the cook, I decided it was a good time to run away from the institute. So after the men left the room, I went to the lamp and twisted it sideways. The bookcase opened up, leading to a long tunnel. I found a lantern by the tunnel entrance and a flint to light it. After following the passage for a long way, I found several tunnels that intercepted it. I picked one and followed it until I reached a set of stairs. I climbed them and found a sliding panel to peek into a room. Inside, His Holiness the Cardinal and two other men sat around a table. I overheard his plans to promote me to agent since I had several talents needed for an assignment."

He looked over at Lois. "I knew if I became an agent for the Church, I would have an opportunity to make money and one day marry you. So I found my way back to the school and waited in my room as if I'd never been gone. The cook saw me at dinner, but because the headmaster had singled me out for a meeting with the Cardinal that evening, no more was said about my addition to his soup. Even the headmaster complimented the man for using more spices." Theroux paused and glanced from right to left down the two tunnels. "After my first successful assignment, I explored every tunnel over the years until I could come and go whenever I chose."

"You never told me." The tone of Lois's voice held more disappointment than anger.

"I planned to show you when we ran away together, but that didn't happen." Theroux's tone matched hers.

"You two can discuss your pasts later. How do we get to the castle?" Julianna's impatience equaled John's.

"Shu-ush." Theroux pressed back into the tunnel. They all stood silent and listened. Voices echoed from the right tunnel, amplifying the sound.

Lois and Julianna turned down the wicks on their lanterns and sat them on the dirt floor behind them to diffuse the light as much as possible. Both women readied their weapons.

"The boss ain't happy. He fears the king may already know of 'is plans." The man's voice sounded congested and nasally. "I hate these tunnels. They make me head ache and me nose run every time I 'ave to come down 'ere."

"Oh, stop yur moanin'. In two days you'll not hav' to use 'em again." The second man chuckled.

More voices interrupted. "Hurry, we've got a lead on our escaped princess and her aunt. We've found the donkey and cart at the stables. Since you're both good trackers you can find which way they've gone." The sound of men running away from them grew dim, then disappeared.

"That was too close." Julianna murmured, the lavender scent capturing John's attention, so he almost missed her words. "I thought these were supposed to be *secret* tunnels?"

"Once they were used only for emergency by the most trusted of the realm. On occasion, the king and his family members used them as a secret escape. King John started using them to spy on any who he thought were disloyal. Since then I've had to dodge the headmaster and the king's henchmen as they patrol these corridors, spying for their own purposes." Theroux headed left, away from where the men had gone. "I recognized the men's voices. They're guards at the school and won't risk being seen anywhere near the castle for fear the king might suspect their motives."

Theroux's pace was slow because of his injury, and they followed in silence for the next ten minutes. Theroux ignored several tunnels that splintered off of the one he had chosen. More voices and lanterns dotted the next intersection of tunnels, coming toward them.

Theroux turned suddenly and drew the ropes that bound his wrists along the sharp edge of the sword Lois carried, freeing him from his bonds. Faster than she could react, he jerked the blade from her grip and swung it in front of them.

She dropped the lantern, but it remained lit. "Give that to me!" Her no-nonsense tone had no effect on Theroux, other than to make him smile. He swatted her hand away when she tried to retrieve the weapon.

"Sorry, my love, but you need to fulfill your mission. And to do that, I need to mislead those coming this way." Theroux bent down and kissed Lois, keeping her between him and John and Julianna. "Follow the tunnel and avoid the next two or three passages, until you come to the one that veers sharply to the right. Follow it to a set of stairs. The stairs should lead you to the king's private office."

"You are coming with us, Theroux." John stepped around Julianna and pointed his staff at the freed assassin. He kept his hand on the carved ring, ready to release the hidden blade.

"Please, you must come with us. I know the king. He'll listen to me." Lois put a hand out to stop John from coming closer.

"No, my love. With my injury, I will only slow you down. If you are to succeed in delivering your proof, you must go now. These men have to be stopped. I can't let them get past me." He glanced up at John. "Monk, I know you have no reason to trust me, but thanks to you, I'm not afraid to die. For the first time in my life, I have peace." The lantern light distorted his features, but John saw the sincerity in his eyes. "You must go with them in case there are more obstacles in your path."

The voices behind them grew nearer, the echoes off the walls distorting the words. Whoever it was had no fear of being overheard, a boldness that could only mean one thing. Their pursuers had tracked them into the passages.

"I'll wait for you in our special place after we've both fulfilled our assignments." Lois reached up and kissed him hard on the lips. "Stay safe, my love."

"You had better not fail her, Theroux." Julianna put a hand on Lois and nudged her forward.

John tapped him on the shoulder as he passed. "God will be with you if you do what is right in His sight." He still wasn't convinced Theroux would remain loyal to his word, but John was relieved that he wasn't faced with the task of turning him over to the king's jailers to be tortured and hung.

The three hurried forward following Theroux's instructions. John paused only long enough to glance down the tunnel behind them. Several lights bounced off the black stone walls. If Theroux was sincerely right with God, hopefully they'd all survive this day to talk about it later.

John feared he'd lost count of the tunnels they passed, but the one they followed made a sharp right turn and inclined until they reached a steep set of stairs. No matter where it led, this was an exit and John was ready to get out.

Lois went first, then Julianna. John glanced behind to confirm there were no signs of light or echo of voices. So far, so good.

"I found the release lever." Lois set her lantern down to use both hands. She manipulated something John couldn't see from his position, but he heard a sound of metal sliding against metal, then the creak of hinges.

Daylight shone through the opening. It was as if he could once again draw a deep breath. There was nothing like the sweetness of fresh air.

The women escaped the dark dungeon into the opening, leaving their lanterns behind. As soon as they cleared the stairs, he made haste and stumbled through the exit bumping into Julianna's back and shoving her two steps forward.

"Who are you?" A woman screamed. "Guards!"

"I am Julianna, Lady Hampton. Don't you remember me?" Julianna rushed forward and reached out her hand to the woman. "Remember? You promised to help me if ever I had need."

"You?" The woman's eyes grew large and her hand went to her throat. "Julianna? Have you been sent to kill me and my husband?" She staggered back against a desk, and tears filled her eyes.

"No! Oh, no. You are safe." Julianna smiled. "I keep my promises."

The woman sagged with relief. "I nearly didn't recognize you in that nun's habit. What assignment has you masquerading as a member of the Church?" The sound of feet running in their direction caused the woman to gasp. "Hurry, hide behind this screen."

With a wave of her hand, she sent the trio behind a large ornate silk screen decorated with Asian designs of lotus flowers and people walking in a garden. Lois reached out and turned the wall sconce to close the passageway, then joined her friends. The large bi-folding piece of art was angled where it hid them from the doorway, but didn't block the view of their hostess.

The door of the library slammed open.

"Your Ladyship, are you in danger?" The guards' heavy tread stomped into the room.

John could almost picture the men as they glanced around expecting an intruder, their hands tightened on their weapons and ready for a life or death battle.

"Oh, silly me. A mouse ran across my foot. It gave me quite a fright." The woman giggled and fanned herself. "You can put away your weapons...unless you see that vile creature, of course."

"I don't see anything, M'lady." The guard's tone sounded annoyed.

"I'm fine, as you can see. Thank you for your prompt appearance. My husband will be quite pleased with your diligence." Lady Hampton waved her would-be rescuers away.

She stood still until the library doors closed. "Oh, my. The guards are already convinced I'm too highly strung, for I've had three other instances recently where I feared for my life. Thankfully, each occasion turned out to be a false alarm." She glanced over at Julianna. "With the increased tensions around the castle, my nerves are frayed." Her glance narrowed. "Why are you in the secret tunnels and why did you come here?"

"We were looking for the tunnel to the castle. We're scheduled for an audience with the king and were shown into the passages to avoid the crowds, but our guide disappeared, after giving us poor directions. We must have taken a wrong turn." Lois reached out her hand. "I'm Sister Margaret and you are?"

"Lady Gloria Hampton, the wife of the king's chancellor." She glanced from Lois to John. "And you are?"

"Brother John. We have most urgent business with the king. How do we find him?"

"You won't be safe to continue in the tunnels. The king has ordered all tunnels and entrances to be sealed. This one my husband simply hasn't remembered to deal with. The guards roaming the passages will surely find it and secure it from that side."

She waved an arm toward a cozy settee and a silver tray set with tea. "Sit. I can have more cups brought."

"We can't stay. Please, we must see the king immediately." Lois stood.

"I see." She glanced from Lois to Julianna, then to John. "I'll have my carriage brought around immediately. The king's guards know it by sight and should admit you into the castle's courtyard, but I'm not sure how you'll escape the palace guards once you arrive." Lady Hampton wrung her hands. "The king is more paranoid than ever after the attempts on his life. No one is allowed near him without his guard in attendance, not even my husband."

"If you can get us to the castle, we'll take it from there." John brushed the spider webs and dust from his robe, and the women did the same. An audience with the king demanded a certain amount of tidiness, at the very least.

"Of course." Lady Hampton walked to the door of the library and opened it. "Carlton, have my carriage brought around to the side entrance, at once." A mumbled reply could be heard from the hall. As John glanced outside, no unusual activity appeared to be going on in the garden. The sky had darkened, threatening a heavy downpour.

"Looks like rain." John paced back to the middle of the room. He pulled the silk screen in front of the closed door to the tunnel's opening. Maybe he was being overly cautious, but at least anyone trying to enter by the secret entrance would have to move the screen, giving John and the women time to escape.

Lady Hampton hurried back into the room. "The carriage will be here shortly." She glanced at them. "Would anyone like to freshen up before you go?"

"Yes, please." Julianna stepped forward with Lois close behind. They followed their hostess from the room, leaving John to ponder if he should have also gone.

The library doors flew open.

"Who are you?" An elderly man still wearing his traveling cloak stomped into the room and stood before John, waving his cane. "Did you think I wouldn't find out?"

"Sir?" John's heart pounded. He could easily disarm and disable the man, but should he wait until he found out who he was and what he thought he'd found out? "I'm Brother John, a sojourner from Brighton Castle to a monastery just north of London." He reached out his hand and looked the man in the eyes. "Lady Hampton has been very kind to me and my party when she found us stranded without transportation."

"Lady Hampton is my wife. I am Lord Hampton and chancellor to the king." He reluctantly shook John's outstretched hand when he didn't lower it. "I find it hard to believe a tale of my wife being party to any unselfish act of kindness."

"Geoffrey, that's untrue and you know it." Lady Hampton stepped up beside the older gentleman and stroked his cheek. "Let me introduce you." She turned to Julianna. "This is Sister Sarah and this is Sister Margaret. They've traveled a long ways to pay homage to the Pope. They suffered an unfortunate loss of their carriage by highwaymen." She grinned at the old man and he smiled back.

"I'm sorry, monk, that I misjudged you." Lord Hampton rubbed a hand over his balding head. "What can we do for you?"

"Oh, darling, I've made arrangements for our driver to take

them in our carriage to their destination." She gushed over the man as if it was his idea, and he responded as if it was so.

"With the Pope arriving within the week, the town is filled with riffraff wanting an audience with His Eminence." Lord Hampton removed his traveling cloak with the aid of his wife and, with the use of his cane, made it to his desk chair. He sat with a huff, as if exhausted. "Have you a place to stay while you're here?"

"Yes, sir. The Church will care for us and our needs. All we must do is arrive there in one piece."

"Is that all of the luggage you have with you?" Lord Hampton's tone was once again suspicious when eyeing John's kit and Julianna's small case.

"Yes, unfortunately this is the only luggage that survived the robbery." Julianna stepped up and smiled. "We are grateful for even these few items they deemed not worthy of taking. We have very little need for ourselves."

"Then you should teach my wife how to be grateful for fewer things in her life." His grin took the edge off his comments, but his wife frowned. "Where did you say you're from, Sister?"

A knock sounded at the door and a servant stepped inside. "The carriage is ready M'lady."

"We must go." Julianna smiled at the old man and then glanced over at his wife. "Thank you for your help, M'lady. You are indeed a woman of your word."

CHAPTER 19

Julianna settled into the carriage next to Lois. John's long legs brushed hers as he leaned back and closed his eyes. His lips were moving silently in petition to God for their safety. She had learned to read lips as a technique for spying. It was a relief that they were covered in prayer for what they were about to face.

"We left the tunnels too soon." Lois stiffened her posture. "Theroux wouldn't deliberately send us in the wrong direction." Her words didn't match the doubt in her tone.

"By the distance the carriage is taking us to the castle I'm not sure we were anywhere close to the king's private study." John rubbed his temple. "I fear I allowed an assassin to escape." He leaned forward with his elbows on his knees. "I suggest we avoid mentioning our encounter with Theroux to the king."

"I agree." Julianna could see no good coming from revealing their connection to the man who charmed his way back into Lois's life, only to steal her sword and disappear again.

The carriage stopped as the castle gates were opened to let them pass into the courtyard of the keep.

Once inside, the footman opened the door and helped her

and Lois climb down, then stepped aside while John exited the conveyance. They were immediately surrounded by five castle guards.

"Who are you and why have you come in the chancellor's carriage?" The captain of the guards walked up to them with his hand on his sword. He glanced up and made eye contact with John. "Lord Stanton! Why do you wear the robes of a monk?" His eyes narrowed and his stance stiffened as if prepared to challenge.

"Captain Henry Brummel. It's good to see you again after so long a time." When the man didn't meet John's greeting with one of his own, his tone turned serious. "We found it necessary to come cloaked in these robes to escape assassins set to stop us from delivering some urgent news to the king." John pushed back the hood of his robe and straightened to his full height to address the man before him in the more authoritative manner of Lord Stanton. Gone was the humble posture of Brother John.

It was hard for Julianna to connect the two aspects of the man she had grown to respect and...love. She shoved down those thoughts.

"Please, there is no time to lose." Julianna's plea and John's reputation seemed all the captain needed to assure him of the truthfulness of their mission.

"Give leave to the carriage driver to return to Lord Hampton." The captain gave orders to his men, then turned back to John. "Follow me." He led them up the castle steps and into the entry. "Wait here." He disappeared down a long hall on the right.

"We are not safe standing here in the open." Lois took the valise filled with jewels from Julianna and clutched it to her chest. She kept her right hand on her dagger still hidden within her cloak. Raised voices sounded around a corner. "Go." She pushed Julianna in the direction the captain of the guards had taken, and the three of them sprinted that way. Hopefully, the guard had been going to the king's study. They arrived just as the door opened and the captain stepped out.

"I told you to stay put." The frown on his face made it clear his message to the king hadn't gone well.

"King John! It's Julianna and Lois with urgent news!" Julianna tried to shove past the captain. "Please, Your Majesty, your life is in grave danger." The guard grabbed her arm in a firm grip. She glanced at John with silent desperation. They were so close to completing their mission.

The captain turned to John for confirmation.

"It's true. You must prepare your men for an attack on the king and the castle. These women have vital information that's uncovered the identities of the traitors, even those in the king's own court." Unwavering, John met the captain's gaze. "On my word."

The captain released Julianna and let her pass, then stood aside as Lois and John entered into the study, followed by the captain.

King John stood and motioned them closer. "I had almost given up on you returning. I feared you had been murdered or turned traitors, as happened to my other spies. What have you found out?" He sat and left them standing, glancing up at John. "I don't remember sending for you, Lord Stanton."

"No, Sire, but he saved us from assassins and aided our return." Lois stepped up closer to the desk, but was halted by the king's personal guard. He raised his sword as a warning and a barrier. "We wouldn't be here but for his help."

"You may stay." The king waved his hand and his guard lowered the sword to his side, but he kept his focus on the group.

John's frown of determination, and clenched fist around his staff, left no doubt there would be bloodshed if anyone tried to remove him from the room.

She hurriedly unfastened the leather pouch from her middle and handed it to the king.

"Within this pouch are papers that prove you were correct in suspecting the Earl of Arnsberg as a leader of the Black Guard. But you also have traitors within your ranks. Your chief advisor, Frederick Compton, was also at the earl's manor to meet with the men plotting your assassination."

"What!" The king stood, his face turning a bright shade of red.

The door to a side room off the study opened.

"She lies!" Fredrick Compton stepped in, pointing a finger at Julianna. "I never left London." When he glanced at her, the wickedness of his grin sent a chill down her back. He must have traveled night and day to arrive when he did.

John started forward, but Captain Brummel put a hand on his arm and shook his head.

"Read the papers, Sire." Lois pointed to the documents now spread across his desk. Then she turned to face Lord Compton. "Besides Julianna and myself, you were seen by several servants and members of the Black Guard. Once they're arrested, how many will swear to the truth if only to save their own miserable lives?"

Lord Compton frowned and tugged on his collar, as if it had suddenly tightened. "I have my own witnesses who will swear I never left London." The evil grin was once again in place. In his arrogance, did he really believe he could deceive the king with lies?

"Put them all in the dungeon until I can determine who is telling the truth." The king waved his hand toward them.

John stepped forward. "Sire, you know my parents. I served in your army until severely wounded. I would never deceive you. I've pledged my loyalty to the Crown and the Church." He waved at Julianna and Lois and raised his voice with the urgency of the situation. "These women are telling the truth.

They saw their driver murdered, fought off brigands hired to stop them, and faced all manner of peril in their quest to get these papers to you. The ruthless men who seek their lives will stop at nothing to keep them from giving their eyewitness account of who they saw and what they heard at that meeting."

John took a knee, his voice lowered, but the intensity of his words demanded attention. "Those papers identify each member of my family and every person with royal blood who could legally claim the throne after your death. They are all to be assassinated in the next two days if we don't do something immediately to save them."

"Poppycock!" Lord Compton's voice rose in a desperate shrill of denial. He waved his hand in dismissal of them.

"There!" Lois reached forward and grabbed Compton's right sleeve and tore the fabric, exposing a black bird tattooed on the inside of his wrist. "This is a sign of the Black Guard."

"Strike the king now!" Compton yelled to the king's personal guard and jerked free of Lois's grasp.

"No!" Julianna grabbed a tall candle stand next to her and swung it, deflecting the guard's sword from striking the king.

With the sword pushed to the side, King John drew his dagger and plunged it into the guard's heart in quick retaliation.

The same door Compton had entered into the study now swung open, and three more men dressed as castle guards ran in.

"Get them, you fools!" Compton screamed at the intruders as he drew his dagger and lunged toward Lois. She deflected the attack with the valise she wielded as a shield. Compton turned on Julianna, who came to aid Lois, and punched her hard enough to send her staggering back into the wall, dazed from the blow.

John knocked out one of the traitorous guards, then turned and swung his staff in a low arc, dropping Compton to his knees with a bone-crushing blow to his legs.

Captain Brummel took on the second assailant, overcoming the blackheart with a single blow to his chest.

Lois loosed her dagger, striking the final attacker's gut and knocking him to the floor writhing in pain.

Julianna rubbed her jaw, which ached from Compton's closed fist punch. She inhaled a deep breath, and clenched her fists, ready to return the favor.

"Drop your weapon or die, Compton." Captain Brummel pushed the point of his sword in harder, until the man cried out and dropped the dagger he had pulled from his waistcoat.

"When did you first know Compton was a traitor?" The king glanced over at Lois.

"Besides seeing him at the earl's manor, the black bird tattoo is identifying proof on the wrist of every member of the Black Guard. They wear it so they can be recognized in the fight that is to come in the next two days." Lois pointed at the traitorous advisor. "He knows every detail of what is planned. I suggest you use whatever methods your head jailer thinks best to get him to reveal all he knows."

"No! I'll tell you whatever you want to know." Lord Compton's whimpering submission rang hollow.

"I highly recommend checking every guard and servant in the castle for the sign of the black bird." John spoke to the king, but with a gaze, which included Captain Brummel.

The captain turned to the king and raised his sleeves to prove he had no black bird tattooed on his flesh.

"We'll need loyal men to carry the warning to all on this list. Their lives depend on it." The king stepped over the body of his former bodyguard. "I need two honest men, one to take this traitor's place to protect me." He turned to John. "You could take the place of my former advisor."

"That's an honor Your Majesty, but I must decline, for I need to make sure my family is safe from this coming battle." He turned to Julianna. "You can come with me."

Julianna's heart sped up at the thought of meeting John's family. What would they think of her, a spy with no heritage worthy of their son?

"No. Agent Julianna and Agent Lois must remain here and give me and the chancellor the full report of their findings. A plan must be set in motion to foil the Black Guard. There isn't a moment to lose." He waved a hand at John. "Go. You've served me well. Save your family while there is time."

While the king and Lois went over the stolen papers in great detail, Julianna watched and listened from the window above as Captain Brummel walked John out and ordered a fast horse be brought to the courtyard.

The chances of her and John meeting again were unlikely. They were from different worlds, too far apart. The heaviness in her heart made it difficult to breathe. She had to see him one last time to say goodbye.

"God's speed, Lord Stanton." The captain waved to John, then called several of his men and checked each arm for the black bird. Having found none he gave them their assignments. Two of the men, he sent into the castle to guard the king.

Julianna rushed from the window and out of the room, passing those same two guards, nearly knocking into them in her haste to get to the courtyard before John left.

"Wait!" She waved her hand to get John's attention as the groomsman led a tall chestnut gelding prancing into the court-yard from the stables. John quickly tied his kit onto the back of the saddle.

He had shed his monk's robes for the freedom of the less cumbersome tunic and pants. What did that mean? Was it in case of battle or had he reconsidered taking his vows?

A guard reached out to hand him a sword, but John waved him aside and raised his staff. The groomsman pointed to the darkening sky. John nodded, handed the groomsman his staff and opened his kit. He pulled out his cloak and put it on.

He stepped toward the horse to mount. Julianna called out again. "John!"

He spun, and when he saw Julianna, he charged toward her, running up the stairs. "What's wrong?" He grabbed her arms and searched her face.

To never see him again… A sudden rush of emotions, the kind she felt when her father abandoned her at the institution made her stop and gasp for breath.

"I didn't get to say goodbye." Her eyes filled with tears. "I…"

John released her only to draw her into his arms. He gazed into her eyes then kissed her with such passion, she no longer cared they had an audience. A nun wearing her habit, being thoroughly kissed by a monk, who had just shed his robe, would certainly set many tongues to wagging.

"I shall never forget you." John's voice was husky as he drew back a little. He gently brushed the tears off her cheeks with his thumbs. "Will you take care of Precious while I'm gone? I'm not sure how long that will be." He brushed another kiss across her lips.

"I…" Words threatened to release the dam of emotions Julianna barely held in check. With her nod, he smiled.

"Thank you." His words were soft and low. He drew her tight against his chest sending a ripple of need within her. A shutter bunched his muscles beneath her touch.

"I…I have to go." By his brusque tone and flushed cheeks, his need equaled hers. He released her and ran down the steps. John leapt into the stirrup, and swung a leg over the horse. The groomsman handed him his staff and John raced off, not looking back.

Her legs were weak from such a passion-filled kiss. She waited until he was out of sight before she attempted to return to the king's study and her duties. What did any of it matter when her heart had ridden away with the man she loved?

CHAPTER 20

John's heart pounded with love for the only woman who could make him regret his vow. How had he let it happened?

His steed was strong and agile as they wove between crowds of loud market goers who hindered their progress out of town. From the pushing, yelling, and armloads of goods carried by the people, there appeared to be a frenzy of buying. Perhaps they had heard of the trouble coming their way.

The horse John rode was lean and bred for stamina and speed, which made him able to travel long distances with less need to rest. Those were necessary traits in a mount when delivering urgent orders from the king to his commanders in the fields and far-off posts.

When John finally escaped the city traffic, he allowed his eager mount to stretch its legs, eating up the miles toward the manor where his family would be gathered. Had William made it there to warn them? He couldn't take the chance that something had hindered him along the way.

Within the hour, the sky opened up and the dark clouds delivered on their promise of heavy rain. John was soon soaked to the skin, but the horse didn't seem bothered by the drenching and kept up a steady pace.

Soon the road became a muddy mire, slowing them to a walk. A large sign appeared at the side of the road, informing travelers that the Wild Goose Inn and Tavern was a quarter of a mile away.

The welcome sight of the inn finally appeared through the rain-clouded haze.

"What say we stop here for the night and rest?" John patted the animal's neck, then reined the horse into the courtyard of the well-lit inn. They stopped in front of the stables and he dismounted.

He led the horse inside, removed the saddle, and then found an empty feed sack to wipe down the gelding before leading him into an empty stall filled with fresh straw. The clean stall with fresh bedding was a good sign the inn's accommodations would most likely be clean, too.

He placed his saddle on the rack in front of the stall, untied his kit from behind the seat, then touched the pouch of coins at his waist. There hadn't been time to deliver to the Church the offerings given to him along his journey. "God forgive me for using these coins for my selfish purposes. I promise to repay the Church for whatever I use with interest." For now, he was grateful for the money to pay for a night's lodging for him and the horse, and food for their empty stomachs.

He opened the door of the inn, and the smell of hot bread and stout ale greeted him. The room was large, and a roaring fire in the fireplace warmed his chilled body. There were several tables with people sitting around them eating and drinking. A hush fell over the room with his presence.

"Welcome, stranger." A jovial man wiping his hands on a towel walked out from behind the bar. "Terrible storm to be caught out in, for sure. What can I get ye?"

"Do you still have a room for rent for the night?" John

glanced around to search the faces for overly interested or suspicious characters. He could see only the patron's backs, as they'd returned to their meals and drink. "I left my horse in the barn and would also like to pay for him to be grained and watered."

"Aye. I have one room left. I'll send me boy out to care for yur horse straightaway." He turned and barked an order at a youth in the corner of the room. The lad was talking to two men at the table and looked annoyed to be interrupted.

"Aye, Pop-p-pa." He retrieved the empty mugs and delivered them to the bar, before donning an oiled-skin cloak from a peg and slipping out into the storm.

The innkeeper turned back to John. "Ye look a bit chilled. Would ye like a hot bath before going to yur room?" He lowered his voice. "It's a bit extra, but ye can be the first to use the water."

"Yes, a hot bath would be well worth the extra cost, especially to be the first to use it." John grinned and reached inside his pouch to fish out sufficient coins for payment. His stomach growled loud enough the innkeeper chuckled.

"I'll fetch ye some food." The man left the bar area and disappeared into a room beyond. Moments later, he returned with a large bun stuffed with meat. He handed it to John.

John finished off the well-seasoned roasted lamb and fresh bread in three bites and washed it down with a mug of ale. He wiped his mouth. "That was delicious. Perhaps after my bath, I could have another of these sent up to my room?"

"Aye." The man smiled and motioned for John to follow him. He led him to a small room located on the backside of the fireplace. The heat from the stone wall made it warm and private. Steam rose from a large, wooden half-barrel stationed nearest the rock chimney. An older woman pushed past them, hauling another bucket of hot water, which she poured into the bath.

"There ye go, dearie. It's all ready. The soap's on the shelf and the towel's o'er there." She gave him a weary smile and pointed to a large towel hanging from a hook on the wall. "There's a rack to hang your wet things to dry. If you need somethin' else, let me man know and he'll fetch it right away."

"Thank you." He waited until the couple left and fastened the latch on the door. Stripping off his wet clothing, he hung them along the iron rack to dry and slipped into the hot water. The water was perfect, and he groaned with delight. His plans to reach his family had been hindered by the intensity of the storm. There was nothing more he could do until the storm abated. The arduous journey had aggravated his old war wound, but his aching muscles relaxed in the heated water. He scrubbed away the muddy traces of his travels.

Had Julianna had a chance to relax, too?

It was best he keep his mind away from her. He tried to pray, but every thought returned to their kiss. He shouldn't have done it, but they may never meet again. When he saw her, his only thought was to touch her.

The kiss just happened. He hadn't planned it. Well, he might have dreamed about it and more, but…

Voices outside the door interrupted his ponderings. He was about to tell them to move on until he heard the conspiratorial tone of their conversation.

"It's started early." A man's husky voice rose with excitement, allowing a French accent to invade his speech. "The Black Guard's going to rid England of that crazy king once and for all."

"By the brand on-on its hip and the royal s-seal on the s-saddle and its fittings, the horse in-in the barn belongs to-to the k-king's s-stables." By the stutter, the second voice must belong to the innkeeper's son. "He might b-be the king's messenger with orders for reinforce-m-ments from the garrison."

"Naw. The gent didn't wear nothing indicating him bein' in service to His-Royal-Pain-In-The-Backside. More likely 'e stole it or bought it from ones who did the stealin'." The man with the husky voice was once again hiding his origins. He sounded confident he had John's possession of the Crown's horse all figured out.

John slipped out of the bath and quickly dried off. Fortunately, he had a clean set of clothes in his kit. Leaving his monk's robes behind might have been a mistake if wearing them could convince strangers he was of no threat. But then again, he would have still been suspect, as he would have no reason for riding a horse owned by the Crown.

He dressed in haste and shoved his damp clothing back into the kit. It felt good to be clean and dry for now.

"I sent Rob to find Andre." Smoke from a freshly lit pipe seeped under the door. The man coughed. The acrid stench of the strong tobacco burned John's nose. He covered his nose and mouth with his hand to hold back a sneeze.

"What if he-e can't get-t through? The r-rain's not let up."

"He'll get through or die trying. Until Andre arrives, we won't bother your new guest. I hope the man understands French, for Andre forgets his English when he gets angry." The man with the husky voice chuckled. "Your folks don't know a thing is up, so let's leave it that way. Just keep quiet, and you'll have a place in the new ruling government."

"I'm ready to do s-something more than c-clean, fetch, and c-carry. You c-can c-count on me."

"Good. The French commander told me, once the Black Guard and the king's men kill each other off, our invading army will meet with little or no resistance. Soon, all of England will be under French rule." His chuckle faded as the two walked away.

An invasion by French radicals? John had to get this information back to the king. He prayed God would keep his family safe, for a French invasion threatened all of England, peasants and royals.

He grabbed his kit and staff, then exited the bath. The back door was to his right, where the boy's oiled-skin cloak hung on a peg. *Thank you, Lord.* That cloak would help keep him dry on his journey back to London.

The innkeeper's welcome echoed through the hall, as he greeted another traveler seeking shelter from the storm. The innkeepers were good people and not part of the Frenchman's plot. Only God could keep them safe after the king learned where John overheard the information.

The barn was quiet when he slipped inside. The horse whickered a greeting. John checked the gelding to make sure the youth didn't try to injure or poison it. The horse appeared fit and well fed, so John saddled him and secured his kit. He kept his staff close at hand in case it was needed.

He mounted the horse inside the barn to stay dry. After raising the hood of the cloak, he spread the excess over the saddle covering his kit and a portion of the horse. A loud clack of lightning nearby, followed by more thunder, covered their escape into the night. Thankfully, this horse was well-trained and didn't balk at storms or loud noises.

The torrential rain poured all night, slowing their progress. Swollen creeks etched treacherous, swift-running gullies across the roads, which they had to ford. Strong winds knocked down ancient trees and pelted John and his horse with sticks and leaves. Finally, the wind ceased, leaving only the driving rain in its wake.

He entered the outskirts of the city near dawn as the rain slowed from a downpour to a drizzle. The streets were eerily empty, except for a stray dog or two that ran from him as he rode near.

The sounds of men yelling curses and the clank of metal against metal grew louder the closer he got to the castle. His heart pounded at the thought of being thrust into the middle of another bloody battle, this time without his armor or comrades.

"Looks like the siege has begun." John patted the gelding's neck to calm his own fears. Only his mission to warn the king kept him going forward. He wanted no more battles to invade his nightmares. "Now to find a way into a fortified castle without getting either of us killed."

He rode to the stable behind the cathedral without meeting anyone along the way, though his neck prickled as if he were being watched. When he glanced up, movement shifted in the closed windows, but no one called down to him. The Crown's brand on the horse's rump and the saddle were easily seen in the early light and would label him either an enemy or a friend, depending on where the loyalties of the observer lay.

No horses whinnied greetings when he rode into the barn and dismounted. He took the gelding to the nearest stall and led him inside, leaving him saddled in case he needed a quick escape. He removed his staff and kit.

Tugging off the cloak, he hung it on a hook outside the stall. Each stall was empty along the way to the one where he had left Precious. The cart had been moved outside the barn—he could see it through the open doors that led to the paddock.

No ear-piercing brays to convey her annoyance. One glance into the stall confirmed, the donkey was missing. He hoped Julianna had rescued the cantankerous beast before the siege, and both were safe.

The feed room door was ajar. The broken lock lay in the dirt nearby. He opened the door with caution, for someone could be waiting to ambush him.

The room inside was empty. He released his breath in a rush of relief. The sacks of feed that were once piled high along the walls were gone, leaving trails of grain out the door, where some had leaked their contents. Probably looters taking advantage of the invaders' presence to help themselves to anything not nailed down.

As Theroux had done, John paced off the distance from the

back wall to almost midway. Kneeling down, he found the knot and pressed it. The secret door refused to open. Had the king's guards sealed this entrance?

No! This was the only way to get past the fighting and gain access into the castle. He pushed the knot harder.

Nothing. Closing his eyes, he tried to remember what Theroux had done to get the door to release. He went through each action. *Yes.* Theroux had pressed the knot twice in quick succession.

The wood panel swung open, allowing the stale air of the tunnels to blow into his face. A quick glance around the feed room yielded only a lone half-melted candle, but no lantern. Not the best light, but it would have to do. Hopefully, he would run across an abandon lantern along the way, for he did not relish the thought of being lost inside those endless tunnels in the dark.

His mind flashed an image of his childhood trauma, stirring up his pulse until it pounded against his temples. "I have not been given a spirit of fear but of power, love, and a sound mind." He whispered the Scripture over and over again, until calm replaced the panic that made him want to run from everything —the tunnels, the battle that raged outside, and especially the doubts that plagued him about becoming a monk.

He took a deep breath. There was no other way to prevent the invasion. Duty, honor, and saving the lives of those he loved were powerful incentives to complete his mission.

The vision of Julianna holding the child she had helped deliver, allowed a sense of calm to wash over him. With a flint he found on the workbench, he lit the candle. He drew in and released another deep breath, then crawled into the inky void.

God, please be with me. The walls of the tunnels seemed to close in on him, racing his pulse with a dark foreboding. There had been others besides Julianna with him the first time in the tunnels. He survived then, and would again.

Focused on his mission, he put one foot in front of the other, counting every step instead of listening to the wild imaginations of doom that sped through his mind.

The candle flickered and threatened to go out several times, but steadied when he slowed. He had tucked the flint in his kit, just in case he needed it to relight the candle. Hopefully, that wouldn't be necessary. Striking the flint at just the right angle to produce a spark that connected with the wick would be a challenge in total darkness.

Retracing their earlier path was easy enough, since he'd memorized the way in case they needed to return to the feed room. But at the rate the fire consumed the candlewick, he might not have enough light to make it all the way to his destination.

Water ran down the walls and across the floor of the tunnels. Drainage from the heavy rains seeping underground through saturated soil, made the passages slick and hazardous.

The quiet was broken only by the sound of the splash of his footsteps and the loud thump of his heartbeat in his ears.

"All I have to do is keep going." His voice echoed in the empty void that surrounded him, but gave him a sense of calm to define his destination. "I have to pass at least six more tunnels before I turn left—not right toward the castle." Talking to himself also helped him focus on his task.

A chunk of rock broke loose in front of him, releasing a torrent of pent up water. The gushing liquid struck John hard in the chest, knocking him to his knees. His kit slid off his shoulder, nearly knocking his staff from his grip, but he held on.

The cold water rushed around his legs, making it difficult to hold his position. He kept a tight grip on the lit candle, his kit, and his staff. As the water slowed to a steady stream, he shouldered his kit and used his staff to help him stand.

More rocks started to fall. With a rumble that shook the floor of the passage, a loud groan filled the tunnel. The earth shifted and loosed a whole section of tunnel behind him, sending a wall of water spraying in all directions.

He hurried forward, careful to keep his footing as the tunnel sloped upward. At least there was no standing water here, only streams running on either side of the path. Every step was an act of determination to keep his footing, until the floor leveled off, making his path easier to navigate.

Arriving at the place where they had turned right in their earlier journey, he hesitated. There might still be two lanterns Lois and Julianna had left on the steps leading to the chancellor's home. A detour could gain him a more secure source of light, but it would cost him another thirty minutes or so to gather the prize, and the same amount to retrace his steps. Could he risk the passage being blocked off? Would it be best to continue on?

Faint sounds of murmuring voices coming from a side tunnel behind him gave him his answer. He had to reach the castle. Since the headmaster of the institute was involved with the Black Guard, the man may have come up with the same plan as John's to gain access to the castle without being seen. There was no time to spare.

In spite of the slower pace he was forced to keep, he continued onward. No other passages connected to the one he was on. The voices behind him faded. Hopefully, they were also hindered by a cave in or the rain's runoff, or maybe indecision about which passage led where.

His shoulders ached from his hunched position, having to duck around the runoff and the low ceiling.

Plop! A large drop of water fell from the ceiling, dousing the candle. Instant darkness flooded over him.

"No!" Paralyzing fear squeezed off his breath. "Oh, God help me. I repent of my stubbornness to do things my way." Another vision of Julianna holding the babe flashed into his mind. Calmness eased through him. The iron fist of fear released his throat and he gasped for air. He drew a deeper breath, then another.

I know the plans I have for you. Plans to prosper you and not harm you plans to give you a hope and a future.

John recognized the passage from Jeremiah.

Julianna is to be your wife, John, and you will teach your children and grandchildren to serve me. That is the way you will honor your vow to Me.

The presence of God was as if a thousand lit candles dispelled the darkness. His words loosed the grief and guilt from John's heart freeing him from burdens God never required him to bear alone.

John dropped to his knees on the cold, hard floor of the tunnel and wept.

A person had but to believe. God's words lit John's heart with a flame of hope.

"Thank you, Lord." John's praise seemed so little to convey the gratitude that filled his heart.

Look.

John raised his face and blinked. Light bounced against the walls of the passage, coming toward him.

He stood and grasped his staff, prepared to meet whoever arrived. There was the sound of many feet. At first, he could only make out a man's outline in the glare of the lantern light.

"Lord Stanton!" That was the voice of Henry Brummel, the captain of the castle guards. The man closed the distance between them and reached out his hand in greeting. "Where is your lantern? And how did you get here?"

"Only by God's hand of protection, my friend." He shook the captain's hand. "I must speak to the king."

"We were told there are assassins in the tunnels."

"Aye. I heard voices in the passages, but not for a while." Warmth settled on him, as if a comforting hand was laid on his shoulder—a touch that could only be from God since no one stood behind him. "I don't think you'll have to worry about the enemy finding their way to the castle by way of this tunnel."

A loud rumble filled the passage, and the ground beneath them shook with a force that made them cling to the walls.

"Cave in!"

The captain shouted orders for retreat, and the six guards with him turned to escape the way they had just come. John sprinted after them, the captain close behind him. Within minutes, they came to a large opening where daylight poured in, showing the way of escape.

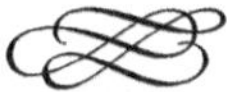

CHAPTER 21

Julianna paced her room, wanting to shout with frustration at having been locked inside while the castle was being attacked by Black Guards. The king refused to allow her and Lois free reign to roam around the castle or check on Precious in the stables, insisting it was for their safety. He had mandated no civilian travel until the danger was over.

It was more likely he didn't want them caught and forced to confess what they knew of the king's counter-attack.

"I am not a helpless female." The more she paced, the angrier she became. "Enough!"

She made sure her dagger was secure on her waist, then strapped a smaller one to her ankle. She reached for the handle of the door, but it was pushed opened. She pulled her dagger.

Lois's face appeared in the doorway. When she saw Julianna's weapon, she grinned. "About time we do something more than twittle our thumbs."

Julianna chuckled and lowered her dagger, leftover alarm still pulsing through her veins. They made their way down the stairs to the main hall, where loud voices came from the king's study.

"They dare to invade our land!" King John's words were followed with a string of curses that would make a low-born soldier blush.

"Sire, I know what to do." John's voice sounded calm and confident.

John. What was he doing back in the castle? She and Lois hovered by the open door. To stay out of sight, Julianna watched through the gap between the door hinges and the wall.

Julianna gleaned by the bits of overheard conversation, that John had a plan to foil, not only the remaining Black Guard outside the gates, but also a hoard of Frenchmen determined to take possession of English lands.

"It's a sound plan, M'Lord." Captain Brummel added his input and a group of men that stood around the room agreed, each accepting their part in the plan. When they began to file out, Lois and Julianna remained hidden behind the door.

"I'll meet you when this is all over." The captain shook John's hand, then strode out of sight.

"John," Julianna whispered. He turned and spotted her. His grin sent warm tingles tracing her spine and fluttering within her chest.

He stepped out of the doorway, and in two strides, he was within reach.

"You're back." She couldn't resist touching his cheek, which was rough with a beard that hadn't been shaved in days.

"I overheard news of a French invasion that sent me back before I got far." He captured her hand and kissed it, making her knees weak. "The captain told me that with your and Lois's help, they've arrested all of the traitors within the castle. They've sent soldiers out with letters from the king to warn the aristocracy about the plot to assassinate them."

"As long as the people are in residence, they'll be warned."

Julianna loved the way he looked at her. His approval was better than that of the king's.

John had an odd glint to his gaze as he met hers. "I've had an encounter with God." He smiled, but Julianna's heart sank.

She would have to forget her love, for this man belonged to God. Who was she to stand in the way?

All she wanted to do was run and hide to release the growing grief pressing against her heart, by his nearness.

She had been trained not to show her emotions, so she steeled herself against her need to flee. "Don't you still need to reach your family with news of the danger from two fronts?" She tugged her hand from his grasp and hid it behind her, his touch still tingling on her skin.

"No, the king has forbidden travel out of the city until this last crisis has been dealt with. I have prayed and believe that William reached them. Also, Captain Brummel promised to send two of his men to check on them and remain until further notice." He smiled, stepped closer, and reached out. "I need to tell you…"

"I'm glad your family will be safe, but I can't talk now. We're needed elsewhere." Julianna stepped away, then grabbed Lois by the arm and led her down a corridor. She had no idea where it led but she couldn't bear to hear John tell her they could never be together.

Before they had gone twenty steps, she could no longer withhold her grief. Sobs racked her body, and Lois led her into a small linen closet and shut the door. Julianna dropped to her knees, pressing her hands to her mouth.

"You love him." Lois patted Julianna on the shoulder. She reached for a royal napkin from a neat stack on a shelf and handed it to Julianna to wipe her eyes.

"Yes-s-s." She couldn't stop the tears or the hiccups they fed. "Why does it hu-rt so much?" With a hefty swipe she dried the tears, only to have others replace them. "I-I love a man-n of God, Lois. How did that happen?"

"I fell in love with a ruthless assassin. The heart dictates who we love, not logic." She closed her eyes. "I don't even know if Theroux is alive or dead." Her voice dropped barely above a whisper.

"Oh, I'm so sorry. I've had only my concerns on my thoughts." With one last swipe of the napkin, she dried her tears and blew her nose. There was nothing she could do about her situation but maybe she could help Lois. "How do we find out if Theroux lives?"

"I don't think this is the right timing to ask for help while the castle remains under siege." Lois opened the door and peered out. She mumbled a few words, then there was a long pause. "The way's clear now. Let's find something worthwhile to do with our time." Lois led the way and headed down a narrow corridor used only by the servants.

"Where are we going?" Julianna hurried to keep up with her mentor. They climbed two flights of stairs and made three turns, which brought them to an area of the castle which Julianna was unfamiliar. They came to a heavy door with large black hinges. The thick steel ring, that would release the latch, required two hands to operate.

"Help me." Lois grabbed one side of the ring and Julianna the other, and they pulled until it turned, allowing the door to nudge open inwardly.

Lois pulled her dagger from her belt, so Julianna did likewise. Were they headed into danger, or was this just a precaution?

"I thought you'd be hiding in here." Lois pointed her weapon at a cloaked figure standing near a window. In the courtyard below, sounds of fighting echoed across the space.

"You were always too smart for your own good, Agent Lois." The headmaster of the institute, Sir Alistair Craven swung around with his own weapon. Where Lois's and Julianna's daggers were simple and marked by the king's weapon's maker, the headmaster's dagger had a jeweled handle and curved blade. He glared at Lois and stiffened as if ready to attack. "How many guards await outside?"

"Enough to deal with the likes of you." Lois smiled and circled to the left of him, while Julianna stood her ground in front of the door. It was a standard bluff taught to all advanced students of the institute, but perhaps the headmaster would think this time it was true. She edged closer to the door, as if waiting for Lois's signal to let in the guards.

Two trunks sat on the floor beside the headmaster. He bent over and slammed the lid of the largest one. The lock clicked, securing it. With the toe of her shoe, Lois kicked the smaller of two trunks, tipping it over. Jewels and gold coins spilled onto the floor. "Looks like you're planning a trip."

"Look what you've done." He screamed obscenities and turned toward her. With a sweep of his weapon, he aimed the blade at Lois's throat, but she easily ducked out of the old man's reach.

While he was off balance, she swung around with a kick to his backside, knocking him to the floor on top of his scattered loot.

"I'll have you killed for this." He gathered the jewels within his reach and stuffed them in his cloak's pockets, all the while shouting more obscenities.

"Open the door, Julianna." Lois grinned and kicked the jeweled dagger out of the old man's reach.

Julianna did as she was told and pulled open the heavy door, though what the older woman had planned next, she had no idea.

John and three guards stood outside, and she waved them in. She glanced at Lois. "How?"

The woman smiled. "I knew by your young monk's expression that he would not be put off by your dismissal. He followed us and waited outside the room to bide his time, for there was no other exit. When I leaned out of the door, I whispered to him to get help then meet us here." She picked up a gaudy necklace of emeralds and rubies. The sunlight from the window high-lighted the many facets in the jewels, sending colored prisms dancing across the floor and wall, before she dropped it back into the smaller case.

Lois frowned at the headmaster. "I've known forever where you kept your treasures. I simply waited until the right time to expose you with them." She grinned and jerked up the old man's sleeve, revealing a tattoo of a black bird on his wrist. She waved the guards near and pointed to the evidence. "Here is the man behind it all, including the Black Guards. The king will want to deal with him personally."

With a wave of her dagger, she pointed the blade at each man. "You know me and my reputation, so know this. If any of you allow this man to escape, I will find you. My face will be the last you see on this earth, and no one will ever find your body. Understand?"

Each man's eyes grew large and they nodded. Two of the guards grabbed the old headmaster with a tight grip, and the third picked up the case filled with jewels.

Lois turned to face Julianna and John. "I'll follow to make sure he and his treasure arrive unhindered into the king's presence."

Then Lois frowned and put her hand to her hip. "You two are to remain here until you speak all that is in your hearts." A knowing smile softened her features. "I'll know if you don't do as I ask." She pointed her dagger at them. "I'll make it my mission to have you both thrown into the dungeon in a single cell until you do. Understand?" With that, she followed the guards out of the room. The heavy door shut with a thud.

"I have no idea what has gotten into her lately." Julianna

walked to the window and looked down. The fighting had ceased. The surviving guards and undertakers were in the courtyard, dealing with the dead and injured.

"Come, Julianna, sit with me." John pulled two satin-covered chairs close together, facing each other. "I will not touch you until we've finished talking. At least, I'll try not to."

The humor in his voice made her angry. She turned and faced him.

"Why are you so happy?" A sob caught in her voice, but she held her hand up when he reached out to her. "All I can think of is…"

"What?" John's grin infuriated her. He was happy and she was dying inside. He must not have ever loved her the way she did him.

"How can you smile when we'll never see each other again?" She swiped away the tears that ignored her determination to make them stop. What had happened to her steel will, which made it possible to ignore her feelings?

"Do you love me?" His voice lowered and his grin disappeared. The intensity of his stare made her heart speed up.

"I don't want to. You're a man of your word who has vowed to serve God all the days of your life." She glared at him. "Can you deny that?"

"No, I won't deny my vow to serve God." His grin was back. "Answer my question. Do you love me?"

"God, please forgive me. Yes." When she met his gaze, she found love so intense, she felt cloaked in it, yet how could that be? "But what good is that for a monk to hear?"

"While I was in the tunnels, trying desperately to get here, my candle went out. I didn't know where I was or how far I would have to go to escape the darkness. I was a child again, lost and alone. I cried out to God and repented for my stubbornness to do things my way." He rubbed a hand over his face, then smiled. "Peace filled me in that dark place, and I realized I was never alone as long as I had the Lord Jesus in my heart. It was then God spoke to me as clearly as we're speaking now."

She didn't understand, but she could feel the anointing on his words and leaned in so she didn't miss what he had to say.

"He told me I could best fulfill my vow to Him by raising my children to honor and serve Him."

Julianna's heart leapt in her chest. "I didn't think monks could marry."

"That's correct, but the Lord told me that being a monk was my idea, not His plan." He reached out and lightly touched her hand. "And that you and I are to marry."

"What?" Shock pulsed through her. Then a glorious hope took its place. She stood, and he rose to meet her stance. "Are you asking me to marry you?" She could barely breathe as she waited for his response.

"That's exactly what I'm doing." His arms were around her, drawing her close. "Will you?"

"I..." Her heart ached. How did she tell him she belonged to the Crown and the Church? She was a bondservant to her master. Even if she were free to choose her destiny, she was illegitimate and unworthy of his position. Though her father was a count and her mother of royal bloodlines, they'd not been wed at the time of her birth. John's parents wouldn't want their only son married to such a woman with her questionable background. Unlike him having been raised in a happy home, learning how to live a good life by a loving family, she had been trained to be a spy...and worse.

"What is that expression on your face? Disappointment? Guilt?" He leaned back and frowned, but kept his arms around her. "Did you lose my donkey?

"No, oh no!" At least he couldn't discern her thoughts. "I managed to get Precious safely moved to the castle's stable shortly before the fighting started. Although she doesn't act like I did her a favor. She continues to bray, bite at the groomsmen, and kick the walls of her stall. I think she misses you." The glint of something shiny on the floor caught Julianna's attention, but she tugged her focus back up to John.

"How about you? Did you miss me?" Humor glimmered in his gaze.

"I...." She sighed with the truth of it. "Yes." But she couldn't let him pull anything more from her. She stepped from his arms and bent over to pick up several loose jewels next to her foot. Straightening, she idly rubbed them between her fingers and thumb.

"And you'll marry me?" He captured her hands and touched her palm. "I may not be able to give you a case full of jewels like these, but I promise I'll do everything in my power to make you happy." He drew her closer and nuzzled her neck.

Her breath caught as warmth flooded through her. "Stop. I can't think when you're this close." With all of the skills she had learned over the years, none had included how to have a happy home. She slipped the jewels into her pocket to deal with later. How many of these precious stones had she and her fellow students earned the headmaster in payment?

She tried to push out of John's embrace, but he gently refused to let her go.

"Julianna." His voice was soft and imploring.

"I can't marry you." There. She said it, though her grief threatened to strangle the breath from her. A sob broke through and she slumped into his arms. If this was the last time she could feel his arms, she wanted to remember every moment.

"What do you mean you *can't* marry me?" John released her enough to stare into her eyes. "Are you already married?"

"No. I am...I mean, I belong to the Crown and the Church... and my mother and father were never married." She glanced down to avoid his reaction.

"I know. I'll deal with the king to free you from your servitude. You saved his life, so he owes you. And about the other thing…" He brushed some stray hair from her cheeks and tilted her face up to look into her eyes. So much love glimmered in his gaze, hope stirred within her. "You told me about your mother and father not being married when we were at the abbey." He smiled. "I had a chance to speak to Lois and she told me your story. You're of a royal bloodline on both sides, and many royals have been born without benefit of a marriage certificate. If that's your only excuse for denying me, then it's invalid." He started to pull her close again, but she resisted.

The joy that sprang up within her was as if heaven smiled, but she had to know what was truly in his heart. "You haven't said you love me."

"From the moment we first met." His voice grew husky, and his eyes darkened to emerald with emotion. "My love for you has been an overwhelming force that refused to be denied, no matter how hard I tried." He paused, but didn't take his eyes off her. "I didn't know such love existed. I can't breathe without knowing I belong with you for the rest of my days." His eyes shone with truth, erasing any lingering doubt.

"All right." She touched his short hair. "But you must promise to let your hair grow out again."

"Agreed." He picked her up and swung her around once, then stopped long enough to kiss her until they were both breathless.

"I'm afraid your mother will be disappointed in getting a trained spy and assassin for a daughter-in-law." Julianna's concern threatened to smother her happiness.

"You'll have more in common than you can imagine, but I'll let her tell you her story." John laughed and hugged her again. "Let's go find a priest. I can't wait to marry you."

"Wait. You don't want a proper wedding?" Relief washed through her. The idea of her trying to persuade her father to acknowledge her and stand beside her in the church always gave her nightmares. Or worse, that he might show up unin-vited and disrupt the ceremony in a drunken state. According to rumors, he spent a great deal of time drowning his life's disappointments in strong drink, instead of tending to his estate.

"I'm sorry. I should have asked. Do you want to wait until the fighting is over so you can meet my parents and I meet your father? I should warn you, since you haven't a mother to help plan the wedding, my mother and sisters will insist on helping. What they really mean is they'd love to take over the entire event. It could be months before they're satisfied they've covered every detail for a properly staged wedding ceremony." John frowned.

"No. I'd much rather find a priest, marry, and then celebrate our marriage with your family later, in a more private setting." She reached up and kissed him, which led to a deeper kiss, until he stepped back.

"Come with me, woman." John tugged the door open and, hand in hand, led her to the king's chapel. They found the Cardinal pacing the aisles, reciting scriptures of protection in Latin. His assistant knelt at the altar praying silently.

The ceremony was briefer than Julianna expected. Perhaps that was because she had a hard time focusing on anything other than John. His posture was that of a soldier at attention and his attentiveness that of a monk. Then he glanced down at Julianna after the final benediction with the look of love and expectation of a new groom. She blushed when he winked at her. His intention was clear.

"Go with God, children." The Cardinal hastily signed their marriage certificate his assistant provided. He waved them away and turned back to his pacing.

"Thank you, your Imminence." John tucked Julianna's hand in his and left the chapel. "I love you, wife." Somehow, those words, above all else made it official.

CHAPTER 22

Married two days and John couldn't believe it wasn't a dream each morning when he awoke with Julianna in his arms. Marriage to this woman was more wondrous than he could have ever dreamed.

"I think we need to go to the stables again this morning and check on Precious. The young groomsman who's in charge of her, sent a message. She's off her feed and is more contrary than ever, though she's stopped kicking the stall's walls." Julianna's concern matched his own.

After a light meal of fruit and cooked oats with cream and butter, they dressed and headed to the stables.

"Make way." A messenger from the institute pushed past a guard and headed to the castle.

"Benjamin?" Julianna reached out a hand toward the young man. She turned to John. "I've known this boy since he was brought to the institute as a child. I helped Lois tutor him through the years."

The lad hurried over to them and shook his head. "It's 'orrible, Miss Julianna." Tears gathered in his eyes.

"What is it?" Julianna tensed. John stepped closer to his wife.

"It's Miss Lois…she's dead."

"No." Julianna paled and leaned into John as he encircled her shoulders with his arm. "It can't be true." Her voice lowered to a whisper, which worried John more than if she had raged and threatened revenge on those who had harmed Lois.

"How did she die?" John kept his voice soft.

"Don't know no details. Just, there's no body to bury. A magistrate signed the death certificate." The boy waved a sheet of paper before them. "I have to give this to the king. He sent her on that assignment late last night." The boy hurried away to deliver the report to a king who hated bad news. The boy, and anyone else unlucky enough to be in the room, would likely suffer the king's wrath after the report was read.

"Wait, Julianna." John kept her from following after Benjamin. "We'll go to the king after the boy has had time to inform him. Let's wait in our room." He put a hand under her arm. She allowed him to lead her to their rooms. Once the door closed, she slumped into a chair.

"I'm numb to the bone." She leaned her head back against the chair and closed her eyes. "While I was enjoying my most wonderful dream, Lois had died alone, still in bondage to the Crown and Church, never having found Theroux."

"The king released you from your bonds, so I don't understand why he didn't also release Lois." John paced their room and finally settled in a chair next to his wife. When he grasped her hand, it was cold. He rubbed it between his palms.

He suspected the truth, from what he knew about the king. With his paranoia, the monarch would never release two such experienced agents.

Since John's family had strong ties to the throne, and Julianna had saved the king's life, the king had felt the pressure to release her or risk alienating those who were important to his reign. Lois would be kept in servitude, for as long as she was deemed useful. The only comfort he could give Julianna was Lois was finally free of her earthly bonds.

~

Since news of Lois's death, Julianna had grieved in the comfort of his arms.

Early the following morning, a knock at their door stirred John to rise and dress. He feared more bad news, as he picked up the folded message that had been slid under their door.

"What is it, John?" Julianna stretched and sat up. "Hopefully, it's not more bad news."

"It's from the groomsman in charge of Precious." He smoothed out the paper. "It asks that we come down to the stables as soon as possible. Though he implies urgency, he gives no reason." John put the cryptic message on the table. "I can go alone, if you want to stay in bed." He went to her side, leaned down and kissed her. "I'll return later and join you."

If the donkey was ill, he feared another loss would be too much for Julianna to bear.

"I'll be ready before you finish your meal." Julianna pulled the cord that summoned the servant with their morning meal, then slipped out of bed. She brushed her fingers across John's cheek and giggled as she deftly escaped his grasp. She disappeared into the closet before he could protest.

Less than an hour later he had finished his meal and considered slipping out without her, but thought better of it.

"I'm done." He wiped his mouth. "Don't you want something to eat?"

She appeared dressed and looking beautiful, at his side. "This is plenty for now." With the deftness of a pickpocket, she slipped a slice of toast from his plate and waved her fingers at him. "Let's go check on Precious."

They walked hand-in-hand through the castle, grinning at

the whispers of the nun and the monk who got married, that followed them. According to the captain of the guards, their union was the main subject of more conversations than the successful repelling of the French rebels from coming ashore, or of the bloody overthrow of the Black Guard.

The young groomsman who had sent the message met them when they entered the stables. "I should have known. All of the signs were there, but she's a donkey and I've never tended one before." The groomsman led them to Precious's stall.

"Oh, John, she has a baby!" Julianna squealed, then opened the stall door and entered. He stepped in after her.

"The prophetess told me Precious had a secret. I never guessed this was it." He rubbed a hand down the mother's face. "Look what you've done."

Precious gave him a "he-e-haw-w," then nuzzled her foal.

"It's a wee jenny, the spit'n image of her mum." The groomsman stepped inside, but when Precious snorted and pinned back her ears in warning, he hurried out of the stall again. "She's still a bit testy, but I'm determined to win her over with my boiled sweet mash."

"We've barely been married three days and we already have an addition to our family." Julianna laughed and hugged the wobbly-legged babe. "She's precious, too."

"Yes, well, this complicates our journey to the manor. A newborn foal needs a few weeks before it's safe to take her on such a long journey." John gave Precious another affectionate pat.

"I know of a wagon that's suitable for hauling livestock and a team fit to pull it, if you want to use that." The groomsman leaned in, only to back out again. "I can pad the wagon with a thick layer of straw to make it comfortable for the mum and babe."

"As much as I would like to take them with us, we'll need to travel faster than a wagon hauling livestock can go. The heavy rains have caused much damage to the roads. It will be treacherous getting there riding a strong horse." The donkeys would be far safer here for a while longer. Even though most of the fighting had ceased, there were still assassins dispatched over the land who could cause more trouble.

Julianna stepped back so John could get a closer look at the baby. He ran a hand down the foal's back and down each leg to familiarize her with his scent and get her used to being touched. The sooner the newborn was touched, the easier she would be to handle and train.

He stood and faced the groomsman hovering in the doorway. "If you think you can manage these two for a little while longer, I'll return when I know it's safe again to travel and take them with me then."

Precious shook her head and stomped her foot, as if she understood she wouldn't be going with him.

"Sorry, girl but you must stay here." He stroked her head and neck. "Besides, you have a wee babe to watch over. I won't forget to come back for you, I promise."

The donkey flicked her tail and pushed John aside with her head so she could reach her foal. She licked her newborn, then nudged the wobbly babe, almost knocking her down. The foal finally began to nurse.

"I think she wants us to leave." John grinned and ushered Julianna out of the stall, then closed the door.

"I'll take excellent care of the two until your return, Lord Stanton." The groomsman grinned, as if eager to accept the challenge of making friends with the cantankerous Precious.

"Thank you..." John reached out his hand to shake the man's hand.

"My name's Benson." The man seemed surprised at the gesture of respect. He ran his palm down his pant leg to clean it before he shook John's hand.

"If you call Precious by her name, Benson, she's more likely to cooperate." He couldn't help but chuckle at the expression of surprise and relief on the groom's face.

"That's good to know, sir." The young man walked with John and Julianna to the barn door. "I received orders to pick you out a couple of good mounts for your journey. I'll have them saddled and ready within the hour."

"Thank you. If the chestnut gelding I rode is available, I'd like him." That horse hadn't been in any of the stalls they'd passed.

"The gelding's name is Charlie. He's having a shoe replaced, but he'll be available in time for your trip."

"As in Charlie Horse?" Julianna chuckled.

"He was named by the head groomsman's little girl, Emmy, and it stuck." Benson smiled. "Charlie's of exceptional bloodlines and has the heart of a lion and the speed of a gazelle."

"I found that out when I had to ride him through the storm. Do you have one his equal for my wife to ride? We've a long journey ahead of us, and the enemy could still make trouble along the way." John drew Julianna against his side. He loved the way she fit under his arm.

"Yes, a gray gelding named Samson. He's well trained, with a good temperament." The groomsman hesitated. "Or would you prefer to pick out your own mount, M'lady?"

"No. We trust you to know your stock best. We'll see you within the hour." John led Julianna back to their quarters to pack. The trip to the manor would take a full day, possibly two, depending on the condition of the roads.

After they stepped into their rooms and closed the door, John drew Julianna into his arms. "Are you still nervous about meeting my family?"

"How can you tell?" She relaxed into his embrace.

"Since you brought your belongings here from the institute, you've changed clothes twice. You've discarded items and replaced them with others, then repacked at least that many times." He brushed a hand across her shoulder and nuzzled her neck. "We'll return and get the rest of your things before we journey to Brighton Castle. I want you to see where I grew up."

"There's so little I can bring on this trip, and I can't decide what would fair best crammed into the small case." She kissed him, then stepped back.

She glanced over the room at the six trunks lining the wall of their room, which were filled with everything she valued. "These four trunks contain books and trinkets from my travels." She pointed to the remaining two with their lids open, which contained her clothing. "In my life at the institute, I was loaned whatever type of clothing was needed to fit my assignments, but none of those clothes were mine to keep." She paced to one of the trunks and sifted through the contents again. "I wish I had some of the fine gowns I had to leave behind on my last assignment, for nothing I have seems ideal to meet your family."

"You realize that when we arrive at my sister's home, we'll need to clean up and change clothes after our long journey, so whatever you decide to wear now won't matter." He stepped back and grinned as his beautiful Viking princess fussed over her apparel. She would be breathtaking in whatever she wore, even a nun's habit.

A knock at the door interrupted his thoughts. Before he could open the door, a missive was shoved under.

Julianna's name was written on the outside, so he handed it over to her. "This is for you."

She tore open the envelope and walked to the window for better light. "It's from Lois." Her voice was a harsh whisper. She sank into the chair nearest her. "She's alive!"

John's pulse quickened as he stepped up beside her and claimed the adjoining chair. The table between them held cakes and a pot of tea, which were still warm, but untouched.

"She didn't die while on assignment for the king?" John had secured Julianna's release from her bondage to marry him because of her courage and bravery saving the king's life, but even after he received the news of her death, the king had remained adamant in justifying his denial to release Lois from her obligations to the Crown.

Julianna's brow furrowed as she read. "Lois says when she was unable to find Theroux within the city, she accepted the king's assignment to gain release from the castle. That way she'd have freedom to search for him." She tensed. "Listen to this.

"I took my most valuable possessions with me, for I will never return. I also took the jewels from the headmaster's treasures, which I earned in my many years of servitude. I shall live out my days in comfort so don't fret for me. Yesterday, Theroux met me at our secret spot. He had been waiting for me."

Julianna handed John the pages of the letter as she finished each one.

"Do not grieve for me, for in spite of the horrors you will hear of the way I died in service to the king, I am alive and well. Theroux is a master of such things and helped me fake my death, so no one will doubt my demise and search for me. Please honor my wishes and don't try to find us. We will disappear as we had once planned long ago."

She looked up at him, tears glistening in her beautiful eyes. "Oh, John. I'm so relieved to know she's alive and well." Drawing a deep breath, she released it with a sigh, then focused on the letter again. "There's more.

"I never told you, Julianna, that Theroux and I were married that night you found us. The timing wasn't right then, but it is now. I'm happier than I could ever imagine, thanks to finding the Lord as our Savior on the boat. We are prepared to live our life to the fullest, having freedom to do good, no longer forced to do evil.

Please thank John for his part in helping us find our redemption. He will make a wonderful husband for you and a good father to your children, which we hope will be many. Though we may never meet again this side of heaven, we shall never forget you. Pray for our happiness as we shall pray for yours.

With much love,

Lois and Theroux.

P.S. I have sent this missive by a special courier who owes me his life, so there is no fear he will reveal the truth."

Julianna handed John the last page and sagged against the chair's back. "She was as close to family as I had, but I never knew she and Theroux were married all those years ago. I feel awful for being the reason they never knew the happiness we've had these last three days." Tears pooled in her eyes.

"No reason to be sad. Lois is alive and free to pursue the happiness she always wanted. It's a relief to know they're finally together." He stood and drew her into his embrace. "We're blessed to be able to enjoy our marriage now and not have to wait."

He chuckled and pointed her to the bag resting on their unmade bed. "Finish packing so we can take our leave before the king finds more excuses for us to stay, or decides you must take Lois's place as his personal spy."

He stepped back and checked his kit to make sure it was complete. "Now that the troops have kept the rebel's invasion forces from landing on our shores, the king has lifted his travel ban. There are still Black Guards to identify and arrest, but that could take weeks to complete, and I don't want to be delayed by it."

"And we have another stop to make before we leave town."

Julianna gathered the pages of Lois's letter and placed them in the fireplace. She watched as they turned to ash, then mixed them in with the burnt logs. No one must ever find out the truth. She returned to her packing and stuffed the last items inside her case and closed it. "I'm ready."

CHAPTER 23

Julianna and John found Keet's boat gone when they arrived at the docks, so they inquired at the nearby tavern. The owner of the tavern could read and write, so sailors often left messages for each other and their loved ones with him to deliver. Keet might have left a message for them before he shipped out.

The tavern was a rough place, so Julianna was content to stay outside and protect the horses while John inquired within.

She kept her hand on her dagger. War brought out the best and the worst in people. The near overthrow of the king would have many with strong opinions, from both sides looking to take offense toward those of opposite views. That she and John rode horses with the Crown's brand could spark violence with the slightest provocation.

John smiled as he left the tavern. He handed her a warm pastry filled with meat and cheese, wrapped in butcher's paper. "I couldn't resist the delicious smell. I thought these would make a good snack along our way out of town." He took a big bite before he rewrapped the pastry and handed it to Julianna to hold while he mounted. She returned it to him as they rode away.

"Did Keet leave a message for you?" She couldn't help a grin as John devoured his snack. She would need to make a list of his favorite foods if she was to keep her hungry husband satisfied.

"Yes." John wiped his mouth with the empty wrapper and tucked it into his kit behind his saddle. "I read it while I was waiting on the food. I also left a message for the farmer Dilbert or any of their village who stop there. They're to take my message to Sister Agnes to let her know what has transpired, so she won't worry about Tommy…or us."

He smiled as he unfolded the piece of paper he'd pulled from his pocket. "The note from Keet says someone on the docks knew Tommy's grandfather and where he was staying, so Keet took the boy to him. The old man had been a deckhand on a fishing boat, but couldn't work for a while after he was injured. He lost a finger and almost his life when he got tangle in a net as it was being thrown overboard. Keet hired him, so now Thomas and his grandfather are safe with him."

"Oh, how wonderful the boy found his grandfather. Maybe we can visit them sometime, for I suspect there's much more to the story than that." Julianna handed him her untouched food.

"Are you not hungry?" His brows arched in concern.

She smiled and shook her head.

John accepted the food and finished it off in a few bites. He gave her a big smile. "Are you ready to put these horses through their paces? We could reach the manor before dark if we ride hard."

"I'd love a good ride in the country after being cooped up so long." She adjusted her seat and took a firm hold on the reins. "Let's go."

The couple kicked the horses into a gallop, but had to watch for dangers in the road. There were a good deal of hollowed out ruts and debris to avoid. Downed trees and broken limbs scattered by the wind. Water still flowing hard out of its banks made for slow going in spots, but they had the road mostly to themselves. The sound of birds singing and the sight of cattle and sheep calmly grazing in the pastures they passed could deceive one into believing nothing was amiss. As if no horrors of war had reached this far from London.

When they passed the Wild Goose Tavern, the barn had been burned to the ground, but the tavern appeared unharmed. There was no sign of anyone around.

"I hope the owner and his wife are well. They were kind, hardworking people. Their son's traitorous behavior could have been the cause of the fire. It will be dark soon, so there's no time to stop now, but the duke will probably know what happened to them."

They kept a slower pace until they found a part of the road that was still smooth, then they allowed their mounts to stretch their legs. This also allowed Julianna to tease John into a friendly competition, with a brief race to the bend in the road where a giant oak shaded the spot.

"I won!" John hollered when they reached the mark, and they eased back to a more sedate pace to let the horses rest.

"It was close, but I'll concede…this time." The exhilaration of the race and the wind blowing through her hair filled Julianna with joy and a sense of freedom she had never known before.

After an hour, they alternated between an easy canter and a walk.

"We're within a mile of my sister's home." John rode close to Julianna's side and leaned over to kiss her soundly. "You can see the manor up on the hill." He pointed to a large country estate, surrounded by green pastures dotted with sheep.

"Is there a place where we could stop for a few minutes so I can tidy up a bit?" She'd need more than mere hand and face washing. Even combing her hair wouldn't make her presentable after their trip, but it would have to do.

"The sun is setting. Do what you have to, but hurry. We have thirty minutes at most before dark." He grinned and led the way to a grove of trees by the side of the road. "They'll love you even if we do show up covered in mud." He swiped his hand down his tunic, which was too soiled from their travels to fix with a dusting off. "

The sound of horses galloping toward them had them drawing their weapons. Julianna held her dagger as John grabbed his staff, keeping his dagger ready at his side.

The eight men rode up to them, all armed and tense, as if ready for a battle.

"Who are you and why are you riding royal horses?" The leader had a scar down the left side of his face and wore the uniform of a king's soldier. Another man also wore an ill-fitting uniform of the king's guard. Both rode horses with the Crown's brand, but neither man had the straight posture or demeanor of a well-trained soldier.

Something was not right. Julianna stepped closer to John, hoping to get his attention, but his focus was on the men. By his tense demeanor, he wasn't deceived.

"I'm Lord John Stanton and this is my wife." John lowered his staff and smiled. "It's good to see you patrolling the roads. Have you had any trouble from the assassins or French rebels?"

"Lord Stanton, welcome. I was told to expect you." The guard ignored the question about trouble, which Julianna could see by John's stiff posture, he had noticed too.

"We need to continue on to the manor, for they're awaiting our arrival." He shifted closer to Julianna to help her mount.

As he gave her a leg up, he whispered. "I recognize one of the men. Expect trouble." He turned toward his own mount and smiled at the men. "We welcome your escort."

Julianna sheathed her dagger, but found it hard to appear at ease. Every fiber of her being wanted to spur her mount and race for the manor, though there could be more brigands waiting for them once they arrived. One glance at John and he shook his head, probably thinking the same thing as she. Waiting for the right moment was something she had been trained for, but waiting was never easy.

They rode at a sedate pace in silence, for the leader of the gang had his men flank them on either side, with two following behind. Julianna glanced toward John in time to see him stiffen when he made eye contact with one of the so-called guards riding beside them. The man tensed, but gave John a slight shake of his head and remained silent. He fixed his gaze on the ground, as if a reluctant participant. Maybe the young man would side with them in a fight.

The gate to the stone wall surrounding the manor was closed. No workers were in the field, and there were no sounds of people.

The hair on Julianna's neck rose in warning.

John would have to make his move soon, or they would be trapped once they reached the estate. They would be used as hostages to gain whatever they wanted from the manor. This would not end well, for John would not allow that to happen.

"You'll be glad to know the king is sending more troops this way to secure the peace in this area." John smiled. "They should arrive soon, since they're not far behind us. There are to be no trials. Their orders are to hang any traitors they find as they sweep through to the border. I've been sent to assure the duke that none of the rebels, traitors, or assassins will escape their punishment."

The leader turned a shade paler. The men around them grumbled.

"Thank you for enlightening us of what to expect, Lord Stanton." The leader with the scar stopped his horse and turned his mount to face them. "I shall relieve you and your fine lady of your valuables and your fine horses, so we may flee this cursed land." He spouted a string of curse words in French, drawing his short sword and pointing it at John. His men did the same.

The sound of a horn blowing reverberated through the air, announcing a charge. Shouts of a hundred soldiers grew louder until it echoed around them. From the manor, four armed guards on horses and a multitude of servants on foot came rushing out of the opened gates. They carried all manner of weapons and charged toward their group.

The men surrounding John and Julianna turned their swords to the hoard of people coming their way, but their eyes were wide with fright.

John raised his staff, released the blade, and pointed it at the leader. "You have one chance to live, Frenchman." He held back on the reins and pressed his heel against his mount's side cuing it to sidestep until he was next to Julianna's. He gave the rest of the men a stern glance. "You can surrender your weapons and live, or you will be hunted down and hung. As I said, there will be no trial for you or your men when you're caught." He barely finished speaking when the imposters spurred their horses and raced off toward the coast, the manor guards charged after them.

Only one imposter remained.

"I-I am s-sorry. I had no c-choice. They tied up my p-parents and t-threatened to kill them if I didn't do as they s-said. I must g-go f-free them." The young man turned his mount and raced back toward the tavern.

"I take it you know him?" Julianna glanced at her husband as they rode toward their rescuers from the manor. The oncoming crowd was now smiling and shaking their weapons in the air in victory.

"He's the tavern owner's son. I'll tell you all about it later, but now I want you to meet my parents." John spurred his mount to reach the couple riding toward them.

Julianna followed John, but she was afraid her reluctance showed on her face in spite of her smile.

"John!" The woman rode close enough to hug him. "We're so glad you're all right." She frowned. "We hurried out to help you after the servants saw the rebels heading toward you. Those Frenchmen came by the manor two days ago and tried to take it by force. Needless to say, they are missing six of their men who didn't survive the attempted siege."

"It's very good to see you, son, though I almost didn't recognize you." The man smiled and motioned to John's short haircut and scruffy beard.

Julianna smiled at the warm welcome and parental affection obvious in the couple hovering on either side of John.

Then the woman turned to her. "I'm sorry. We've ignored you too long. I'm Evangeline, John's mother." She smiled at Julianna, then waved at the man beside her. "This is my husband, Henry. And you are?"

John rode up beside Julianna and put a hand on her leg. "This is my wife, Julianna." He puffed out his chest and grinned like he'd won a prize.

"Wife?" Lady Evangeline squealed with surprise and delight. "We feared you'd never marry. So you decided not to become a monk after all?"

"You knew?" It was John's turn to sound shocked.

"Yes, son, we knew." His father smiled. "We'll discuss it all with you later. Let's get back to the manor so we can introduce you and your new bride to the newest member of our family."

～

The duke dispatched two of his guards to check on the innkeepers. They found them relieved to be freed and not seriously injured. Their son begged for forgiveness and was granted a second chance to redeem himself. The castle's servants returned to their work, no longer afraid to be away from the safety of the manor. A meal was prepared while John and Julianna washed and change into clean clothes. They had been given a room away from the family, a sort of honeymoon suite because of its privacy.

The family's acceptance of her was almost too good to be true. She met John's youngest sister, Hanna, who she loved instantly. Next, she was taken to the private quarters of Sarah and her husband, the Earl of Denham, Trevor Kinsman, who obviously adored Sarah and his new son, Trevor Kinsman III, born the evening before. If the adoration bestowed on the child by everyone was any indication, he would grow up knowing he was much loved.

Holding the newborn, she had the same overwhelming feeling of joy as she'd had on the trail after the farmer's wife delivered. She could hardly wait until she could cuddle her own child.

The evening meal was filled with news of the Black Guard's foiled attempt to assassinate the king and the defeat of the French rebel's invasion. The bad weather that sent strong winds and downpours in the region had also kept the French from landing on English soil with a larger force. The delay gave the king's army time to assimilate a powerful defense. The superior show of force caused their enemy to sail away without an arrow being shot.

"I'm glad William made it to you in time to warn you about the assassins. I assume the two guards sent to you by the king were ambushed and killed, since the brigands wore their uniforms." John placed his napkin on the table, having finished his meal.

"Yes. Once we fortified the manor against assassins, it was days before we heard of the guards' deaths. One of our local farmers found the bodies and brought the bad news. Trevor keeps the peace around this area and acts as the local magistrate when needed, so he warned the villagers to beware of strangers and be prepared to hide until the trouble was over." Henry leaned back in his chair. "Trevor has a half dozen guards living and working at the manor who helped fortify the defenses."

"Aye. It wasn't until after the burial of the king's guards that we noticed the blighters who killed them stalking us, so we retreated to the manor and secured it." Trevor smiled. "It was soon after, that my darling Sarah went into labor." He stood. "Speaking of my dear wife, it's time I return to her and my son." He turned to Henry. "Please continue with the story and take care of our guests. I'll see everyone tomorrow."

The servants brought more tea and removed the empty dishes.

"Forgive me, also." Evangeline stood and tapped Hanna, on the shoulder. The girl had been caught feeding the family dog scraps from her meal, as he hid under the table at her feet. "Didn't we discuss the reason we don't feed the dog from the table?"

"Yes, but he's hungry." Hanna grinned and flipped the last of her bread crust to the dog before she stood.

"It's time this young lady gets ready for bed. Say goodnight." Evangeline waited as her daughter complied.

"Goodnight, Poppa." Hanna gave her father a kiss and accepted one in return. Then she went to John, who stood and hugged her tight, then twirled her around until she squealed.

"I'm glad you're here, Bubbie." John had said she'd used that nickname for him since she'd been able to form words.

Happiness bubbled up in Julianna, as Hanna threw her arms around her and kissed her on the cheek. She'd never imagined it would be this wonderful to be part of a family.

"He used to be sad, but you brought my happy brother back to me. I'm so glad you are my sister." Hanna bounced away with the dog following her.

Evangeline turned to Julianna. "I agree with Hanna. You've

put the joy back in John. Thank you." She motioned to a servant to distract the dog while she ushered her talkative daughter toward their quarters.

When the rest of them settled back in their seats, John's father spoke again. "To continue where Trevor left off, since I wasn't about to miss the birth of my first grandchild to deal with a bunch of French rebels, we gathered all the servants inside the compound and shut the gates. We've remained secured until this morning when the rebels tried to break through the gates. We had a short but bloody battle resulting in only the deaths of the French rebels. None of our people were hurt.

"Once Evangeline helped deliver the baby and declared Sarah and the little one well, we prepared to deal with the rest of the Frenchmen." Henry tugged on his beard and cleared the emotion from his throat before he continued. "Just as we readied for battle, the guards on duty warned me that the rebels were sighted racing toward two people on the road. That's when we saw your capture. Trevor remained behind to guard his family, and commanded three guards to also stay behind. I rallied the servants to make as much noise as they could."

Henry led John and Julianna into the study, where a fire warmed the cozy room, making conversation more comfortable. He settled into a leather armchair.

John drew Julianna next to him onto a comfortable settee. "But what I don't understand is how such a small force could make so much noise that it sounded like the king's army was charging into battle."

"It's a secret." Henry drew a pipe from a glass dish on the desk and filled it with tobacco from a tin beside it. Once the tobacco received the touch of fire, Henry drew on the mouthpiece until a puff of smoke carried a sweet scent into the air.

He grinned, then produced another puff from the pipe. "Apparently, the unique topography of the area, just out from the trees, causes any sound to amplify, as if a hoard of soldiers is approaching from all directions. It is an amazing phenomenon." Henry relaxed into his chair with a smile. "Trevor said it was a trick his great grandfather used to protect the manor from invading armies. And the reason he chose this site to build." Henry took a sip of the drink he'd brought from the dining room. "Those rebels are probably still riding hard to get away."

"Now that we have that mystery solved, tell me more about Elise's absence from our family gathering." John frowned. Julianna knew him well enough to tell he was worried. "And why is William not here?"

Henry frowned and rubbed a hand over his face, a gesture John did also when he was tired or worried. "William didn't arrive until much later, after Elise had already gone." He took another puff from the pipe and blew out the smoke. "Your sister needed supplies to fix a broken gate hinge, so she and I visited the village blacksmith to find the right kind of iron. While at the blacksmith's, she met her old professor from that school in London, Lord Isaac Canterbury. His party had stopped to repair a wagon wheel." By his frown, the memory was not a pleasant one.

"Apparently, the professor is extremely interested in meteorites and droned on about them incessantly during dinner, that night. He had taken leave of the School of Scientifica, where Elise had once attended, to investigate the rumors of a large rock that fell from the sky and landed in a farmer's field. The professor is convinced that the meteorites contain all manner of elements that could be beneficial to mankind. Elise seemed particularly excited about the expedition. The professor, his wife, and her nasty cat stayed the night. Oh, and there were also two assistants traveling with them, both chaps looked capable of defending the group, though we had no reason to assume there would be danger, at the time.

"The next morning, Elise begged to go with them, giving us

plenty of reasons for her interest. So we decided to let her go. It was only to be for a fortnight." Henry stood and walked to the fireplace to stoke the fire and add a log.

"After William came with the news of the danger, we sent him after Elise to protect her, though I doubt if we could have stopped him from going." Henry returned to his chair. "I would have gone with him, but the news also meant I was needed here to help protect the manor. A week later, a paid messenger arrived from William. He said the professor had finally found the site of the rumors. Elise was as excited as the professor about inspecting the stone and its unusual properties. All of their party was safe and would be staying at the farm. William would remain with Elise until it was safe to return."

John took Julianna's hand. "Now that the danger has passed, do you want Julianna and me to find them and escort them back to Brighton Castle?"

She snuggled closer to her husband. Now that she was part of a real family, she would do her part to keep them safe.

"I don't think that will be necessary...for now. You know how Elise gets when she's focused on a project. If they're not back before we're ready to return home, I'll go and retrieve them." He stood and yawned. "I know your mother well enough that we'll be here for a month so she can help with Sarah and the baby. I'd appreciate it if you and Julianna would return to Brighton to watch over everything there until we can return. We'll discuss plans for the future then." He turned his attention to Julianna. "We would like for you and John to stay at least long enough to rest and give us more time to get to know each other, Julianna." He stretched. "It's been a very exhausting day. I must retire and let you two do the same."

Julianna and John stood. She stepped forward, then paused. Would he welcome a hug? Her own father wouldn't have.

As though he could read her mind, Henry reached out an arm. "Come."

His fatherly hug overwhelmed her with the love of family it conveyed. "Thank you for making me feel so welcome." Tears of joy threatened to spill out, so she stepped back.

Swiping at the tear that had escaped, she turned and hurried out of the room. She'd been taught the outward expression of joy, anger, fear, or love was never acceptable. Those and many other lessons would be hard to overcome, but not impossible. With God's help, she could do it. One step at a time.

John caught up with her and took her hand, turning her to face him, his eyes searching hers. "I love you and so do my family." Then he drew her under his arm and led her to their quarters.

He closed the door behind them and turned to her. "I'm glad our future is together." Then he kissed her soundly.

"Me, too." Julianna allowed the tears to fall now, for the love in her heart was too full to contain them another moment.

CHAPTER 24

Ten days later, Julianna and John took their leave and headed back to London.

She'd enjoyed the visit with his family—with her new family—but John had become restless with an urgency to return to Brighton Castle.

First, they needed to return their horses to the king's stable and pick up Precious and her foal. It might be a challenge to find a boat willing to transport the donkeys, in which case they would need to buy a wagon and team to journey back to Brighton.

"I wasn't sure they would actually let us leave." John smiled at Julianna as she rode beside him.

She returned his smile. "I love your family. I'm sorry to leave, but…"

"I know." John chuckled. "It's nice to be on our own again, isn't it?"

"Yes." Julianna kicked her mount into a canter, which John matched.

After a pleasant, uneventful trip, they arrived in London a

day longer than it had taken them to reach the manor because of delays, as severely damaged roads were being repaired. Inside the city, they went directly to the port to try and secure passage for them and the donkeys, but none of the ships in dock had the capacity to haul livestock. So they rode to the stables to return the king's horses.

"Good to see you are well, Lord Stanton." Benson, the groomsman, met them and accepted John's and Julianna's mounts. "Unsaddle the horses, Freddie. Brush them before you stall and feed them." The groomsman handed the reins over to a young boy about twelve, who nodded and did as he was told.

"How are the donkeys doing?" John still had a hard time calling Precious by such a name in front of people.

"Precious is a bit protective of Sweetie, but is in every way healthy." Benson led them into the barn.

"Sweetie?" John grumbled. His tone and frown relayed the extent of his disapproval.

"The stable master's daughter fell in love with the foal and named her Sweetie." The groomsman hesitated. He opened his mouth, as if to continue, but one glance at John's lack of amusement, silenced him. They continued toward the back of the barn without further comment.

Julianna smiled. By her husband's expression, the foal's name would *not* remain Sweetie.

"No noble beast deserves to be saddled with such a demeaning name." John mumbled so only Julianna heard him.

"It's fine for now. Don't fuss and risk offending anyone, please." She put a hand on his arm, and he nodded.

Benson led them to the last stall. Precious and her foal were in a large box stall with a door that allowed the donkeys to be released into a separate enclosure while the box stall was cleaned. Usually, such a two-stall set up was used for horses deemed too dangerous for the stable hands to handle.

"So you've had a bit of trouble with her?" John's voice held concern.

"Aye, she seems to have taken particular offense to being tied up and has gotten away a few times." Benson frowned. "It's a bit of a chore to get her caught and returned to her stall, so I found it safer for all concerned to keep her confined to this space."

"I should have warned you about her talent for escape." John waited until the groomsman unlocked the door. "Do you still have the livestock wagon you spoke of last time we met? Would you be willing to sell it to me to transport these two to Brighton?"

"It's not mine to sell, but I'll ask my brother-in-law if he wants to part with it. When do you want to leave?" Benson waited while John and Julianna entered the stall, then closed the door.

"We must leave today. We've a long journey home and want to start as soon as we can make the necessary arrangements." John reached down and rubbed Precious's head. She pushed into his hand, a good sign she was glad to see him. "And we prefer if our presence is not known."

"I understand. I'll go immediately to inquire about the wagon."

Benson and his brother-in-law returned an hour later with the wagon and a stout team to pull it.

Julianna was a bit surprised John didn't haggle with the owner for a better price than the large sum he asked, but John seemed satisfied. He gave the owner the tidy sum to complete the transaction and received the bill of sale.

While Julianna took the young groomsman's apprentice, Freddie, with her to bring her trunks from storage, John loaded the supplies they would need for their trip. He secured her trunks in the storage area near the front of the wagon. Once they were ready, they loaded Precious and her foal into the back area of the wagon, which had a thick layer of straw added to keep the foal safe during the journey.

With the king busy dealing with several trials of the traitors, Julianna and John moved quickly to ready for their journey, lest they be summoned and drawn into more of the king's assignments. Julianna wasn't sure the king would honor her release from his service since Lois was declared dead and the headmaster found to be a traitor. She was done with the institute and wanted nothing to do with it or its nefarious purposes.

What if this happiness she'd found with John was merely a mirage or a wonderful dream, to be stolen from her like her childhood had been taken?

"Julianna, we're ready to go." John put a hand out to assist her up on the wagon's padded bench. He turned and thanked Benson and Freddie before climbing aboard and taking the reins. They were finally on their way, but she wouldn't find peace until they were well away from the castle and her past.

~

"I wasn't sure if we would make it out of London without the king's interference." John kept the team plodding along at a steady pace that would take days longer to reach Brighton Castle than on horseback or by ship.

"I'm not convinced we're yet far enough away. Let's not talk of it, lest he still send someone to find us." Julianna smiled and turned her attention to the road as they waved a friendly hello to passing farmers and fellow travelers.

John was still concerned about the dangers of being on the road with no escort, but he kept his worry to himself and tried to enjoy having Julianna to himself. After they arrived at the castle, his attention would be consumed with tending to any matters that arose while they were away. Such responsibilities often kept his father busy all day until the evening meal.

After three days on the road, they had settled into a comfortable routine, stopping at inns along the way for comfort and protection for the night. John's dreams were no longer consumed with bloody battles, but happy adventures with his future children as they grew up in Brighton. His favorite dreams were of Julianna. He awoke every morning since their marriage with a smile on his face and his wife in his arms. Life was better than he could have ever imagined.

"Precious and her baby are doing well. At least they don't seem to mind the long trip." Julianna turned on the wagon seat to check on the donkeys.

"I agree." He pulled back on the reins. "Whoa." The team stopped. He secured the brake and handed the reins to Julianna. "It's my turn to take the donkeys out and let them stretch their legs." He climbed down and went to the back and unloaded the donkeys, which they did every few hours.

While Julianna drove the team, he led Precious for a mile or so and allowed the foal to buck and run beside the slow moving wagon. When the little jenny tired, he loaded the pair into the wagon again.

The trip had been peaceful so far. Hopefully, the last few days of their journey would remain uneventful, but he dare not let down his guard.

"Oh, John what a quaint village. Can we stop here and see what they have for sale?" Julianna surprised him with her request, for she had rarely asked to stop and browse the shops along the way.

"And what do you need that you don't have packed in those trunks?" John couldn't resist teasing her.

"I just need a few necessities." She grinned and snuggled against him. He had no thought of denying her request. "And I'd like to buy a few simple gifts for the servants you've been telling me about."

"You don't have to buy them anything to make them like you."

"I know, but sometimes a small gift of appreciation makes a better impression than lavish praises, if they're perceived as ingenuous. I'll save the tokens until I've gotten to know them."

John stopped the team next to a large watering trough in front of a building with a sign nailed over the door. "The Flying Goose Inn and Mercantile. Items for sale from every corner of the known world." Around the door were smaller signs carefully hand printed with the promise of hot food, strong drink, and clean beds. For the illiterate, beautiful pictures of the items had been sketched by the hand of a talented artist. A plate of meat and vegetables was next to what appeared to be a steaming bowl of soup, which made John hungry and his stomach to growl. A large mug of beer with the foam slipping over the rim, and various colorful items displayed in the glass window were intended to lure even the less imaginative shopper inside.

Julianna climbed down before John could go around the wagon and assist her. He had tried to explain to her that his need to help had nothing to do with whether she could manage the task on her own, but was a simple act of a loving husband showing his respect.

"I'm sorry, I forgot. I'll let you *help* me next time." Julianna gave him a cheeky grin and winked before she climbed the wooden stairs and disappeared into the building.

While he waited, John checked the wagon for any potential problems, but all appeared to be in good working order. He rubbed his hands over the team to check for injuries or tender spots while they drank the water, then checked the harness and tightened one of the straps that had come loose.

"Hey, mister, that's a fine rig. Want to sell it?" An older man with a skinny lad at his side approached John. By his scruffy dress, he didn't give the impression he had the funds to purchase a pint of brew, let alone an expensive wagon and team.

"Sorry, but I'm not interested." John tried to appear friendly, but he got the feeling the man expected a negative reply to his inquiry. He glanced to the building where Julianna had disappeared and prayed her shopping would be concluded in short order.

"How about them donkeys?" The man walked up to John while the skinny lad circled close to the wagon and peered in at Precious and her foal.

Before John could respond, he heard the tailgate being unlatched.

"I think we'll take a closer look." The man grinned and pulled out a large knife, then pointed it at John.

"That's not a good idea." John edged closer to his staff leaning against the front wheel.

Precious squealed. He glanced up in time to see her jerk the lead rope out of the lad's hands. The donkey turned and kicked him square in the chest, sending him flying. He hit the ground hard and groaned, clutching his chest as he struggled to breathe.

John grabbed his staff, loosed the blade, then turned it on the distracted older man. "Stealing, or attempting to steal a man's horse and possessions are punishable by death. But since I'm in a generous mood, I'll give two choices. Stay and die. Or leave. Your choice." John took the stance of an experienced soldier and pointed the sword at the man's heart.

"We were just funnin' you. No harm done, mister. We're leaving." The man hurried around to the back of the wagon and helped the boy to his feet, half dragging him down the road and out of sight.

Once John was sure they weren't coming back with friends who might be hiding in the trees, he led Precious out of the wagon so she could drink as the foal nursed. As soon as she quenched her thirst, he put her back into the wagon and secured the lock.

"John can you help me?" Julianna stepped out of the shop

with an armful of packages, followed by a man holding twice the amount.

"Julianna, did you leave anything for others to buy?" He hurried up the stairs and captured several of the bundles as they were about to spill onto the ground. She opened the storage area and placed the items John carried inside, and then added the merchant's collection. She thanked the man for his help and he disappeared back into the building.

"I also bought us some food to eat until our next stop." She produced a basket as they climbed back on the wagon. "I'm sorry I took so long, but they had the most interesting items. I couldn't decide which I liked most, so I bought everything." She glanced at John and grinned. "I couldn't help myself."

"So you married me for my money?" John chuckled when she huffed with indignation.

"Hardly. I used my funds." Julianna frowned, looking offended until he leaned over and kissed her.

He flipped the reins and the team moved forward. "While you were making the merchant rich, I was dealing with thieves intent on stealing our wagon. At least, until the boy tried to take Precious, while his partner pointed a knife at me."

"What?" Julianna dropped the chunk of cheese she'd been holding, and it fell back into the basket. "Are you hurt?" She looked him over, then glanced back at the donkeys.

"We're all fine, but perhaps we should stay alert for further trouble." He smiled. "We're safe for now, and I'm hungry so…" With a glance at the contents of the basket, his stomach growled. "Death-defying adventures give me an appetite." He grinned and reached for the cheese and a slice of crusty bread Julianna held out for him.

"The merchant said there was another inn three hours away, the Fox and The Hound. It's owned by his brother-in-law and sister. Can we make that before dark?"

"Maybe. If we don't stop to shop along the way." John couldn't resist teasing her.

"Ha, ha." Julianna took a portion of cheese. "M-m-m, this is quite good." She glanced over at John when he laughed. "What? I find shopping gives me an appetite." She laughed and handed him another portion of cheese and bread.

CHAPTER 25

After a week on the trail, John was weary with the travel and glad to see familiar sights as they neared the castle.

"We'll be home within the hour." He shifted position again, trying to get comfortable. All he wanted was to push the team harder, but they had been on the road since sunup and the animals were weary too.

"John, I saw someone following us. They're in the trees." Julianna drew her knife and rested the blade across her lap.

"I saw them, too." He flicked the reins and sent the team into a trot. The road took a turn ahead, and the decline would aid the horses in gaining speed.

As they came to the bend in the road, brush had been pulled across to block the path. John pulled the horses to a stop.

"You're surrounded. Don't try and escape." A crowd of people armed with pitchforks, axes, and saplings sharpened into lances, poured out of the forest. A man dressed in peasant's clothing limped out into the road and stood with his arms crossed. Silence hovered over them. Even the birds of the forest had quieted.

John leaned forward and recognized the man glaring at

them. The glimmer of humor lit the man's eyes. John grinned. The peasant burst into laughter.

"Angus!" John jumped from the wagon and was surrounded by people from the village, laughing and slapping him on the back, all talking at the same time.

"Enough." A priest made his way through the crowd to reach him, and the crowd quieted.

"Father Alvin." John reached out to shake his hand.

"It's good to see you." Father Alvin tugged on the sleeve of John's tunic. "I see Lord Stanton has arrived and not Brother John." He smiled and glanced up at Julianna, who remained seated with her hands on the reins. "And you are?"

"This is Julianna, my wife." John grinned and slapped the priest on the shoulder. "I guess you were right. God did have a different plan for my life…a far better plan, as it turns out."

"I want to hear all about it, but first we must let you continue on to the castle. We'll speak tomorrow once you've had a chance to settle in." Father Alvin turned to the people. "Let's clear the road so Lord Stanton and his bride can be on their way. Everyone can go home, and I'll see you all at mass in two days' time." He raised his hand and praised their quick response to the call to arms, then proclaimed a blessing on them. As soon as the brush was dragged off the road, he waved the wagon forward.

"My heart nearly stopped when so many people came out of the forest and surrounded us." Julianna's dagger remained in her palm. "Are we truly safe?"

"Yes. I recognized most of the folks, and even Angus looks like a new man." John leaned over and hugged his wife tight. "There's our home." He pointed to the small castle built into the rugged hillside. The midday sun highlighted the limestone walls and parapet, making it a welcoming sight. Glancing across the green pastures dotted with sheep grazing contently, a sudden wave of peace washed over John, filling his soul with contentment he'd not experienced since before he joined the king's army.

"Julianna, we are truly home." He stopped the wagon and drew his wife into an embrace. He gazed into her eyes, then kissed her. "I can hardly wait to see what God has planned for us next."

~

Chapter 1

1207
ENGLAND

*L*ady Elise Stanton bent down and scooped a handful of soft earth. She stood and released it a little at a time watching the direction the dust drifted. The breeze blew it South and a little East.

Perfect.

She wiped her hand down the front of the borrowed tunic. She would wash it and the pants before returning them to the stable boy who lent them to her. The pants were a bit baggy but a piece of rope worked well as a belt, and also held her dagger.

She lifted the nine foot length of the wing's edge and ran her fingers over the seams checking for tears or gaps that could affect the experiment. Everything appeared smooth and the linen covering the willow frame remained taut. According to her calculations, the frame had to remain flexible but the surface must remain tight if it was to carry her weight in flight.

If her calculations of updrafts and wind currents were correct, she should be able to sail safely over the deep ravine and remain airborne long enough to glide down to a grassy knoll not far from the castle moat. The area was large enough to give her room to stop…she hoped. The moat was a vile open cesspool and not a place she would want to land.

Finding an updraft, while in flight, to take her high enough to land in the courtyard would have been her first choice but perhaps a bit too ambitious for a first flight. She smiled at the thought of the tower guards' wide-eyed alarm as she sailed by them.

She glanced down at the wing. It was beautiful in its simplicity. Her heartbeat sped up with the excitement of fulfilling months of studying large birds of prey in this area. There was no logical reason why man, or in her case, woman could not also learn to fly…with the proper equipment, of course.

She paced off the sixty-nine steps down the slope to the cliff's edge. If she were not in flight before she reached the last ten-steps, she would have to abort.

The locals didn't call that spot *dead man's leap* for naught. The ravine was lined with large, jagged boulders and falling into it would not turn out well for her or her apparatus. As an added precaution, she anchored her favorite yellow, silk scarf under a rock to mark the spot. The loose end flopped and waved in the breeze.

She climbed back up the steep incline to the large wing where she'd left it lying on the ground. Doubt thumped in her chest before she cast it away and bent down. She grasped the center of the wing and lifted it until she was able to stand with it extended over her head. It wasn't terribly heavy only awkward to keep level. The breeze was already pushing and tugging against the broad surface.

Long leather straps dangled from under the wing to her left and right. Walking her fingers out to grasp the strap on the left, she wrapped the loop around her wrist until it was tight then repeated the process on her right. The straps would keep her secured to the wing while in flight. Dropping from the height she'd predicted the flight would take her could be catastrophic.

She ignored the sudden chill of negative possibilities that prickled her skin to stay focused. Science wasn't advanced by cowards.

Besides she had prepared. She'd practiced hanging by straps around her wrists from the largest oak tree in the garden several times over the last three weeks until she built up her strength and could do it for over the fifteen minutes she projected it would take for her maiden flight. Those practices had revealed the need for padding around her wrist like she wore today to reduce the swelling and irritation the suspension caused.

Fear tightened around her chest, as she braced herself against the push of the wind. What if… She closed her eyes.

"Lord you are the author of witty inventions and this one has such wonderful potential…if I can get it to work. Please keep me safe. Amen."

Her heartbeat sounded as loud as thundering hoof beats in her ears.

A sudden gust tugged at the wing forcing her to plant her feet to keep from being pushed down the slope before she was ready. Something was off. She adjusted the wing until it was balanced and centered. "Maybe I should do a trial flight with the present size dimensions and substitute my weight with a sack of potatoes."

She huffed. Talking to herself was almost as good as writing down a thought. Visualizing the sketches on her workbench helped to justify this trial. "The smaller models of the wing flew fine after a few modifications to the width and design. Besides, I've already made all of the adjustments from the previous tests to the current design." Her thoughts turned to Cook, and she would certainly complain and might even tell Elise's mother, if she asked for anymore vegetables for her experiments.

If she was going to do it, now was the time. Her parents were occupied with visitors as was the castle's staff. If she was gone much longer she'd be missed and her father would send her brother, or might come to find her himself. The thought of what he might do if he saw the experiment before she completed her flight successfully made her cringe. There would be no words of explanation that would soothe his wrath if he felt she had endangered her life.

She shook off the thought and stepped forward gaining momentum on the slope. The yellow scarf grew larger in her sight.

"No!" A rider raced toward her. She heard him but couldn't see him.

"Wait!" His voice grew loud and demanding.

Her vision was blocked by the length of the wing but it didn't sound like her father or her brother.

Too late to heed the horseman, the wind caught the wing and lifted her feet off of the ground.

She was actually flying!

Butterflies fluttered in her midsection. The air tore against her, as if trying to tear her loose. The wind pulled her forward gaining speed. The wing shuttered then smoothed out again when she shifted her weight to compensate for the increased angle. The ground grew farther away. Fear shrouded the thrill of it, but she was determined not to abort the experiment for as long as she could.

The gust gained force tugging at the wing dragging it ever higher. She sped toward the cliff's edge. The scarf was almost beneath her waving frantically as if to warn her off.

Strong hands clasped her legs and pulled her relentlessly downward. The wing resisted, whipping hard from the right to the left, like a dog shaking a rat.

The rider's horse screamed with fear fighting the rider, as the wing fought against Elise's need to control it.

She was caught firmly from below by the unyielding would-be rescuer, making her unable to balance the wing or wiggle free.

"Unhand me!" She kicked with all her might to no avail.

"Stop fighting me, you daft woman!" The man tugged her down until he grasped her waist. In swift succession, he cut the leather straps freeing her wrists.

Freed from her weight, the wing shot up like a giant winged beast, until it blotted out the sun. The rider got the frightened horse under control and stopped at the cliff's edge.

"Let me go!" Elise struggled against her assailant, then stilled. She watched in anguish, as her beautiful creation sailed out and over the cliff without her.

Suddenly, the wing stalled in midair, as if caught between two opposing currents.

She held her breath.

The same force that held it captive suddenly released it and the wing sailed straight up. The hope that quickened within her allowed her to take another breath and release it with a soft plea. "Please fly." The wing dipped then sailed higher. Just as quickly as hope bloomed, the wing stalled and plunged toward the earth.

"No..." Elise wanted to look away, but she had to know its fate.

The air current that bore the wing aloft was over ridden by a stronger down flow current that slammed it onto the rocks below. The horror of it left her speechless and limp.

A sob caught in her throat.

"That could have been you." Her brother's best friend, William Degraf's voice was gruff with anger. His heart thumped fast and hard against her side. "What were you thinking?"

She glanced over at the man who held her so tightly she could barely draw a breath. "I would've been fine." Her voice was a hoarse whisper. Another glance into the ravine was evidence of the truth. That could have been her crumpled on the rocks. "Let me down, you're crushing me." Her demand was louder this time, as she pushed against his hard, muscled chest and strong arms that held her prisoner.

He swore something under his breath, bent over and set her on her feet then dismounted. His jaw muscle ticked with pent-up anger.

"You ruined my experiment. My flying wing is destroyed. It will take weeks to fix, if it's even repairable." Her body trembled as she glanced down again at the wreckage scattered out over the sharp rocks below. She refused to accept the defeat as her cause, but his.

"By the Saints." William ground out a curse and scrubbed his hand over his well-trimmed beard. She'd known him all of her seventeen years. His reaction was a familiar one whenever he was vexed beyond words, but she'd rarely seen him this angry.

"Why are you here?" She watched him try to calm his emotions by pacing away from her, stop, turned her way, open his mouth then shut it again and pace some more. He was tall, strong, brave, and handsome. She had loved him for as long as she could remember, but once she had reached a marriageable age, he had refused to encourage her interest.

He drew a deep breath and let it out before he turned to face her.

"I needed to see you…" He halted, as if he hadn't planned to say whatever had been on his heart. She could see the surprise in his eyes briefly before he dropped his gaze. He cleared his voice. "Your mother sent me to find you and bring you home." Without asking permission, he reached out and cut the protective wrap of lamb's wool that covered her wrists then frowned when he saw the whelps that had formed.

"Why didn't she send John or father?" Elise glanced at the bruises that also lined her wrists. It was evident she would have to create a better way to protect her skin the next time. She refused to rub the burning sensation, as the shock wore off and the feeling returned. To resist the temptation, she hid her hands behind her back.

"I'm here because I'm a better tracker than your brother and your parents have guests that have come to celebrate his commission in the king's army." His voice was deceptively calm but his hands were fisted at his side. "John and I are leaving day after tomorrow." He glanced up at the sun's position in the sky. "My family is expecting me for the same reason, and I don't want to be late."

"You needn't wait for me. I arrived here on my own and I can get back the same way." She pointed to a wagon and a team of horses tied beneath a large shade tree. "I need to retrieve my wing before I go." It would be a difficult climb down and a harder one climbing up with the extra weight and awkwardness of the wing. It might even take multiple trips to gather all of the pieces.

He stepped toward her and stopped, as if seeing her for the first time. "What are you wearing? Does your mother know you dress like a peasant when you're traipsing around dangerous places without escort or guards?"

"No, and you mustn't tell her." She met his gaze and tilted her head giving him her most beseeching smile. "Please,

William." She motioned toward the wagon. "My dress is there. I'll change back into it before I go home."

"But what were you going to do once you *flew* away? Your clothes are here?"

She hadn't thought of that. Rather than giving him the satisfaction of knowing she'd forgotten that minor detail she remained silent. It would have to be put on her list.

His eyes lit with amusement, but he refused to smile. "Go and change and I'll retrieve that mangled mess if you promise me you won't try to *fly* it ever again." His tone remained serious as if he had a right to give her orders.

"Nay. I'll get it myself, for I have every intention of recreating that wing and it *will* carry me safely into the sky...as long as I don't have any further interference." She raised her chin with stubborn defiance then turned toward the cliff scanning the rocky edge to find a safe way down.

With a grim expression, William stepped in front of her, his fists on his hips. She recognized the intent in his eyes a split second before he reached out and hauled her over his shoulder then stalked toward the wagon leading his horse behind him.

"Let me go this instant." She squirmed against his unyielding hold and knew she could get free by using the more aggressive measures she'd been taught since childhood. Her parents were diligent to teach their children to defend themselves in case of kidnapping...or worse. Hands unbound, she could reach the dagger at her waist. She didn't want to harm him—though she was sorely tempted to poke him with the tip of her dagger just to show him she was able to get free if she so desired. The idea was forgotten as fast as it had come. She didn't feel like being dumped on the ground, for she had bruises enough from her adventure.

William heaved her into the back of the wagon without speaking then tied his horse at the back. The expression of pinched lips and deep scowl he gave her when she got to her knees, was a warning that left no measure for misunderstanding, he would not stand for further interference in his plan to take her home.

In silence, he untied the team, climbed up to the driver's seat, and set the team in motion with a snap of the reins.

"William, please. I can't leave my creation out there. I spent too much time on it to let it be destroyed by the weather or animals." Her plea was ignored.

She heard something that sounded suspiciously like, *good riddance*, but he kept the horses headed toward Castle Brighton.

She had no intentions of being the subject of a lecture on proper attire for a lady or to embarrass her parents in front of their guests. There wasn't much time if she wanted to change back into her houppelande before she reached home. The long shapeless gown boasted of overly long sleeves which would hide the bruises already forming dark purple bands on her wrists from her short flight and from being yanked out of the wing.

If William told where he found her so far from the castle without escort or guards, she would no doubt be subjected to the usual lecture and warnings of leaving the castle without protection. Perhaps she could persuade him not to mention the part about the flying wing.

If she were on her best behavior and helped with the guests, perhaps all would be forgotten. With her noble upbringing, she knew how to act the dutiful daughter and be gracious to visitors when the need arose. Thankfully living in a remote area that bordered Scotland and England, there wasn't often the need to play hostess, though her mother insisted she would need such practice when she married.

She glanced at William's broad back and smiled. Such lofty rules of etiquette wouldn't be necessary as a soldier's wife.

With him facing forward, she gathered her dress around her

and pulled it over her head. Once hidden within its layers of fabric, she tugged off the soiled tunic then raised her arms and pushed her hands up into the sleeves of the dress.

The dress caught and wouldn't budge. No matter how hard she twisted or pulled, she couldn't tug it down or push it up to escape.

She was stuck.

The oversized hair comb she'd worn to keep her long hair out of her face had caught in the fabric. Her arms ached being hopelessly caught in the lengthy ornate sleeves. Her back muscles burned and a cramp had formed in her neck at the awkward position her limbs were stuck in above her head.

She swallowed hard. There was only one way to resolve the issue and she hated it.

"William." She waited but he didn't respond. "Please, I need your help." There she'd said it. Tears of humiliation clog her throat.

"What?" His weight shifted on the seat and she heard the spring give as he turned around. "What the…" He laughed.

"It's not funny." She couldn't keep the growing panic out of her voice. "I think my hair comb is caught and I can't move to free it."

"I should deliver you to your mother like that and let her help you as you explain why you're stuck in a dress and wearing man's breeches."

"But then my parents are going to wonder what part you played in my situation." That small measure of satisfaction wasn't worth the fear that scenario produced in her thoughts.

He cursed and stopped the team. His weight rocked the wagon as he climbed into the back with her.

For a man who rarely cursed, she seemed to have provoked him to do so several times in the short time he'd been with her.

He knelt beside her. "How can I help?" His voice was solemn, though a hint of humor edged it. She could feel his gaze on her.

"Reach inside the open neck and see if you can find and pull my hair comb free." She held still. "I think it's stuck on some lace." The ache in her shoulders and arms grew ever more painful until she wanted to shout for him to hurry. "Don't look. I already took off the tunic."

"How am I going to find the comb without looking?"

"William."

"Fine." His grumble made her smile. He was a good and honorable man and had protected her in worse situations as they grew up.

His hand groped her head mussing her hair as he explored the fabric. "I found it, but it's not coming free." He blew his breath out in frustration. "I have to look, Elise or risk tearing your dress and then what do you think your parents would say?"

"They'd probably demand you marry me to protect my honor." She chuckled but he stiffened.

"They'd more likely have me hung than have you marry a lowborn innkeeper's son who had just joined the king's army." His tone carried disappointment. At least he hadn't laughed at the possibility of marrying her.

"William Degraf, you know well that my parents count yours as their equals." She knew the separation between noble and lowborn was considered by both classes, as an impossible chasm to cross and too dangerous to challenge the status quo, except in private and special circumstances. Her mother and his had been best friends since childhood, which defied such social laws at least at Brighton.

"There." He dropped the ornate comb in front of her and climbed back to the driver's seat. The wagon pulled away nearly toppling her off her knees and onto her backside. She hurriedly tugged the dress fully on and shed the pants.

Once she had her hair and dress in order she stood and

moved to the front. She nudged him over and climbed onto the seat beside him.

They rode in silence until she could no longer stand it.

"I'm sorry you had to take time away from your family to come and fetch me." She was repentant now that she'd calmed down and could appreciate how valiant he was in rescuing her. Even if she hadn't needed his help, he hadn't known that.

"Good thing I did." What was that in his tone?

"Are you still angry with me?" She couldn't stand it if the last time they were together, he was at odds with her.

"You scared ten years off my life with that reckless stunt." He turned and gave her the half-smile he allowed when something amused him but he wanted to keep to himself. "I must say, it was one of your more interesting inventions. It nearly pulled me out of the saddle when I grabbed you. I'm glad we both survived." With a flick of his hand on the reins, the team sped up. "Time to get you home before your father sends out the guards to hunt for the both of us."

"How long will you and John be gone?" She missed him already.

"We've signed for two years with an open-end contract to stay longer if we're needed, but we'll have leaves to come home for short visits periodically."

"I know the king's edict makes it compulsory to serve, but my mother was disappointed that John didn't hire a substitute to take his place, as is custom by many nobles. Instead he chose to serve in the army himself. I know she would have rather he stayed home and found a bride." She leaned closer to William to block the wind. It seems to have increased as they drew closer to the castle. That would need to be added to her notes for the next time she tried the wing. A chill ran over her...if she tried it again.

"I think your mum blames me, because John decided to join

after I did." He shifted closer to her. "My father joined the army at my age of nineteen."

"I heard your father joined to try and forget your mother. After she married, he couldn't stand the thought of seeing her with another man when he knew she loved him." She felt the familiar flutter of longing when she thought of a man loving a woman so much that he joined the army to deal with his broken heart.

"From what my father said, it was more to keep from doing great bodily harm to the old man who took advantage of my mother's love for her mother to trick her into marriage. The blackheart was old enough to be her father's father. The old man promised to buy my indentured mum and gran'mum's freedom so she could live out her days a free woman." He stiffened. "That blackheart promised whatever he needed to get my mum to marry him, not out of love or to do the good thing but to have a slave for life. He owned her with the small price of her papers and a priest speaking marriage vows over them." His tone softened. "I'm glad he died, for he left my mum the inn. My father had a place to return after he served his time in the army and came back to marry her. They're happy."

That was probably the most conversation she'd heard out of William for months. Maybe because he was leaving soon that the memories were stirring within him. She placed her hand on his arm as a gesture of understanding and the muscles flexed beneath her touch.

Was he also leaving because of the love of a woman he thought unattainable? There was a twinge of jealousy when she tried to think of which of the village girls that mooned over him would stir him with such passion. None came to mind. She smiled with satisfaction.

Once back at the castle he accepted her parent's thanks without mentioning where he found her or about the wing. He left without another word to her, though he glanced her way and winked before departing. As always, her secrets were safe with him.

She wished she had more experience with matters of the heart. He was her perfect match—too bad he refused to acknowledge it.

GET FOR ***THE STONE AND THE SECRETS*** AT YOUR FAVORITE RETAILER.

Did you enjoy this book? We hope so!
Would you take a quick minute to leave a review where you purchased the book?
It doesn't have to be long. Just a sentence or two telling what you liked about the story!

Receive a FREE ebook and get updates when new Wild Heart books release: https://www.wildheartbooks.org/newsletter

Book 3: The Stone and the Secrets

ABOUT THE AUTHOR

Jan Davis Warren is a mother, grandmother, and a young-at-heart great-grandmother. Her wonderful husband passed away the same year she won the ACFW Genesis Award for Romantic Suspense. That win and many others are encouraging reminders that God wants her to continue writing even in the tough times.

Learn more at www.janwarrenbooks.com.

ACKNOWLEDGMENTS

To my father, Warren Davis, an avid story teller and highly decorated soldier. He joined the Army as a teen and fought for our country during WWII. He was captured on Corregidor in the Philippines where he survived multiple death marches and spent three-and-a-half years in Japanese prison camps. He suffered torturous treatment at the hands of his captors, which left many physical scars but he never allowed hatred to dominate him. Raised during the depression in a Christian home, he contributed his survival to faith in God and prayer, both his and his family's. The night before his scheduled execution, he was made to dig his own grave. His camp was liberated the following morning. His survival was truly a miracle.

As I grew up, I don't remember him focusing on the hardships of that time, but of stories of gratitude and forgiveness, like the time a Japanese guard shared his meager lunch with my starving father, knowing that if he were caught he would be killed for aiding the enemy. And about the Pilipino resistance who risked their lives to sneak food and medicine to the POWs. After coming home, meeting my mom and getting married, they had me and my sister. He worked as a carpenter to provide for his family and help rebuild the country until his retirement. He died at age 90, not long after he finished writing the story of his life. I hope to publish it so my family will have a tangible reminder of God's saving grace, and of a hero's sacrifice, perseverance, faith and love that passes all understanding. Virtues very much needed in our world today.

Scars are the proof of survival. Let God heal you of the grief and unforgiveness caused by your scars.

John 3:16 KJV For God so loved the world that he gave his only begotten son that whosoever believeth in him shall not perish but have everlasting life.

John 10:10 KJV The thief cometh not, but for to steal, and to kill, and to destroy: I am come that they might have life and that they might have it more abundantly.

Matthew 6:9 KJV (The Lord 's Prayer) Our Father which art in heaven, Hallowed be thy name. 10 Thy kingdom come. Thy will be done in earth, as it is in heaven. 11 Give us this day our daily bread. 12 And forgive us our debts, as we forgive our debtors.13 And lead us not into temptation, but deliver us from evil: For thine is the kingdom, and the power, and the glory, forever. Amen. 14 For if ye forgive men their trespasses, your heavenly Father will also forgive you: 15 But if ye forgive not men their trespasses, neither will your Father forgive your trespasses.

Thanks to my readers: Psalms 91 My prayers go out to you and yours. May the Lord bless you and keep you. In Jesus Precious Name.

Want more?

If you love historical romance, check out the other Wild Heart books!

Marisol ~ Spanish Rose by Elva Cobb Martin

Escaping to the New World is her only option...Rescuing her will wrap the chains of the Inquisition around his neck.

Marisol Valentin flees Spain after murdering the nobleman who molested her. She ends up for sale on the indentured servants' block at Charles Town harbor—dirty, angry, and with child. Her hopes are shattered, but she must find a refuge for herself and the child she carries. Can this new land offer her the grace, love, and security she craves? Or must she escape again to her only living relative in Cartagena?

Captain Ethan Becket, once a Charles Town minister, now sails the seas as a privateer, grieving his deceased wife. But when he takes captive a ship full of indentured servants, he's intrigued by the woman whose manners seem much more refined than the average Spanish serving girl. Perfect to become governess for his young son. But when he sets out on a quest to find his captured sister, said to be in Cartagena, little does he expect his new Spanish governess to stow away on his ship with her six-month-old son. Yet her offer of help to free his sister is too tempting to pass up. And her beauty, both inside and out, is too attractive for his heart to protect itself against—until he learns she is a wanted murderess.

As their paths intertwine on a journey filled with danger, intrigue, and romance, only love and the grace of God can overcome the past and ignite a new beginning for Marisol and Ethan.

~

Waltz in the Wilderness by Kathleen Denly

She's desperate to find her missing father. His conscience demands he risk all to help.

Eliza Brooks is haunted by her role in her mother's death, so she'll do anything to find her missing pa—even if it means sneaking aboard a southbound ship. When those meant to protect her abandon and betray her instead, a family friend's unexpected assistance is a blessing she can't refuse.

Daniel Clarke came to California to make his fortune, and a stable job as a San Francisco carpenter has earned him more than most have scraped from the local goldfields. But it's been four years since he left Massachusetts and his fiancé is impatient for his return. Bound for home at last, Daniel Clarke finds his heart and plans challenged by a tenacious young woman with haunted eyes. Though every word he utters seems to offend her, he is determined to see her safely returned to her father. Even if that means risking his fragile engagement.

When disaster befalls them in the remote wilderness of the Southern California mountains, true feelings are revealed, and both must face heart-rending decisions. But how to decide when every choice before them leads to someone getting hurt?

~

Lone Star Ranger by Renae Brumbaugh Green

Elizabeth Covington will get her man.

And she has just a week to prove her brother isn't the murderer Texas Ranger Rett Smith accuses him of being. She'll show the good-looking lawman he's wrong, even if it means setting out on a risky race across Texas to catch the real killer.

Rett doesn't want to convict an innocent man. But he can't let the Boston beauty sway his senses to set a guilty man free. When Elizabeth follows him on a dangerous trek, the Ranger vows to keep her safe. But who will protect him from the woman whose conviction and courage leave him doubting everything—even his heart?